AF580783

what lies beneath the flowers

NATASHA DÍAZ

DELACORTE PRESS

Delacorte Press
An imprint of Random House Children's Books
A division of Penguin Random House LLC
1745 Broadway, New York, NY 10019
penguinrandomhouse.com
getunderlined.com

Editor: Bria Ragin
Cover Designer: Liz Dresner
Interior Designer: Cathy Bobak
Production Editor: Colleen Fellingham
Managing Editor: Tamar Schwartz
Production Manager: Tracy Heydweiller

Library of Congress Cataloging-in-Publication Data
Names: Diaz, Natasha (Natasha E.) author
Title: What lies beneath the flowers : a novel / by Natasha Díaz.
Description: New York, NY : Delacorte Press, 2026. | Audience: Ages 12 and up | Audience: Grades 7–9 | Summary: When Estella Aubergine, a teenage socialite, goes missing, seventeen-year-old best friends Pippa and Bidi set out to find her in hopes of claiming a hefty reward that could change their lives, but their investigation forces them to question both their morals and their friendship.
Identifiers: LCCN 2025034390 | ISBN 978-0-593-12434-5 (hardcover) | ISBN 978-0-593-12435-2 (ebook)
Subjects: CYAC: Mystery and detective stories | Missing persons—Fiction | Social classes—Fiction | Friendship—Fiction | LCGFT: Novels | Detective and mystery fiction
Classification: LCC PZ7.1.D499 Wh 2026

The text of this book is set in 10.8-point Warnock Pro.

Manufactured in the United States of America
1st Printing

The authorized representative in the EU for product safety and compliance is Penguin Random House Ireland, Morrison Chambers, 32 Nassau Street, Dublin D02 YH68, Ireland, https://eu-contact.penguin.ie.

To the mothers, especially Cora Deliz Andrade Thomas.
You worked all the time to never miss the rent.
Thank you for delaying your dreams so I could chase mine.

Floral Guide

Linnaea borealis

Paeonia lactiflora

Antirrhinum majus

Lamprocapnos spectabilis

Mandragora officinarum

Lonicera periclymenum

Nerium odorum

Conium maculatum

Then

This Is the End, Almost

Sharp blood tickled her nostrils as she inhaled what she had done. She tried to think back and pinpoint her mistake—the moment she'd changed course to end up here, alone and abandoned. Her new life had started out so beautifully, but maybe she shouldn't have dreamed. Maybe she shouldn't have dared to love. Maybe she shouldn't have strayed so far from what she knew. Now, at the age of nineteen, she was already too familiar with the reality of how much space existed between hope and home.

Movement on her chest disrupted her thoughts, and she looked down at the newborn in her arms. A daughter. She was the mother to a daughter, and now it was her job to keep her alive, if she could do the same for herself.

The apartment seemed so fragile now, as if she could roll it between her fingers until it was a tiny ball of nothing. She leaned against the wall just under the window and tried not to let her life slip between her fingers. Seconds felt like hours as she tried to keep her eyelids from closing, but the blood continued to gush.

The baby nuzzled her. *Miracles aren't predictable,* she reminded herself, and despite the circumstances, this *was* a miracle. A miracle she had to protect, but how could she do that when the strength to keep herself upright was waning rapidly?

She let out a shriek that mixed with the electric currents of the ocean and the crackle of the bonfires on the beach outside. *Someone will come. Someone will help us*, she thought, and screamed again, but no one did. If she could get out into the hallway, she could get the baby to a doctor, to a clean, safe hospital. Wasted time fell piece by piece before her eyes, rice grains too tedious to collect. Too tacky with drying blood to sweep.

"I'm sorry," she whispered to the tiny body now resting in her lap.

She took off her shirt and placed it on the ground. The plants leaned against the walls, lush and green, with small purple posies beginning to bloom. She lowered the baby onto the shirt on the floor, then dragged herself across the room.

"Help!" she screamed toward the door.

Her voice, shrill and desperate, woke the baby, who then added to the chorus. Footsteps out in the building hallway rocked through a wave of pain in her stomach; another came when the door opened, and a blurry figure ran in.

They rushed past her to the newborn.

"Help us, please!" she whispered just before her head rolled to the side and the light left her eyes and the ocean crashed outside the window and pulled her away.

National Missing Persons Tip Hotline Transcript Excerpts

4/24/1987 Caller: Hello, my son Miles, he's an addict. He fell off the wagon again. We are in Washington Park, Chicago. I need help finding him. The cops won't help. Please call me back. 312-555-7766.

9/17/1999 Caller: Hello, my name is Candy Jenkins. I'm calling from Sheffield, Missouri. My daughter Shana has this boyfriend, who's too old for her, and they fight a lot. I told her while she lives in my house, she can't see him anymore. She walked out last week. I haven't been able to get ahold of her since. I called the regular emergency line for a wellness check. They said they knocked, and he said she wasn't there. I checked her phone location; it's still there. The police won't do anything. My number is 415-555-9988.

1/7/2008 Caller: Ola—um—H-hello, she's here in San Francisco. Meu bebê. A mother knows. I have to find her. I have to find her.

Now

CHAPTER 1

Pippa

Floral families are the same as ours, broken down into layers. First a genus, and then a wider ancestry, some herbs and fruit. Even legumes should be considered, or at the very least not discounted, as part of the extended genealogy. Some flowers span continents tied to each other by nothing more than DNA. Some may never meet, not in a garden or a bouquet. Some may be plucked; others shrivel up from drought. And yet, of all shades, of all heights, of all petals, they are family. Whether they like it or not.

The nice thing about flowers is they can't talk.

They can't guilt or manipulate you. They can't feel. Flowers could spend their entire existence growing beside a sibling seedling, but it would make no difference to them if they were seven thousand miles away instead. They can't fight or abandon; there's no pressure to feel loyalty. Even if it defines you, when you are a flower, "family" is just a word.

They don't know how lucky they are.

The ground squeaks as worn rubber meets wet blades of

grass, and I move down the hill of the cemetery. I come to the graveyard for the distraction but also for the sunflowers and lilies whenever I spot them, some chrysanthemums too. I pick through the bouquets bought by strangers and pull the flowers that still have a chance to live. You can tell a lot about the dead from the flowers a person's people leave, like the fact that they came at all.

A bouquet of tea roses sits between two plots a few rows down. The stems are fresh, springy, exactly what I need to finish a batch of crowns. Any flowers left over will be in my next sculpture. The piece that could get me into a private arts university or discovered. The first step toward my future.

At the cemetery, not everyone comes back for you, so I come here to sit among others who have yet to be claimed. Here, surrounded by whole lives reduced to names, I whisper my mother's name to them.

"Sofia Santos."

It is easier to grieve the mother I could have had than to accept the waste she turned out to be. If she is dead, that would explain every second she's missed.

"Pippa."

I say my name the way my mamãe is supposed to, as though I am a gift she made for the universe. I speak to the sunrise just before the day breaks its shell to spread the sun across the city.

"*Pippa*," I say again. I twist misfortune into grace, into refuge, and together, we are reborn.

"PIPPA?"

This time my name bellows out of my pocket. I pull out my phone and am greeted by an up-close Ziwe-esque eyeball.

"Pippa, it's weird just staring at the inside of your pants listening to you breathe."

My best friend, Bidi, shifts the phone to a normal distance from her face. Her braids are wrapped up in a rainbow-tie-dyed scarf and pulled away from her face while she peels off a Korean mask. It doesn't matter how busy she is—Bidi's deep brown skin is going to be dewy and flawless. She moves in and out of frame and around her kitchen.

"You are the one who demanded I FaceTime you every time I stop by the cemetery!" I shoot back. Bidi grabs a knife and jabs at the screen.

"You're lucky I don't institutionalize you for wandering around dark-ass graveyards like a necrophiliac. Being the subject of a Netflix original true crime series isn't the goal, Pippa—it's actually meant to be avoided at all costs."

"The whole point is to be still. Cemeteries are quiet," I explain for the hundredth time.

"Yes, that's because flesh rots silently, Pippa." Bidi sucks her teeth like she bit into a sour cherry.

She moves the phone to the table, where she sets down a smoothie and preps a lunch box for her younger sister. Bidi has more plates in the air than seems possible, and she has never dropped one, or if she has, she glued it back together so well no one ever noticed. She is the only other person I know who willingly wakes up at the crack of dawn. The difference between us is that she's up because she is organizing and fundraising for local youth programs. Bidi is up because every step she takes has been calculated toward her run for city council as soon as she's eighteen next year. Her big plans have been in motion since the first breath she took on this earth. Meanwhile, I'm up before the sun so I don't dream that Mamãe is chasing after me like a loose petal blown from her fingertips, always just out of grasp.

"All right, so . . . do you think it's time to wrap this up or . . ." Bidi nags again, eyes burdened.

She doesn't want to get off the phone; she wants to change the topic. I forgot today is the day Bidi receives the official acceptance letters for two prestigious internships, and I was supposed to be there with her.

"I'm the worst," I admit.

"You aren't the worst, but you are very bad at sticking to plans and generally remembering things," Bidi confirms.

I have spent a lot of time wondering why Bidi loves me enough to stay around even though I am always messing up. Somehow, she wakes up every morning and chooses to keep me. We have been so close for so long that there must have been a moment when it made sense. Now so much time has passed that there's no point trying to remember what happened and when.

"So, have you opened the emails?" I ask.

She shakes her head. One of the offers will be from the current city councilwoman's office, and the other is from the state page program. Whichever she chooses will define her campaign next year. Bidi's looking for the AOC to her Zohran. She already got assurances from both the city councilwoman's office and the page program that she had been selected, but the official notices are being sent today. She hasn't decided which one to accept.

"You do know that seeing the words will not trigger some divine advice from the unknown to guide you toward your truth, right? You still have to be the one to decide," I remind her.

Caroline, Bidi's five-year-old sister, juts her hip out in the corner of the phone screen. "Bidi, this is boring, and I'm hungry."

Bidi marches Caroline to the table, where she laid out her breakfast, then returns.

"Can you just come over?" Bidi whines.

The sun above me shifts and hides, swallowed by gray chunks of fog now hanging above the seven-by-seven-mile stretch of soul and grit that makes up the city of San Francisco.

"I can if I catch the next bus. I'll run," I say, and hang up just as Caroline launches her bowl of cereal at Bidi's head.

The flowers poke out of my open backpack slung in front of my chest to avoid damage on the journey home. I make it a whole fourteen steps before my first detour. A girl no older than nine is on the path a few feet in front of me. She lies flat on her back to block my way.

"Um . . . sorry, small child, can I get by?" I ask.

She lifts her arms above her head so the grass tickles her skin, waving them up and down like she is in flight. Her head turns away from my toes to look up at the clouds before she speaks.

"My mom is dead."

I pull a couple of chrysanthemums out of my bag, orange and red. They wind around each other to make a quick, twisted tiara. I bend down to hand it to her, but she doesn't move to take it.

Stubborn. Good, she'll need that to survive in this world.

"Have you ever heard the saying 'Make lemons out of lemonade'?" I ask. She shakes her head.

"It's a Beyoncé quote. It means things are only as bad as you let them be. You never know; it could be a blessing in disguise! This could be your lucky break. I mean, I wish my mom was dead."

Shock ties itself around her neck and pulls her upright; tears stream down her cheeks before she starts to scream.

"Daddy!"

She bounds over to a man twenty feet away crouched before a gravestone. Typical. I try to be honest, and now I'm the villain. He moves in my direction, so I throw the headpiece I made for the girl onto my head and run.

"Hey, get back here!" the man shouts.

An exit appears to my left, and I go through the open metal door onto the street, where I flatten myself against the outer wall of the cemetery. I know what kind of rage grief inspires. I don't need anyone else's. His feet rush right past me and farther into the graveyard, so I look up to figure out where I am. The street is not one I know, and I would remember. I've walked the enclave of mansions nearby, but somehow, I've missed the estate in front of me.

I cross the street to the ironwork that encases the private garden where honeysuckles stifle the air, cloying and ripe. A massive purple mandrake peeks out through the slats, bold and violet, a streak of sunrise caught on a branch. Mandrakes never grow on the West Coast, and this is the largest one I have ever seen. I lift my hands to pull down the mass of purple petals to add to my graveyard bouquet collection, but the gate of the estate creaks open, and I drop down to hide behind the bush beside me. I would be weirded out if I found someone staring into my yard at this hour of the morning.

Through the cracks in the leaves, I watch as Estella Aubergine walks out to the curb, wrestling a loose curl from her bun into submission. A San Francisco darling, Estella found her way into the spotlight through a mix of accolades and social prowess. The point being, you don't have to know her to know her, which is how I know someone messed up. People wait for Estella Aubergine, not the other way around.

She scrolls through her phone, foot tapping until she looks up and moves her gaze toward the bush I am crouched behind. I hold my breath but the silence between us is overtaken by the engine of a black car with rose-gold rims rounding the bend. The rear door swings open, a wall blocking my view.

"You're late." I hear the imprint of Estella's voice on the brisk San Francisco morning breeze. Someone steps out of the car, but all I can see is the top of a black hoodie pulled up over their head, barely peeking over the SUV door.

"No!" Estella shouts.

Instinctively, I rise from the shrubbery, and we lock eyes, just before Estella is swallowed inside the car along with the hooded person. The SUV peels off and silence replaces it.

Great. The last thing I need is to be the poor kid in a rich ass neighborhood at the wrong time.

The urge to leave plays tug-of-war with my concern. I run back the tape in my head. Before the car pulled up, she was calm, no distress. She was waiting and she knew who pulled up. Estella has been known to get into dramatic public spats with her on-again, off-again girlfriend, Bettina.

I force my worry to wane. People like Estella always land on their feet in custom Louboutins.

In Estella's wake, the scent of the honeysuckles hits again. Their perfume spreads out to shield delicate noses from the fragrance of piss and desperate hope that wafts from the San Francisco sidewalks. This garden could have been an oasis if it had not been so badly ignored. I stare at the tangled web of overgrowth, so ill-maintained it feels like a personal attack.

My phone vibrates in my pocket. Not Bidi this time but an alarm: **Shift.** I pull the maps app up on my phone to navigate to the bus.

Seventeen-year-olds like Estella spend their summer weekdays interning and their nights drinking and dating. Drenching themselves in the city. Dancing in their strappy heels down Mission Ave. They tiptoe around cracked vials and piles of shit, past rows of tents—homes of those displaced by their rich parents. They hop from party to party, bar to bar. They come back and burrow into their thick, fluffy fantasies, only to wake up again and drag themselves back out into mysterious vans early in the morning. Bidi's voice rings in my ears. *"Estella is fine—she lives for every minute."*

Us? We work.

My alarm buzzes again, the second reminder: **Shift.**

The bus gags to a stop in front of me, ten minutes past its scheduled time. I climb aboard with the late shifts ending and the early shifts still getting ready. Wind flies in every time the accordion door opens at the back of the bus, too rough, too bold, too willing to tussle. Snapping at my skin like Bidi does when someone gets in the way of her ten-year plan.

We drive away down into the city, past the Victorian homes bathed in majestic pinks and purples. Past the Mission and Potrero Hill and the Fillmore District, halfway to Bayview Hunters Point. All neighborhoods like mine, still holding themselves tight. Bidi says the louder we are, the better. It's not easy to make someone disappear when everyone is looking, and as we barrel down the streets, past La Taq and Bernal Heights Park, all I see is us.

I rise from my bus seat when a tattered awning comes into view. *H* and *I*, the only letters still intact on the sign, greet me as I step down onto the sidewalk.

"Hi," the accidental word, throws fists from the sky like I didn't hear it the first time. The door to the Bahia Padaria swings open from the inside for me as I approach.

"Get to work; you're late."

I catch my Tia Jo's reproach along with the mop thrust in my direction and run inside so that she can lock back up. The Bahia Padaria opens every morning at seven-thirty. Just in time for the coffee crowd. The "enough time to trade dirty nursing scrubs for a shower and fresh nursing scrubs" crowd. The "I need to get my lotto numbers" crowd. The "put it on my tab, you know I'm good for it" crowd. The "stretching rice and beans like rubber bands, always have a story, always ask you how school is going, always leave with a smile even though life is tough" crowd.

Jo says that their pain is not our business. Our business is the shop, and every morning before the early crowd, we clean. She sifts through a pile of mail and marches into her office while I clean my way through the store.

I work with my hand holding tight to the mop as I do to every ounce of resentment for my mamãe—Tia Jo's twin sister, who promised she would return for me and never did.

Jo says San Francisco is the sister city to Rio de Janeiro (and sisters love to fight). Jo says I am like a cloud riding on the tail of the wind, impossible to escape.

Jo says beaches are not supposed to be cold, that you go to beaches to be warm, to sweat out the day, the ocean dancing on your toes. She says the Bay doesn't have the beach. San Francisco has "the water." She used to tell me how much Mamãe loved the beach. Probably more than she ever loved me.

Jo says we do the best we can with what we've got. We move forward. We stay quiet. We don't ask for more than we need. We don't dream, because in our dreams we are haunted by our mothers. We are abandoned over and over. Hands cracked from bleach and Pine-Sol-stained, we empty the buckets. We wipe the counters. We scrub the floor and dust the shelves. We clean to keep our souls fresh. To keep our feet on the ground, our heads above water.

Clean, like we were never there.

Jo crosses the shop to open the door. The crowd has just started to form, and she lets them in. Customers flood the space, freeing me from cleaning duty to rush over to the fourth knuckle of the space, my corner. I take a seat on my crate and pull out the flowers and review my bounty. The best flowers in the graveyard know I'll fight with the bees to give them a second chance. They'd make us more money if I could present and store them properly, but Jo refuses to get a flower fridge. She'd rather stock the shelves with Guaraná, because my flower crowns are the number two best-seller, but the Brazilian soda is number one.

The whole day passes as I make crowns in between reorganizing the chips. And moving the milk that's about to expire up to the front and adding discount stickers. Same with the cheese and the cold cuts. All the while Jo sits up at the front greeting her customers, gossiping. Not lifting a finger. She sits on that stool, and she offers an ear for every customer from the neighborhood who comes in to talk. Jo listens; she absorbs their pain. Then she drinks and unloads it all onto me.

"Pippa, the garbage is overflowing," Jo clucks from the front.

Her job is to oversee, to be seen. Jo's knee vibrates on the edge of the stool behind the counter. Slurping her coffee along with the tea that keeps flying through the door.

"Did you hear that Juanita really left Randy? Finally walked out on that useless loser."

"Meu deus."

"That new restaurant that opened a few blocks north had the nerve to call the cops on Jimmy. Jimmy was just sitting on the corner like he always damned does!"

"Meu deus."

"Miss Annie had a bad fall, but looks like she's going to make a full recovery, God willing."

"Meu deus."

"Jo, you notice the weather's been acting funny. Loud almost?

Funnier than usual for the Bay, and that's saying something. My grandma used to say when the weather acts like that, it means something big is coming."

"Meu deus."

My phone buzzes in my pocket. Bidi's name flashes when I pull it out, but Jo shoots me a glare I'm not willing to go up against by answering a call during my shift. I move deeper into the store to reorganize the toilet paper and text Bidi, but as I'm building a small wall of Cottonelle to hide behind, a finger taps my shoulder.

"Can you help me? I'm looking for the owner?" a woman in Alexander McQueen boots asks.

"That's me," Jo says from halfway down aisle one.

This white lady smells like money and new leather and Chanel No. 5. She turns her back to me and walks toward Jo. I follow, along with everyone else in the store.

"I'm here about an opportunity," she says.

People like her like to come to the neighborhood because then they can say they have been here. They can say they have lived. They can say they made things better. They can say they understand. The naval base contaminating our water kept Realtors and developers away for a good while, but even that disaster has a price someone can pay.

"Look."

She holds up her phone and shows us a few images of a new neighborhood, all metal and glass. She power-washes everything we've known away with each swipe.

"Nope, not interested." Jo's voice is cold and hard.

“You won’t be able to hold on to this place much longer.” The corner of the lady’s mouth flies up.

Bidi steps inside the store as if summoned, all power. “Hey! Don’t threaten her.”

The crowd encircles Jo. We know about the nicknames real estate firms create to make neighborhoods sound like a pocket of the city they only now just discovered. Ladies like her have been coming around for a minute, and we smell them a mile away. The woman pulls an envelope from her Birkin. When Jo doesn’t move to take the note, she places it onto the counter. “My cell is on there. You should consider my offer, take a leap.”

Bidi takes center stage like she always does.

“Leave!” she bellows at the lady, and the whole pack behind her chimes in.

“Leave! LEAVE, LEAVE, LEAVE.” Their cries follow her out the door, and while she still has their attention, I grab the envelope and open it.

The lady used nice paper. The heavy type you can’t see through even if you hold it up to a light, which is good because the amount written on it is a block of lead. An offer so big I whisper it out loud to make sure it’s real. Five zeros are more zeros than I have ever seen, even with just a one at the front. This offer is more than Jo will ever make. Enough to change everything. Enough to pay for art school and get my flower sculptures in front of the right people.

Jo snatches the paper from me. She balls it up and launches it, then stands arms raised, ready to conjure a tornado. Our customers huff, validating her righteous anger. They pay for their snacks and their sandwiches with the pride that, today, they held on to their normal.

"We should celebrate," someone shouts.

The masses file out and pull Jo along with them. They leave me behind with the crumpled offer letter, our chance to be free, thrown onto the ground.

CHAPTER 2

Bidi

Pippa walks across the store and picks up the piece of paper from that lady.

"Can we goooo?" my little sister, Caroline, whines at my side.

I rummage through my purse for a ziplock bag of sidewalk chalk and hand it to her. "Here, go draw; stay by the window so I can see you."

Caroline takes the chalk outside while I walk up to the counter.

"You good?" I drop the groceries in front of Pippa.

"I hate that question," Pippa notes, and begins to ring me up.

"Yeah? Well, I wouldn't mind hearing it every once in a while," I snap.

She stops punching the register and looks at me, her negligence for the second time today registering across her face.

"I'm sorry, Bidi. I meant to come by this morning, but this kid in the graveyard was, like, having a nervous breakdown, so I offered her some life advice, but then her dad got all emotional and then I saw this flower and then that influencer walked out and almost caught me stealing from her garden and *then* I was late, and Jo was in a mood—"

Pippa covers her tracks in chaos I don't even try to follow. "Anyway, which internship did you choose?" she asks.

The reminder stings as badly as it did the first time. I pull my phone out for Pippa to see what she would already know if she had thought to check in on me earlier.

> Dear Ms. Jones,
>
> We regret to inform you that, despite your impressive application, we cannot offer you a position in the summer page program.
>
> Sincerely,
> Allen Hopper
> State page program

Pippa's face falls. She stitches words of comfort together.

"Damn. Well—uh, that's good, ya know? Now you don't have to worry about making a choice. You just go with the other one—right?"

I shake my head.

"Both emails were like that." The truth sticks my tongue to the roof of my mouth.

"What? How can that be?" Pippa's rage soothes me. My loss is hers too. Always has been, both ways.

"Didn't they tell you the letter was just a formality?" she asks.

They did, in so many words. I nod. For once, I understand the idea of the cemetery, the way the silence probably eats the things you can't cope with or say out loud.

"Well, they don't deserve you! Seriously, Bidi, screw them. I'm sure you have better backups anyway. You always have something lined up. We should make sure they know it." Pippa's spit flies through the air.

She's right; I normally do have a plan C. But plans A and B both offered me the position in the interview room, and I had to finish the paperwork to get school to approve working on my own campaign as an official elective for senior year. I had to watch Caroline in the evenings. I had to study for exams. I had two promises, so, for once, I didn't do more.

Pippa looks back down to the letter from that woman we just chased out. I switch the focus from my problems to hers.

"For a second, I thought you were hesitating about selling this place," I say.

"I mean . . . it is a lot of money, Bidi. Come on, what would you do with it?" Pippa admits.

"Nothing. I don't want to owe anyone anything." I pull a small jar of minced garlic from the shelf closest to me and place it onto the counter with the rest of the items Mommy asked me to pick up.

Pippa begins to fill my cloth bag as she talks. "Imagine! You could do whatever you wanted!"

"You mean *you* could do what *you* want, Pippa," I clarify.

Pippa thinks her dream is to be famous. She wants to be the artist of the moment. The cultural shifter. Not like the posers and transplants who come to San Francisco and cover our city in whack honey bears, their gentrifier pop art. She wants to set a standard. She wants wealthy people to fawn over her work. She wants to make a splash so large it turns into a tsunami of fame and fortune. She thinks that's her dream, but really, she just wants her mother to see her. Pippa doesn't want to be found by her mother, not anymore. She wants to be unavoidable. An inevitability. She wants to be the one haunting dreams.

"This isn't about me. I am serious, Bidi! You wouldn't need to worry about those dumb internships. You could fund your own campaign. You could do it your way," Pippa pushes.

"The internships aren't dumb, Pippa," I correct.

"They are if they don't want you!" Pippa declares.

If they did want me, I would be accepting one of those positions. I wouldn't be here, panicking. I have never had to panic, not until now.

"Well, thanks, but that doesn't track. I wasn't good enough, and now I'm screwed." I hand her cash for the food.

"You're never screwed if you have money," she teases.

"That's not even funny, Pippa. The neighborhood is already getting picked apart. We can't lose more of us."

"I am part of 'we,'" Pippa reminds me.

"Not if you're gone because you sold this place," I snap back.

My father works so much that the whole summer could go by and I won't see more than the shadow of his back as he creeps out the door after four hours of sleep. Mommy does twelve-hour nursing shifts and takes extra when she can. We don't want for anything, and I pick up the slack when I have to. But I have seen firsthand what it takes to chase a dream with nothing. I've seen the way it tears someone down to do everything right and still be empty at the end of the month. I believe if we stay local and block out the noise of the rest of the world, we can save our pocket of it.

But I get why Pippa wants what she wants.

Money is what we've been taught to crave. That doesn't mean I'm going to let my best friend get sucked away from me without a fight. Especially not because of a woman who abandoned her. Not when I've been saving Pippa's ass from herself damn near our whole lives. Her mother is never going to get caught up in her giggles. She's never going to watch her eat four mangoes in one sitting, down to gnawing on the pit. I am. She doesn't deserve Pippa. It sounds like maybe Pippa's mother knew that about herself too.

Pippa's face twists like cords of earphones that were wrapped neatly and placed in your bag, then reemerged a knot. "You saw Jo. We aren't taking the offer, but I'm allowed to dream."

Not everyone gets to dream. Pippa does, though. She makes mistakes and follows her heart to the graveyard because people like me plan and keep a schedule for her. We take care of everyone else and ourselves with a smile. Always the example. Always responsible for the behavior of entire other humans we did not birth or agree to raise.

Roars from the bar down the block, where Jo and our neighbors are celebrating, burst through the summer evening. Pippa already worked the day shift, and now that Jo is out, she'll be on the night one as well.

"I have to get back home," I say. "See you later?"

She nods before I head outside to collect Caroline.

Our house is only a block away, but we race back because if there is anything more stressful than being Pippa's friend, it's being Malika's daughter, especially when she needs to make dinner.

"Finally!" Mommy throws her hands up as soon as we walk in.

"I need to get dinner finished. You just missed your father," Mommy says from so deep in the grocery bag, she's half upside down. "Mo is coming. Where is the garlic?"

I take the bag from her, and she goes back to the stove to survey the simmering pots.

"Let me find it—wait—Mo?"

"Yes, Mo, your cousin."

My cousins sprout like oregano from Mommy's herb garden. They show up unannounced and come for the summer or the winter. They move in. They move out. They come back. I could go anywhere in this city and have someone related to me within a three-block radius. Mo was more than that, though. He practically lived with us every summer, every holiday, spring break, and then last year, he got into a private school and vanished. Never even sent a text.

Mo and I had been the youngest in the family until Caroline was born twelve years after me. We had to fend off our older cousins, but at least we had each other. Plus, Mo often got the brunt of it. He was easy to mess with. I don't know how many times I tricked him into doing my chores.

"What do you mean, he's coming? Like, for dinner?" I clarify.

"For the summer, Bidi."

Mommy takes the bag from my hands and removes the rest of the items, still no garlic, like that's the biggest concern right now.

"Mommy. For once, can you just say no?" I beg.

I know she won't. She works more than she breathes to own this home, and as long as she does, she's going to open her doors. Mommy always finds a way to make it work, even if that means making it harder for me.

I have to prepare for college applications and build a platform for my campaign for a local election. And now I also have to come up with a summer project to make up for the fact that I didn't get any of my dream internships. If Mo moves in, he will become another thing I am responsible for. It doesn't matter that he is technically older than me by a few months; his mistakes will be my mistakes, and right now, I'm at capacity.

A sinking dread flows through me.

"Wait. Mommy, where is he going to sleep?"

She sorts through the spice cabinet in search of a replacement for the missing aromatic and speaks the one word I need her not to say. "Downstairs."

After years of sharing the room upstairs with Caroline, I was promised the downstairs as long as I kept my grades up and paid for the redecoration myself. After saving and working and countless hours of scouring Facebook Marketplace, I finally got the approval to move in this month.

Before I can begin my defense, Mommy holds up her hand. She's the judge and the jury, and the decision has been made.

"It's just for the summer, Bidi. It doesn't make sense to cram him upstairs when you are already set up there. Speaking of which, do you know what your summer schedule is going to be yet?" Mommy asks.

"I'm weighing my options but planning to be quite busy once things take off."

I manifest an opportunity to fall from the sky. Instead, I get a jail term.

"Mm-hmm, right, okay. Sounds like you've got time to watch Caroline, at least until you've figured it out. You cannot do screens all day. That goes for both of you." Mommy goes back to seasoning.

The only thing I can do is sink into the pit that keeps digging itself deeper beneath me.

"What is going on with you? Is this about Pippa? You always get cranky when you two fight."

I shrug and brush it off, but it doesn't matter. Mommy always knows when something's up, even when she's focusing on everything but me. She takes her phone and plays some music—Selena serenades us from the speaker.

Bidi bidi bom bom.

Mommy goes to the kitchen counter and starts cutting onions in quick, even slices.

When she's done, she puts a pot of water on a burner to boil, then rinses some rice and pours it in. She takes marinated chicken and moves it onto the stove.

"You know the night you were born, I listened to this same song over and over?"

Mommy's feet get caught up somewhere between a shuffle and a stomp. She two-steps my way and places a hand on my back and takes my hand in her other one, and then she guides me and sings along softly in my ear.

Bidi bidi bidi bidi bidi bidi bidi bom bom.

"You were kicking and ripping me half open. I didn't think I was going to make it, but I needed the paycheck. Our neighbor's dad had a restaurant, and he paid me pretty well to do dishes a few nights a week to get me through nursing school. He let me take home any food that was left over, so I didn't need to spend time or money on groceries. That shift I knew you were ready to come out, but I needed the paycheck, and when this song came on, you calmed down. I played it on repeat, hips moving and hands cleaning, over and over and over until I could leave. I went straight to the hospital and ate my dinner on the way."

Mommy glides us around the small room, away from the rice bubbling off beat with the onions and chicken in the neighboring skillet. She scoops her hips side to side through exhaustion, same as she did when I was in her belly.

"You came into the world exactly who you are today. It's a blessing to know your purpose, but in some ways it's also a curse because you have to wait for everyone else to catch up. I'm not going to lie to you, you can't do anything but let them go try to figure it out and hope you like whoever they are when they come back."

Mommy keeps dancing. Her arms lead my body, and her feet keep the pace.

"What if they don't come back at all?" I ask her.

"Then you keep on going, the way you always have."

Her hands cup my cheeks, rough from the years of scorching-hot dishwater she had to train herself to bear at the restaurant. The same pain that built up her tolerance to survive the night shifts as an ER nurse. I steal the lead to dance her back over to the empty chair by the small round table covered in onion peels and avocado pits. Mommy takes the seat, and her apron flies over her neck and around mine in a single motion. She closes her eyes to rest.

Bidi bidi bom bom.

On the other side of the room, the kitchen sink is half empty. I fill it up to the top with hot water and plunge my arms deep down to my elbows, the way Mommy used to. I hold my arms steady under the heat of the water to see how long I can stand the pain.

My phone buzzes on the counter just as I go numb, and a siren ring blares. Cool air hits as I lift my arms from the water to silence the noise and let Mommy rest. Once I've muted the sound, I read the statewide Amber Alert.

A girl my age is missing.

CHAPTER 3

Pippa

Bidi's judgment sits on my shoulders long after she's left. The truth is, I don't *want* to sell the shop—it's my home, but if I had the chance, I would take that money and run.

You won't be able to hold on to this place much longer.

Bidi's voice isn't the only one I can't get out of my head. The real estate lady said it like she was picking a scab on Jo's skin. Like she knows Jo is hiding something, and if there is something to know, I need to find out what it is. Jo always has a mess hidden in a closet, ready to pour out the second I open the door. I grab the crumpled offer letter and take it to Jo's office, where expired mango hair oil sits somehow rotting sweeter. Worn-out bands used to slim waists, waste upon waste. Old bottles line the perimeter of the room, one habit after another. Her office is an addict's graveyard.

Papers sit in a disheveled mess on her desk, where it's completely impossible to differentiate between what's junk and real. I try to sort through to make any sense of them, but they tumble, and a monsoon of bills falls to the floor.

I grab a loose piece of paper from my feet where two large words printed over the rest in bright red stand out against the wooden floor: **Past due.** I pull another envelope from the mess that reads the same. Red notices cut diagonally across the pages. Envelopes crunch when I slide the chair back under. There is barely any space with all the piles of envelopes. I gather them up an armful at a time and drop them back onto the desk. The internet? **Past due.** The electric bill? **Past due.** The vendors? **Past due.** The company credit? **Past due.** The mortgage? **Past due, past due, past due.**

You won't be able to hold on to this place much longer.

This is what Becky with the Good Paper meant. "Past due" is about to be more than a letter my aunt ignores. We won't have a choice but to take the offer. I do the math. Once we pay off Jo's debts, we would end up with just more than nothing. My heart starts to pound, fast and deep, against my rib cage. The hammering reaches my skull to remind me that here I am, seventeen, about to get thrown out of the only home I have ever known because my grown-up had to grow up right beside me. The sound is so loud the walls shake. Jo's skeletons doing their best to break free from inside the shop, the coffin she built for us. What's the difference between skeletons and real estate developers anyway? I gather Jo's lies and carry them back to the front, where they fit in my bag, now empty without the stolen graveyard flowers. Then I sit on her stool and wait.

Quiet shops are bad luck, and since Bidi walked out, the Bahia Padaria has been frozen in time. Quiet as if there hasn't been a word said for years since Jo's lies stared at me from the floor. Bidi may hate me for it, but selling the shop is the only way to have enough money to get Jo out of her mess and me away from here. Because if there is one thing my mother taught me, it's that if you keep moving, you don't have to answer for what you've done.

I begin to roam the aisles and jog down each one to check for missing items I can restock as unease starts to settle. Jo says in Brazil, padarias are loud. They are meant to be cramped and spilled on and smeared, no matter how often you clean them. They creak, and they belly laugh, and they sizzle. *A quiet shop is a bad-luck shop,* I think as I gather the flowers I had sitting in the back and make my way to the front.

Roses and tulips—nothing could make for a worse combo, but perhaps it's still salvageable if I use the bird-of-paradise leaves as well. I make braided, waxy green ropes for a base, then a crown wall with pockets for the tulips and roses, so all that peeks out are bursts of yellow and white. There might as well be beauty if it's going to be so quiet.

Bang.

The front door announces Jo, who steps inside smelling like she swam in a distillery.

"What are you looking at? You think I don't see you for the spoiled, ungrateful girl you are?"

Jo points to the spot where the real estate lady stood. She makes the walls shake as she storms to her office and returns moments later with a bottle of cachaça cradled in her arms. From afar, someone might think she had an infant bundled close.

"I'd say your mother would be disappointed in you, but she invented disloyalty, ah!" Jo grabs at her chest with one hand. She stops walking and grips the alcohol bottle tight with the other.

Jo says there is this twin connection. She's had it for as long as she can remember. Her and Mamãe both do, supposedly. She still feels Mamãe occasionally—that's why she believes she's still out there. It's not telepathic, just a feeling, one she knows isn't hers as soon as it comes on. Jo says sometimes it is a burst of joy or warmth, but mostly, a strike of lightning in her chest. "Sofia," she whispers.

Once Jo has recovered her senses, she throws one more jab my way.

"You will never know what it means to have to rebuild your life brick by brick, garotinha. You are not my baby; this is. They cannot rip this from me; they cannot take my home," Jo snarls. She unscrews the top of the bottle for a quick sip.

It's a sickness, I know. I know, I know.

But if she gets to be sick, I get to be angry. That is a sickness too.

"If we lose this place, it will be because of you! Lock the door!" I shout. The bell rings as she walks back outside before I can throw the proof in her face. Better to wait; she's not in a state to have a real conversation.

Jo keeps a mini TV from the '90s on the counter to watch her telenovelas when the shop is slow. The screen crackles on when I turn the knob for some background noise, an episode of *Avenida Brasil* filling the air. No need to tempt any more silence in this place.

I kill the fluorescent lights and walk to my corner to pull the crate from where it is pressed against the wall and slide open the loose panel where I keep my secret things. A stack of Post-its beside pencils I chewed on, now riddled with teeth marks. Indents of my anxieties and hopes. Once I've collected it all, I replace the panel so it is flush with the rest of the wall and slide my crate back in front.

When I was little, before Jo gave up, we had good weeks. She took over a corner store and morphed it into the Padaria. Sometimes, she would wake me with cinnamon-sugar toast on stale, unsold bread she brought home after her shift. As the butter was bubbling under my nose, she'd say, "Está na hora de falar com a lua." It is time to talk to the moon. She would hand me a flower and a pencil with a Post-it. She'd ask my wish, tell me to write something I wanted, and then we would walk until we found soil. Jo would remind me not to waste my wish on my mother. "Why would she come back for something she threw away?" she'd say. But I never listened.

Too bad Jo's not here. I'm finally making a new wish.

The store provides me with what I need for the ceremony. The letter to buy the shop rests on the floor surrounded by tea lights to make up for the lack of the moon. I close my eyes.

"Please, let Jo take the offer."

Maybe Bidi is right. Maybe I am a sellout.

Maybe I am no different than Mamãe. I often dream about making an escape. I imagine myself with her, chewing on sugarcane in Brazil, on the beach in Rio. Her teeth are pearls against her skin, brown like the eye of a sunflower. Brown like everything beautiful mashed together. I close my eyes, and I am anywhere but here, kneeling on the floor, praying to a Post-it. I wish for Jo to take this deal knowing it won't fix everything. Once we accept, I will still be her problem, but that's how it's always going to be. Mamãe is the only one who truly knows how to get away.

Ding.

The bell on the door rings, and footsteps interrupt my bootleg intention ceremony. Jo didn't lock the door. I'd curse her house if it weren't mine too, for now, at least. The footsteps move fast.

"We're closed!" I rush out to the front just as a long black hooded coat flies out and the bell on the door dings, announcing the figure's swift exit.

"It's looking blustery tomorrow, Phil."

I face the local San Francisco news anchor on the mini-TV. But when I turned it on, Alexandre was professing his love to his ex-girlfriend's mother, Teresa. This is a whole other channel.

"Unexpected cold winds will be sweeping down from the Napa Valley. East Bay will be getting the majority of the chill, so don't be surprised if you need that extra layer, especially in the evening."

"You heard it here first, folks—it's sweatah weathah."

Bidi would roll her eyes at their terrible vintage *SNL* impression if she were still here. The anchor bends down and holds her earpiece to focus on whatever incoming message is being relayed internally. The Emergency Alert System logo flashes across the screen.

"All right, it looks like we have to switch gears here. We've got an important emergency announcement. Correspondent Martina Abreu has the story."

The reporter is stationed before the mess of a garden I stood in front of this morning. I freeze.

"Yes, thank you, Phil. We are here at the Aubergine estate, where police are gathering to investigate the disappearance of teen socialite Estella Aubergine."

Estella's face fills the screen. Perfect white teeth, deep brown skin. The photos of her full, rich life take over. Her viral fashion posts interspersed with the many honors and accolades she's received, but the message the correspondent reads behind the images falls to the floor like a sack of marbles. Some words are lost in the impact.

"Estella Aubergine is missing . . ."

"Mother's worst nightmare . . ."

"Impressive young woman . . ."

Martina Abreu reappears on the screen. A silky chin-length bob frames her face; her hair is thick and black, stark against the ten-foot-high wisteria behind her. From the angle of the camera operator, the flowers look like tarantulas poised to clamp their pinchers around her neck.

"We can confirm Estella exited the premises early this morning. Security footage shows an unmarked black SUV driving by and sitting idle for approximately nine seconds before driving away. After which, Estella is not seen again."

They play the footage along with the narration. If the camera tilted twenty degrees, they'd see me dive into a bush and then pop back out to do nothing as she disappears. Dread seeps from my every pore.

Martina Abreu splits the screen with the now-frozen security footage.

"Anyone with information regarding this vehicle should contact SFPD. Estella is a black female. She is seventeen years old and five feet two. She has a unique birthmark in the shape of a crescent moon encasing her left eye."

Ding.

Jerrod from down the block walks through the door, and other people stream in after him. They come in all at once, asking for pão de queijo, plastic spoons, and change for a fifty. So much for being closed.

"If you see or think of anything related to Estella's disappearance, please use the hotline number below. A reward of two hundred and fifty thousand dollars is being offered for information that leads to her recovery."

"Damn, that's a lot," Jerrod says, laying cheese and bread and relish on the counter for me to ring up. The guilt I felt moments ago fades away.

"It sure is," I confirm to Jerrod, and hand him his change.

Maybe even enough to save the store.

Ding.

Ding.

Ding.

People keep coming in and crowding the space so much I can't think straight. But that is exactly how Jo designed the shop, as a place that always has everything you need: cherries bobbing in syrup, an Easter-themed tablecloth, the scratch-off that's gonna change everything, the coldest water you can find, and perhaps an opportunity worth more than I could ever imagine.

"Yo, P?" Jerrod pokes his head back inside the doorway.

I look over the evening customers at the counter, one man hunched over while trying to find the channel for the Giants game. "Yeah, what's up, Jerrod? I'm a little busy."

"You dropped one of your flowers."

A flash of purple arches over his head as he waves the giant mandrake from the morning back and forth. My blood freezes solid.

"Where did you get that?" I ask.

"It was out here." Jerrod points to the street in front of the store. He brings the flower to the counter before leaving.

The petals have wilted since I saw it still attached to its lifeline this morning, but the purple remains vibrant and magnificent, nonetheless. The security camera might not have caught me at the estate this morning, but whoever left this knows I was there, and they want me to know they know. They want me to know that they have been here, to my home. That black hoodie who got out of the car just walked out my front door and left this. They probably even changed the channel on the TV to the news report.

"EVERYONE OUT!" I scream into the shop.

My customers shuffle out, grumbling that they weren't finished. After the last person leaves, I grab the glass jar of garlic Bidi left on the counter earlier and lock the door to the store behind me.

The smell of dinner wafts from Bidi's windows. Nose drunk off her mother's cooking, I almost forget the mess I am in.

"'Scuse me—"

A duffel bag knocks me in the side and back to the moment. The jar of garlic hops between my hands—I barely catch it.

"Hey!" I shout.

A giraffe with eyelashes and cheekbones that curl up to pray to the sky stares down at me. His headphones are loud enough I can hear the treble even before he pulls one off to speak. The sounds vibrate off his smooth dark brown skin.

"My bad." His voice is low and gravelly like raked, raw soil littered with pebbles and rocks. The door swings open before I have time to ask what he is doing. He steps inside and into Malika's arms.

"Pippa! Is that you? Bidi didn't mention you were coming over!"

Malika releases the tall man and pulls me in.

"Pippa?" Bidi stands behind her mother, confused.

"Come, let me make you a plate." Malika urges me toward the table. She never knows how many people are going to be over for dinner, and yet somehow, she always makes enough.

"Oh, Malika, thank you. It smells delicious, but I'm not, I mean, I can't—I just needed to talk to Bidi. She, um, she left this."

I hold up the garlic. Malika takes the jar and replaces it with a plate.

If there is one thing you aren't going to do in this house, it's tell Malika Thomas what can and can't happen in her kitchen.

I help myself to everything and then head to the small table where the giraffe boy sits, scraping the sauce with the edge of his fork.

Bidi makes herself a plate and sits between us. I can tell she is still annoyed about the offer for the shop. Bidi doesn't want to accept that eventually things are going to change between us. She rejects the idea that everyone won't just fall in line with her vision for the future. Us here forever. Bidi truly does want to save our city. I think she will, if she ever figures out how not to take everything so personally, and right now, she needs to get over it and simply listen to me.

I switch gears, distract, and then engage.

"Who is that?" I whisper, and nod to the tall guy, who rises and walks over to the stove for seconds.

"Mo." Bidi picks up a chicken leg and takes a bite.

"Mo? That is not Mo." I bite my bottom lip to keep my jaw from dropping down to my chest when he looks back at me. He used to stay over at Bidi's all the time, but back then, he was hiding under long greasy hair and swimming in sweatshirts, not towering above us with muscles rippling under his tee. "Are you sure that's Mo?!" I repeat louder than I intended.

"I'm pretty sure I'm me?" he responds.

Amusement sits on his tongue as he breaks open a wing and sticks the flat into his mouth for a single, clean bite.

Mo looks me up and down. "Have we met?"

His words sear across my cheeks. Of course we've met. Bidi's older cousins used to torture Mo. I would sneak him into the coat closet sometimes for a break. I let him cry on my shoulder.

I can't believe I felt sorry for him then. Now I'm sorry I didn't give him up and let them dunk his head in the toilet. I used to think he had a crush on me, the way his eyes would linger when I walked across the room but maybe I was wrong. It was silly to think anyone other than Bidi could see anything but an annoyance or a burden in me. "Where have you been?" I ask.

Bidi scoops up her rice with the drippings from the chicken, fallen soldiers drowning in a pool of gravy.

"He's been at Beaumont avoiding us because we aren't good enough," Bidi says.

Mo rises with a huff and walks down the stairs.

"He's sleeping downstairs?!" I shout.

"Yes," Bidi spits.

"You are supposed to get downstairs. This is outrageous!"

"Thank you!" She throws her hands up in gratitude. I seize the moment between us and run with it.

"Bidi, listen, I really have to talk to you."

She shakes her head and rises. "Pippa, can I have what is left of this one day to only worry about myself? I lost the internships and my room. I need to find something quick before I get stuck watching Caroline full-time this summer!"

Bidi mutters to herself as she storms over to the counter to do the dishes. The failure to secure a summer position is causing her to malfunction. Malika rushes back into the room in freshly pressed scrubs. She takes me into her arms and squeezes, then speaks over my body to Bidi.

"Bidi, make sure Mo gets a blanket and a towel. You know the schedule for tomorrow?"

"Yes, Mommy," Bidi says. I catch her eye for acknowledgment. Bidi made the schedule.

"Oh, and you two, be careful. I don't care if you are fighting or what; you walk together. A girl just got taken."

Malika blows coconut-scented kisses to us both before she walks out, headed back to the hospital.

"Have you seen the story? The one your mom is talking about?" I ask Bidi. She wants to hear what I have to say; she just doesn't know it yet.

"I got the Amber Alert—" Bidi says.

"I was there," I interrupt Bidi.

"You were . . . where?" Mo says from behind us. He holds a giant bag of Lay's and throws a few into his mouth.

"At Estella's house," I say to Bidi.

"What are you talking about? You were at the cemetery, Pippa, remember? We were on the phone."

Bidi holds the back of her hand against my cheek the way Malika does when the kids say they feel sick.

"Do you see spots? Does your tongue feel heavy? Are you experiencing a headache?"

"What? Bidi, no. I'm not having a stroke; please listen. After we got off the phone, I saw this messy garden and this gorgeous purple mandrake—"

"None of this sounds normal . . ." Mo cuts in again.

"Who asked you?" I snap.

"Seriously," Bidi backs me up.

We conjure enough force in our glares that Mo shuts his mouth and slips his oversized headphones over his ears rather than taking us both on.

"Just listen to me, Bidi! I wanted that flower, the mandrake, so I was reaching up to get it when Estella Aubergine walked out of the house. So, I hid in a bush and then that car they showed on the news came around the corner, and it stopped and someone got out and Estella started to argue with them and I stood up and she saw me and then . . . she was gone."

CHAPTER 4

Bidi

I should just sign up for the fire rangers because all I seem to be drawn to is flames. Everywhere I turn, there is another blaze to put out. But for once, whatever mess Pippa has made or plans to make can't be my problem. My problem is my future, one I won't have if I don't get this summer under control. I need to find something revolutionary to accomplish and I am simply unavailable for anything else. Period.

I walk over to the sink, where somehow even more dishes have accumulated, and I need to finish them before I can get back to me.

"For real, Bidi, there's a reward—"

Here it comes. The big idea. The thing that will be self-sabotage if I don't step in and stop her. But like I said, I am unavailable, especially if Pippa's going to pick up and leave the second she gets the chance. I know what I saw in that store with that real estate woman, and it wasn't just Pippa dreaming.

"Bidi! If *we* find her . . ."

"Pippa."

I say her name like the curse that it is, but she doesn't stop.

"Don't you see the signs? I was there the same moment Estella got taken! Bidi, come on!"

"Why were you outside Estella's house at five-forty-five in the morning?" Mo reenters the room, not minding his own business.

This kid ghosts me last year, and all of a sudden, he's my roommate and a spectator.

I ignore him and try to reason with Pippa. "Was she in distress?"

"It's hard to say because I was in that boxwood bush and the leaves are actually quite dense because the boxwood is one of those plants that can thrive in partial sun or shade, plus the angle wasn't great. But I felt like she was looking at me even before the car came. I stood up to get a better look, to make sure she was okay, and she froze. It was like her eyes got trapped in mine for a second."

"And how did she seem? Scared?" I ask.

"Nope. She didn't scream for help or fight back . . ." Pippa says.

"Sounds to me like she was yelling at an underpaid Uber driver for making her late to wherever she was running off to . . ."

"Bidi! The security tapes missed me. It's like the universe is telling me to do this! To find her! *If* she ran away, even better, right? Less trauma than a kidnapping. A happy ending!"

Mo snorts.

"You need to worry about cleaning these dishes and stop listening to our conversation." I throw the wet sponge at him and we walk into the living room.

"Bidi, if we find her, we'll be heroes. Plus, this solves your issue! The case is something *you* can sink your teeth into. Don't you see? You don't need an internship, not if you find Estella. You want to be in local government? You want to help the neighborhood? You do this, you have clout." Pippa's arm flies around the air.

Mommy always says, "You can't argue with fantasy." Pippa isn't operating in the real world; she's on a different planet. People go missing and never get found. Pippa should know that better than anyone.

"We're losing the shop."

Pippa's whisper hits like a stone.

"What do you mean?" I ask.

"Jo is behind on everything. The bills, the mortgage. I didn't know until today. Either we take that offer or—"

"We do this?" I finish her sentence.

Pippa's head bobs as slowly as the last ice cube in a room-temperature Coke. Maybe I was wrong; maybe she doesn't want to leave. But even if she wants to stay, this plan ain't it.

"Estella's already got an Amber Alert, Pippa. She's probably already been found!"

"I set a Google Alert, and she definitely hasn't been yet!" Pippa exclaims.

"Well, what if she doesn't want to be found?" I ask.

"That's a 'her' problem! Bidi, you can take your portion of the reward and help the community. Nobody's saying you have to keep it for yourself if you don't want to but think about it! You do this, you have at LEAST local attention, if not coastal recognition," Pippa spouts.

My chest fills with oxygen as I take a five-second deep breath. Pippa isn't proposing this because it's a good idea for me. She's not considering what will happen if I waste my summer on a completely ridiculous idea.

"There are one million reasons why you can't do this, Pippa."

"I know I can't do it alone, but *we* can. Bidi, come on. Jo dug a hole so deep, even the sale is barely going to keep us going. You keep saying you want to make some real change. This is how we do it."

Pippa waits for me to say thank you for showing me the light. Instead, I shake my head no. Her hands fly up to her hips.

"Okay, Miss Save the World, how is helping a missing promising young Black woman not a good thing?"

"Because she doesn't need our help, Pippa. She's rich. They gave her airtime. In addition to the police, every amateur investigator and true crime enthusiast in the Western Hemisphere is probably looking for her. Meanwhile, how many girls from around here have disappeared? They turn into gossip on the corner until they are forgotten entirely."

"Bidi?" Pippa's plea is dipped in gold flecks of desperation.

Pippa's trauma response is to add chaos onto chaos. I have seen GoFundMes for cat anxiety meds. There are other ways to save the shop. More realistic ways. She just needs to sit in the fantasy until the excitement wears off. By tomorrow, I'll have a plan. Multiple plans. I simply need a moment to figure it all out.

"Pippa, give me tonight, all right? Promise me you will drop this for just tonight."

"But—"

"Promise me, Pippa."

She pouts, and I half expect her to fall into a tantrum, but she slowly sucks her lip back in.

"I promise," she concedes.

I hold the door open for Pippa and wait for her to shuffle her way out.

"Text me when you get home," I call out as she slowly walks to the curb.

A red-and-blue crochet blanket lands on Mo's lap, where his laptop is positioned on the couch downstairs. I cozy up in the recliner and turn on the TV.

"What are you doing?" He looks at me, confused.

The bottom floor is set up like a den, but there's a nook for a bed and a full bathroom. I already mapped out how I was going to organize the campaign corner.

"Oh, you thought you were getting a private suite? Nuh-uh, this is communal territory until it is returned to its rightful owner," I explain.

Mo spreads out, staking his claim. He's so long, the couch becomes more of a love seat. "So . . . why are you here?" I ask.

Mo shifts, like he wasn't prepared for an interrogation.

"My mom got a job for the summer out of town, and it didn't make sense to keep paying rent in that dump we've been in, and your mom said it was okay for me to stay . . ."

He thinks he can answer without answering the real question.

"Where have you been, Maurice?" I clarify.

"You know where I have been—at Beaumont," he answers matter-of-factly.

"Aren't you supposed to be some kind of genius? You need me to spell it out? Where have you been in my life? You practically lived here, and then you went to that school and didn't call. You left me on read for a year."

Mo runs his hands through his hair and twists his neck. "I, uh, yeah, I figured you wouldn't—"

"What? You thought I wouldn't be able to keep up, because I go to the same local public school our parents did? You and Pippa. Both of you are so obsessed with money and status. Those people will never be your people; you know that, right?"

"Yo. Chill, Bidi. You don't know what you are talking about."

He thinks I can't see he's been brainwashed by his rich, spoiled new friends and wants to spend the summer hanging out and living his best rent-free life.

"Anyway, what is your plan this summer?" I get down to business.

"I mean, I'm working on something," he responds, aloof.

"Well, I need help with Caroline while you are here."

Mo rearranges pillows, and he shimmies his shoulders on the way down, really cozying in. "I'm not sure about that. Besides, I heard your mother say that was your job."

The rage bubbles out of me. "Well, you heard wrong. I am busy—"

"With the internships you didn't get?" Mo burns me with the question.

"No! I'm working on my campaign—"

Mo shrugs. "It's not my fault you let yourself get wound up so tight in everything else that you lost sight of your actual goals. I get you have a lot to take on, but you also do way more than you have to. Sometimes you gotta go for what you want, Bidi, even if that means inconveniencing everyone else. I worked hard to get into Beaumont. I'm not apologizing to you for that and I'm not available to do your little babysitters' club."

My head explodes. Brain bits rain down on both of us, littering the rug. This is the clown I used to find hiding in the back of the coat closet with Pippa. The one who let me trick him into telling me where he kept his Halloween stash to steal and sell back to him after I had eaten all the Nerds and Skittles and Peppermint Patties.

"I'm not asking. You will help with Caroline, or you are out of here," I talk through my teeth.

"Yeah, yeah, we all get it, Bidi. You like to be in control, and you push people away the second you realize you don't hold the reins," Mo taunts.

"That is *not* true!"

"Isn't Pippa your best friend? Y'all have always been inseparable, and you practically threw her out."

"I thought you didn't remember her?" I snap.

"Of course I do, and she's still as self-righteous as she's always been." Mo's eyes fall for the first time since he picked this fight. "Anyway, people like you think making a mistake means the end of the world. All that happens is you pick yourself up and keep going."

Everyone is allowed to make mistakes; everyone but me. I'm the one who keeps the peace, who follows the rules. I watch the kids, I help the neighbors, I save Pippa. I fill in the gaps Mommy can't get to. I'm the one everyone expects to have the answers. But without something noteworthy to do this summer, I will have no legs to stand on in a public campaign for office. No connections on the inside who will support me, the youngest candidate in history.

Finding a missing rich girl might help with that.

Pippa's voice interrupts my thoughts, and my teeth grind because for once she really is not wrong, but she's still a liability. The likelihood of finding Estella is practically zero, but maybe Mo and Pippa have a point. Maybe taking the safe route isn't what I need anymore. Maybe it is finally my turn to take a risk. Plus, I need to come up with a plan for Pippa and the shop, which means I have to rule her idea out before I can come up with a new one.

"What's Estella like?" I ask Mo.

"Oh, now you too? Listen, Bidi, Pippa has no clue what she's talking about with her little idea to find Miss Perfect." I taste the venom in his voice from across the room.

"What, did you date her or something?" I push back because his reaction sounded personal.

"Do you live under a rock? Estella Aubergine dates girls. Powerful, snarky, bossy girls." He pauses to give me a once-over. "You'd be her type, actually."

"So you do know her?" I ask.

"Everyone knows Estella; don't bother." Mo snaps his headphones over his ears.

Mo's pushback nags at me even more than Pippa did. Against my better judgment, I pull my phone out and type Estella's name into the search bar because nothing makes me want to do something more than a boy telling me not to.

CHAPTER 5

Pippa

My bedroom windows showcase the gray outside, the way the San Francisco sky likes to be at this hour of the morning. I check the clock—5:24 a.m., another night of no sleep, but I made something of it. The Polaroid shoots out a photograph of the flower sculpture I built, a cornucopia with loose petals cascading out.

I stick the photo to the wall beside the rest of my creations. It took years to build and photograph enough sculptures and crowns to paste to every inch of my space. In person, they rot and dry; they fall apart in days. That is what I love, the impermanence, the tease of it all. I don't want anyone else to keep them. Which is why I don't put them on social media. In the end, I am the only one who gets to live with what I have made. I take the mandrake left for me last night and pin it on the wall as well. The petals are wilted enough that when I position it vertically, they hang down and almost look like a rib cage.

I prop up the pillows on my bed and rearrange my body to sit upright. Bidi barely let me get a word in last night, and I forgot to mention the hooded stalker who left the floral warning on my doorstep. I promised her I would drop the idea of finding Estella for the night, and I did, but now it's a new day.

The only way for me to get anything done is to empty my brain of the million thoughts constantly swirling around. My fingers type rapidly into Google.

> What does bankruptcy mean? *(Not good.)*
>
> How long does it take to be evicted? *(Depends.)*
>
> How do you make someone love you? *(You can't.)*
>
> Can you get a loan from a bank if you are under eighteen years old? (*With a guardian with good credit signing off. So, no.)*
>
> How can you tell the difference between someone who is missing and someone who doesn't want to be found?

I search every question I can think of; then I type in her name: Estella Aubergine.

Estella is practically a household name in the Bay. It's hard not to know everything about her; she's everywhere you turn. TikTok fit checks and cross-influencer posts with reality TV stars and young models. She's at every event and restaurant in the city. Always glossy-faced, charming her followers. Witty, gorgeous. The perfection is all quite boring until you realize the story—her fame—all starts with her. She's rich in cash, but her social capital is lacking.

What we know is that Estella lives with her mother, Amelia Aubergine. The first record of Amelia in the Bay Area is from seventeen years ago, right after Estella was born. Ms. Aubergine appeared one day in San Francisco with her child, but from where? We know only that the purchase of their home was the largest cash deal in the city at the time. You can scour the internet up and down, and Ms. Aubergine does not exist prior to that sale, and since then, she has rarely been seen outside the property.

She was in the press some when she first came into the city. There have been all sorts of rumors and conspiracy theories about her, the lady behind the gate. Some think she is a Russian spy sent to keep tabs on the burgeoning tech hub of the US. Some think she could be some nobody from nowhere who got lucky with the lotto and decided to give herself a brand-new identity. In the end, it doesn't matter who she really is. As soon as Ms. Aubergine loosened her grip on Estella, no one cared about her anymore. They took hold of their it girl.

Unlike her mother, Estella doesn't hide from anyone. From what I've read, she seems to get high off the cameras. Ms. Aubergine still keeps a low profile. She's got no social media presence. Her feet are so rooted down in her estate, she couldn't go elsewhere even if she tried.

There is a photo of the mother-daughter duo at the bottom of one of the articles. Ms. Aubergine and Estella don't share much in appearance—opposites, really. Ms. Aubergine is tall. She is white, pale, and lanky. Her deep auburn hair is untamed, but she is otherwise muted. Estella is short, thick, with strong curves. She has flawless dark brown skin and a light birthmark around her eye. Estella's diamond-shaped face blooms from under her curly bangs.

My mamãe is the shade of brown you see when a shadow comes across the trunk of a redwood tree. Her fraternal twin sister, my Tia Jo, looks more like me, sucked dry of melanin and left a pale yellow. It's nice to see a family like mine. Just because you don't match doesn't mean anything.

Ms. Aubergine's and Estella's eyes, however, bear resemblance to each other. Not the shape or color—what they share is the gaze. Whether they are forcing a smile or straight-faced, there is a crackle behind their pupils, a warning. The thing you get from your mother when she sticks around to give it to you.

My phone buzzes: **Shift.**

The clock reads 8:30 a.m. I got sucked into Estella's world for hours. Hopefully that study session was enough for me to get started. I just need proof of concept to get Bidi on board. Something she can't deny. Coffee brews in the kitchen, and I stack the piles of unpaid bills in three towers for Jo to see when she stumbles back home from wherever she ended up. The crumpled offer letter for the shop sits beside them. A message to tell her that I know what's going on and we need to talk later.

I make myself breakfast in the store before I open. One fried egg, one slice of fried salami, avocado, lettuce, tomato, onion sliced thin enough to see straight through, on a Portuguese roll, toasted and buttered. The mini TV is still set to the local news when I turn it on. Midrate anchors chat about a Little League baseball team that hasn't won in ten years but is now set to win the championships. The mood shifts when Estella's face fills the screen. The man shakes his head as he reads the prompter.

"Still no news regarding the missing person investigation for

Estella Aubergine. Sources tell us the SFPD worked around the clock to make headway."

The anchor holds a finger to his ear mid-sentence. He listens and looks back at the camera.

"We're getting word that Estella's mother is going to join us from her home."

The screen shifts to a press conference outside the estate. On the screen, Amelia Aubergine's face is all sharp angles; her blush and lips are slightly too sharp for the shade she chose. She looks small. Not small, but frail. Not frail, but light, light and fading like a photo that's been facing the sun. Not bleached, but drained. In need of a good night's sleep, maybe two, and a meal, something warm. A bowl of feijoada with white rice and shredded greens and a nice, sweet orange slice.

"I am not sure exactly what to say—"

Her voice is full of air, barely loud enough to carry through the cameras and screens. She looks into the camera. Her eyes pierce me.

"I want whoever is with my girl to know I will not stop searching for her."

The threat steadies her, emboldened; the love behind her rage fills her cheeks with color.

"And Stella, honey, I want you to know that I'm here. I'm here where I've always been, and I'm not going anywhere. Anyone who has any information about where my daughter is, please, come forward."

For one second, I am listening to my mother say the things I have always needed to hear. I feel the way I imagine it might feel to have someone like Ms. Aubergine wonder how I was when we were apart. I may never know, but maybe I can save her from my same fate. Ms. Aubergine chokes on her sadness.

"I'll see you soon, my Stella."

She walks off-screen, and we return to the studio, where the anchor faces the camera.

"Estella is thought to be wearing a custom piece of jewelry: a gold peony pendant embellished with pink diamonds."

An image of the custom jewelry takes over the screen. That alone could save this dump.

"Estella is a rising senior at Beaumont Academy, the most prestigious school in San Francisco."

Beaumont. The idea hits me so hard I drop my phone. It's summer, but I bet there's a janitor or something who can let me in. Bidi may think I can't do this, but maybe it's time I remember I am my mother's daughter. I know how to disappear too. Behind the pulse on the other side of my lashes, inside my chest, on the side of my thumb. Beating like my footsteps, heavy like the sheet rain. Hungry, like quicksand. Hardened, like a secret. I lock up the store before it opens and keep my back to the heavy sighs. To the impatient feet. To the grumbling tongues. And I run.

Then

What Happened Before

When Melissa finally reached room twenty-six at the hostel, she was ready to pass out for days, but the door swung open to reveal a bunk bed and a young woman around the same age as her, leaning against the window frame. A heliotrope reaching for the sun.

"Sorry, I think this is supposed to be a private room," Melissa said to the unexpected houseguest.

"There are no private rooms; you got scammed." The woman laughed.

Melissa started to head downstairs to the office to figure out the issue immediately. The woman jumped up and tried to block her.

"Hey! You won't get your money back. Plus, most hostels put three to a room and have communal washrooms. At least we've got a private one." Her roommate's finger pointed to a metal toilet behind a half-open shower curtain in the far corner. Suspicion gouged Melissa's gut.

"Why do you want me to stay so badly? I could be a murderer!" Melissa asked.

The stranger looked back at Melissa, mischief spread across her face with each bat of her eyelids.

"They keep sticking me with creeps, so I'll take a 'maybe murderer' for a change."

Everything until this moment had been predetermined for Melissa. This was her first decision out on her own. A stranger in a strange place trusting another stranger, or not. Melissa couldn't place the accent on this woman, but neither of them was a local. They were two loose seeds hoping to take root. *This is a chance,* she thought. Why did she leave her home and come here if not to take a chance? The woman reached out her hand to take her luggage, and Melissa let her. She placed the suitcase in the corner of the room and turned back to Melissa.

"Do you want to eat?" she asked. "I'm always hungry after I travel. If you still want to leave after, I can try to help you get some of your money back. No promises, though."

Melissa hadn't known she was hungry until the word unlocked a pang in her belly.

"Yeah, sure," Melissa said, and followed the woman into the hallway, down the stairs, and out the front door.

"Restaurant" was a generous title, as the whole space was nothing more than two tables, a few scattered stools, and a cook in a galley kitchen who moved so quickly, the food appeared as if by magic. Melissa could barely breathe, let alone chat as plates rained down onto the table before them. They fell into a rhythm with their forks until finally there was a lull and one of them had to take the leap. Melissa stared at the woman and contemplated her proposal to stay with her in that hostel.

"I don't think you ever told me your name," Melissa said to the woman.

"I could say the same about you," the woman said, "but you know what? I came here to be something different. I think we should choose new names. Don't you?"

"Mm . . . right now?" Melissa asked. The stranger nodded excitedly.

Melissa wasn't the name of an adventurer. She searched her brain for a name that would feel familiar enough to be hers and different enough to be worth it. There had once been a tutor, a young woman finishing her degree who always brought her little gifts and candies. She'd given her a nickname.

"Missy." Melissa tried it out and found she quite liked the new flavor on her tongue.

"Great. So, Missy. Why did you come here?" the stranger asked her.

"Hmm?" Missy was caught off guard.

"No one ends up at that hostel without a reason, so what is it?" the woman urged. Missy froze. No one had ever been interested in her interests, only in what she had to offer—Missy stopped herself. She couldn't reveal too much. She was not here to look backward. She was here to start over, whatever that meant.

"I don't know," Missy answered finally.

"That's no way to live!"

The chef banged some ladles in the kitchen. A warning to quiet down.

"It's the only way I know how," Missy whispered.

"Let me show you another way. Stay at the hostel with me."

Missy had given herself a second chance.

Friends never seemed to work out for Missy—jealousy had always gotten in the way. But that wouldn't happen with this woman. She'd make sure of it.

"Wait! You never told me your name," Missy reminded the woman.

"Wrong. *You* never told me my name. You pick." She dropped some cash on the table.

Missy had never met anyone like her.

"I trust you. Just look at me and decide who I am," the woman urged Missy.

The name of the tutor who'd call her Missy when she was young popped into her head.

"Amelia," Missy heard herself say.

"I like it. Nice to meet you, Missy," Amelia said.

Missy felt a pull so strong she couldn't tell if it was their will or the wind boosting them into their future. The walk back to the hostel took over an hour because they went in circles, planning. By the time they finally made it back, they had the road map to start a life. Within two weeks, the young women secured jobs cleaning the lobby of a building in exchange for a studio apartment.

They worked all morning, and then during their breaks in the afternoon, they walked over to the botanical gardens to eat their lunch. In quiet moments, Missy would sometimes remember her old world. She would wonder what her parents would do if they knew their daughter was mopping floors to make rent, but then Amelia would bust through the door with her wild laugh and pull Missy into an adventure, and Missy would realize that she had all she needed. A friend. A home. She had taken a chance, and she had chosen right.

Teen Vogue Intern Spotlight: Estella Aubergine Transcript

Estella Aubergine hails from the San Francisco Bay Area. She holds various highly esteemed roles, such as class copresident and debate club captain, at the prestigious Beaumont Academy. Estella volunteers with Alzheimer's patients around the state. In her free time, Estella has cultivated over a quarter million social media followers, who tune in to her accounts for her bold and innovative fashion leaps and takes, which got the attention of designer Christian Siriano. He then invited her to walk in his show for New York Fashion Week. She also caught the eye of the editors here at *Teen Vogue* and landed herself a fashion internship.

TV: So let's get to know Estella Aubergine. Estella, what is your favorite bite of food?

Estella: I wish I could be mysterious and say it was too hard to choose or that I'm still hoping to find it, but there is this Thai restaurant in the Mission, Hawker Fare. They have this dish on the menu called the "chewy beef dish," it's got texture and spice and acid–that's my absolute favorite.

TV: You've sold me. I'll check them out.

Estella: You won't regret it.

TV: What does self-care look like for you?

Estella: Mmm, it depends, but a manicure and a long walk, maybe? I guess I would also say getting to know myself better. I think focusing on being the best, most authentic version of myself feels like the ultimate way to take care of myself these days. I am getting deeper into who I really am.

TV: We can't argue with that. What is the code word you would send in a text to let people know you had been taken?

Estella: Probably something about nature or camping—protect the earth but keep me out of her. Honestly, I think if I got taken, I'm either getting killed or abandoned by whoever took me. I'm not going to be texting; I'm going to be driving them mad.

TV: Is there a fashion trend right now you are really into?

Estella: I don't care what you wear, but just do it with intention. I walk down the street, and I am often distressed. Where are the risks? The color? Give me severe or beam me up to the planet where fashion still exists.

TV: What can we expect from you in the future? Do you have any senior-year plans?

Estella: I don't want to jinx anything, but I've got some big things planned.

TV: Well, we can't wait to cheer you on.

Now

CHAPTER 6

Pippa

The bus rattles away from the Bahia Padaria and the neighborhood toward Beaumont. It takes fifty-nine minutes to get from my world to Estella's, and along the way, we drive by houses drenched in purple and blue. Local historians say the original owners painted the houses bright colors to highlight the unique Edwardian architecture. I think San Francisco has always been extra, and these houses would've been purple no matter who designed them. We turn the corner at a lavender Victorian with gold detail on the moldings. Lavender bushes last a while without nourishment, rationing a single watering to survive, even through a drought. I could use some of that energy right now. *Lavender,* I pray, *become her.*

If Bidi were with me, there would be a plan in place, but she's not, and I'm going with my impulses. Beaumont is the type of school to hide secrets inside, and I am going to dig up Estella's. The bus screeches to a stop at the steps of Beaumont Academy.

A few dry leaves circle my feet like puppies, desperate for a hug. Their soft scratching against the cement is the only thing to be heard. Just as I hoped, no cruel girls and moody heartthrobs. There are no golden-eyed theater nerds singing a cappella in the courtyard. No cloud of marijuana smoke hanging low over skater boys on the steps. Just me walking up some stairs, like Beaumont is where I was meant to be all along.

"ID?" A guard I wasn't expecting holds his hand out on the other side of the front door.

"Mmm, like my state one . . . ?" I stall.

"School ID. The event is private." He bristles.

"Event . . . ?" My mouth moves ten steps before my brain. "Yes, of course, well, I forgot my ID. It's the summer, ya know . . ."

"Excuse me," a familiar voice interrupts from behind me. I turn to see the green sleeveless tee that shows off Mo's arm muscles. Not overdoing it, just teasing. It's a shame that such a specimen is attached to this insufferable soul. "Mo?"

"Mr. Mo." The guard reaches over me for a dap. Mo obliges.

"I think I misplaced my ID, Henry—"

"No problem, Mr. Mo."

"Now, Henry, I told you enough with the 'mister' stuff. Please," Mo says.

He steps around me and into the school. The guard rises and hands me a green visitor sticker.

"I didn't realize you were with Mr. Mo," Henry apologizes to me.

"No—no—" Mo starts to protest, but before he can tell Henry otherwise, I walk down the first hall I see. Mo chases me and cuts me off.

"What are you doing here?"

We say the same thing at the same time, and my cheeks get hot at the sound of our voices together. I pinch my palm.

"I'm not answering until you do." My arms cross over my chest to prevent my fast-beating heart from ripping a hole in my shirt.

Mo's eyes dart around to make sure no one is listening, and then leans close, his lips parting. His left front tooth is just slightly longer than the right; they shine bright white. "If you want to waste your summer on this ridiculous investigation, that's your business." He whispers so close, his lips tickle my ear.

I swat at him like the mosquito he is, but Mo catches my hand and pulls me closer. For a second, he seeps into me. His minty toothpaste and musky deodorant.

"Gross." I pull myself away.

"Why are you here? Did you steal my idea to find Est—"

Mo cuts me off. "You didn't invent the idea of finding a missing person, Pippa. But no, you seem to have forgotten that this is my school. Don't come messing around in my world."

"Or what?" I taunt.

He offers a smirk and turns back down the hallway. This new man smell of his stays behind.

A school like Beaumont is the status quo for most of the students who attend. But for someone like me, it could change the trajectory of my life. It did that for Mo. If I was in his shoes, I'd want to protect that too. I just wouldn't be such an ass about it. I walk in the opposite direction; no need to be around his stuck-up self anyway.

The royal-blue lockers line the off-white walls and complement the earth tones in the Spanish-tiled floor. Windows into closed classrooms reveal 3D printers and a robotics lab. An art studio with a darkroom and photography gallery. A music room boasts glistening horns and slick wooden guitars. The "money can't buy you happiness" crowd is in its flop era—this is even more amazing than I expected it to be. Our public high school is lucky if we get lightly used textbooks and a grant for an art class. I stop outside a door and stand beneath a plaque that reads DRUMMLE LIBRARY.

"Can I help you?" A woman in her late thirties with an eye patch over her left eye and a tight low bun stands. A box sags in her arms.

"Oh, uh—hi—" I stumble through the interaction.

"My coffee hasn't kicked in yet; look at my manners! I'm Ms. Magwitch, the interim librarian for the summer. I haven't met many students yet."

My school never even had a librarian, let alone a backup one for the summer.

"Do you think you could grab the door for me?" She nods to the handle and I open it for her.

Ms. Magwitch walks inside. She drops the box onto the counter and places her purse on top.

"Thanks! What was your name again?" she asks.

"Uhh, Pippa."

I probably shouldn't give my name to anyone in this building, but the interim librarian feels low risk.

"Be right back," Ms. Magwitch says, before she wheels away a half-full cart.

Even though this library is more pristine than any I've ever been to, they're all the same. Libraries always feel like aging gracefully or secrets hidden in the back of the closet. Soft fuzzy leather that hasn't been properly maintained. The consistency is refreshing. Libraries are something I can count on, places that know their place. Living records.

Jo used to deposit me at the library whenever she couldn't watch me on school breaks, or on holidays because she still had to work or when she said she needed a break because she couldn't take it—me—anymore. Libraries were practically my second home until Bidi and Malika started inviting me to spend all my time at their house instead.

I lift the purse from the top of the box Ms. Magwitch carried in and open the flaps. Beaumont yearbooks stare back at me. I slip one out and into my backpack. It can't hurt to get an insider look at the school.

A massive key chain falls from Ms. Magwitch's purse when I place it back on top of the box. One of the keys is twice the length of the others and made of a thick iron.

"That's the skeleton key. It opens every door in this whole building," Ms. Magwitch says from behind me.

"Sorry, I didn't mean—"

She steps closer as I hand the keys back to her.

"There is a faculty tradition for the key to be in our care. I guess no one thinks the librarian is going to cause any trouble." She laughs one of those high-pitched, singsong laughs that begins in the belly and bursts out. Ms. Magwitch's eye flits over her shoulder to her office door, which sits slightly ajar. She studies me, unsure if there is something more she needs to figure out.

"I should probably get going." I start to back away toward the door.

“It was nice to meet you, Pippa,” Ms. Magwitch says.

I nod. The carpet swallows my footsteps on the way to the door.

Libraries always sound the same. Like the moment just before an orchestra erupts, or the stillness in the trees before a bear rears back to unhinge its jaw and roar. The sea of silence that washes over me just before I fall asleep, unsure if I will be reunited with Mamãe in my dreams.

In the hallway, my shoes echo off the floor as the door clicks back into place. Thrust out of the quiet and into the rest of the world, I walk to the end of the hall and continue on.

CHAPTER 7

Bidi

"Where are you, Mo?" I shout into the phone. He wasn't on the couch when I woke up. Abandoned ship. More like dead man walking.

I try to even my breathing as I rush down the street toward the stairs of Beaumont Academy.

"I told you last night that I needed your help with Caroline. I got her a last-minute spot at the Y day camp, but she needs to be picked up at one-thirty p.m. My friends are working there this summer and are doing me a favor, so whatever you do, make sure you are there."

The Beaumont doors swing open once I hang up. I came to prove to myself that my gut instinct was right: that this mission was foolish, and I should be spending my energy elsewhere. Or maybe I came here with the hope that a clue to the mystery of the missing rich brat would fall out of the sky and save us all. The electric rush at the idea makes me dizzy. This is why I don't dream; the highs are high, and the lows knock you off a cliff.

The ID that I snuck from Mo's backpack while he was sleeping slips out of my pocket. I wave it in front of the guard as I walk in. My thumb covers the face and name, but all he looks for is the school crest.

After a Google crash course in Estella Aubergine last night, I uncovered that two things can be true. For example, Estella Aubergine is the most beautiful person to ever walk the earth, *and* she seems like the worst kind of trouble, worse than Pippa. She's too perfect, too pristine. Exactly like this school, shiny and beautiful, the image of what has been hammered into my head my whole life about what I'm supposed to aspire to.

Beaumont exists to remind me of what I can't have and what I don't deserve. But these people don't know what I've already got. They don't see the back door to the supermarket in the neighborhood where clerks hand out misshapen pastries first thing in the morning. They don't see the barbershops handing out free fades and trims to any kid who brings in their report card in the spring and again in the summer. They don't understand that for those of us whose bloodline built this city, the upward mobility takes a bleach pen to our history, erasing our past selves once we come into real money. They don't want girls like me to see that our story can be anything we want it to be if we just hold each other down.

Estella Aubergine is not holding me down. She's taking every opportunity she can and not turning back. She's apolitical. She appears to wield fashion and pettiness as weapons of destruction. She breaks hearts and then basks in the aftermath, but people still want to be her. They want to wear Estella like last year's Versace, and she lets them think that maybe one day, they can.

Well, I know I can't, but that's simply because I don't want to be anyone but me. That doesn't mean I wouldn't also fall in love with her if I had the chance. I breathe deeply through the knot in my stomach at the crush I developed overnight. Again, two things can be true.

The lobby of the building is built like an X; four corridors jut from the corners, each forging its own adventure. Some Beaumont kids posted about an event on Instagram, a call for the student body to come together in this time of need and confusion. A sound comes from across the space to the left. Farther down that hall, I hear it again, something human. I peek through the small windows on the doors until I get to the gymnasium.

Inside, kids sit on bleachers and face the floor, where a woman in a bright orange top and a man in a tweed jacket and jeans with a waxy handlebar mustache stand. He steps forward and speaks with a fervor unmatched by his audience.

"I am always proud to be your principal, but tough times are when Beaumont really shines. We are a community, and that means we will get through this together!"

Keep our secrets, and we will keep yours, I translate his message in my head.

He throws his arms out, and the room does not welcome his embrace. Students stir on the metal benches. They whisper and pull out their phones. The internet told me more than I needed to know about Principal Ruben Pummel, whom, based on the public LiveJournal he has yet to deactivate, I feel very confident in categorizing as ordinary.

The three relationships he has been in ended with such a lack of passion or fury. The last breakup felt almost like a hiccup, a nuisance that seemed to last a lifetime when it had been only fifteen minutes. Despite personal mediocrity, he ascended (through the most prominent Bay Area schools) to Beaumont Academy (the pinnacle of San Franciscan academia), where he fed off the acclaim of his students (three times a day) because power is the only meal he had been taught to enjoy.

But Ruben's mid-ness is catching up to him.

He has run this prodigious institution into near disaster. Estella's disappearance isn't the first scandal to grace the Beaumont halls since Ruben took the reins. According to my extensive overnight research, there has been some significant staff turnover since his tenure began. Most notably, six months ago, the school counselor of over twenty years resigned and self-published a tell-all book. When multiple legacy alumni family scandals were outed, they pulled their annual gifts and removed the school from their wills en masse. The public hit to the endowment was brutal.

"The kitchen has prepared a full lunch service for you, rather than the limited summer options we have been providing for those participating in our summer courses. Thank you again for coming in today. Ms. Brodsky here will be holding walk-in hours all summer, and as I said, we are in this togetherrrr." Pummel channels an Oprah moment and holds the last syllable, but the students' feet thunder down the bleachers and overpower him. They march toward the double doors I am standing behind. I barely make it into the room across the hall before the principal and counselor exit behind the students. Something passes between them, a tension. Cold and gruff, Ms. Brodsky turns her back to him and they head in opposite directions.

Once they're gone, I continue on to my next stop: Estella's locker.

CHAPTER 8

Pippa

My nose awakens when I detect a sudden smell of fresh bread. I should have asked that librarian for a map. Every turn I take lands me in front of a new hallway or stairwell, but if I must die here, I will do so well-fed. I follow the scent of gluten and stop in front of new double doors.

"Behind you!" a voice shouts, and I jump sideways to make room.

A chef carrying a giant wooden oar covered in oval loaves struts into the cafeteria. Kitchen staff bustle around and chatter while students scroll on their phones. I join the line at the counter and collect a steel tray to inch toward the buffet. Working at the Padaria means I know that the best time to get information out of someone is when they are waiting for their food, and Beaumont is no different. In line, they talk.

"You think it's a stunt?"

"If it is, she's taking it too far."

"I wouldn't be surprised if Bettina was behind it all."

"Come on. Bettina is a bitch, but she's not a murderer or kidnapper—oh my God, is Estella being trafficked? Should we, like, be fasting in protest or something?"

"Do you think Pummel is acting weird?"

"Of course he's acting weird; he is *weird. Did you see the leak of his LiveJournal?"*

"Millennials are so tragic. Like, who has a public internet diary anymore?"

"At this point, she better have been taken, because if this was some sort of popularity stunt, it's going to backfire. Someone is going to steal her crown any day, and then she'll never get it back."

"Unless she really was taken—"

The students I've been eavesdropping on in the buffet line peel off. I try to tail them, but I can barely lift my brunch. I was so focused on listening that I didn't pay attention to how much food I loaded up. My meal now requires a second tray and two trips to get situated.

Everyone seems on edge, waiting to see if anyone is willing to walk through the doors and take Estella's space, to restore social order. And while they do that, I eat.

Pistachio-nectarine scones, mezcal-smoked salmon, quiche Lorraine, a breakfast pizza made to order with a sunny-side-up egg in the center and yolk glazing the bubbling cheese, sweet potato home fries, dragon fruit, guava, English muffins with boysenberry jam, beet-and-kale juice, and a matcha latte.

"Hello?" A red-haired kid stands before me wearing a neon-tangerine-colored short-and-tee set.

"Um, hi?" I swallow a piece of guava with a cartoonish gulp.

He holds his finger out to stop me like I am the one who interrupted his free feast. He pulls out his phone and shakes his head in frustration. The sound of alerts and texts swoosh from his phone. His fingers move so fast they blur.

"Are you available? She wants to speak to you," he asks.

"Me?" I look around.

He snaps his neck up and scrunches his face like he just inhaled a fart. "Yes, you."

"Um, yeah. I guess I'm available—"

"Well, come on, then."

He leads me through the cafeteria despite never glancing up from his phone.

"So you are . . ."

"Two." He speaks through the steady rhythm of clicks.

"As in . . ."

"Number twooooo." He holds the sound of the vowel. "As in, second-in-command."

"Right, of course. So who are you handling all of this for . . . ?"

Two stops and meets my eyes. His hair is soft and curly, and he has the type of dewy, poreless skin most of the world can only dream of. He's pretty and knows it.

"I don't know what you have that she wants, but she is delicate. She's an artist. They say her eye captures every inch of the room in seconds, then breaks it into one million possibilities and figures out the handful of shots that work. Her photography is renowned."

Renowned. I snort to myself. *These people are delusional.*

Two's eyes burn greener than a chrysanthemum. I must have

done the thing where the thoughts I have in my head somehow shoot out of my mouth.

"Just answer her questions, do what she wants, and then get out of here."

Two shoves me toward the farthest table in the cafeteria, where Bettina Drummle, Estella's sometimes-girlfriend, sits. She lifts up her hand and wiggles her fingers in the air. Students sitting with her scatter. Bettina's eyes capture me, each blink like a camera shutter. They scan me until I'm a few inches away.

Neither of us speaks, and I'm sure as hell not going to be the first one.

Bettina kicks a chair beside her out from where it was tucked under the tabletop. It slides across the small distance between us and scrapes the floor amid the hush of our onlookers all focused on their princess regent.

"Sit." Bettina nods to the chair as she pulls herself up onto the table.

The tan over-the-knee Stuart Weitzman boots she wears swing back and forth. She's picture perfect—every line, every hair, every curve, not a molecule out of place or off-kilter.

"Why are you here?" Her eyebrows form a question mark.

"The same reason everyone else is—"

"I've never seen you before." She cocks her head, trying to place me.

"Is that a crime?" I counter.

Two leans in to whisper into her ear, but Bettina holds her finger out to shush him. He shoots me a glare like I forced her to do it.

"So you know Estella?" She grabs my arm and digs into my skin.

I nod. "Know" is vague enough that I can get away with it. A pounding at the back of my head starts up. Slow but steady. A warning. I pick at my fingernails to stop myself from running out the door. Bettina snaps her fingers, and Two hands her a phone, which she passes to me.

"Put your number in."

"Why . . . ?" I ask.

"I just feel like we should stick together, you know? Those of us on the inside dealing with the mess she left. I should know. I dated the girl for years, but you know that, being her friend and all."

"So, you think she left?" I ask.

If Estella is behind her own disappearance, which is my current theory, I'd understand why she did it. I want to get away from these people as quickly as I can, and I've only been here for an hour. They all look so hungry, even in a room overflowing with Michelin-star-quality food. Like they will never have enough to feel satisfied.

"It's not my job to worry about Estella anymore," Bettina snaps.

Sometimes Jo's eyes narrow after a long night, when she can't pull a thought from where it is buried in her mind. That's how Bettina looks now, like she's searching for something deep inside, but she's not sure she wants to find it. Maybe something she wants to make sure no one else finds out about.

My number saves to her contacts, but a door slamming open startles me, and Bettina's phone crashes to the ground from my grasp.

Three sets of shoes move toward us and stop right in front where I bent down to pick the phone up. I rise to two uniformed police officers and a man in plain clothes sporting a huge mustache. They must have sensed an interloper. I've been made.

"Miss, we need to speak with you in private," one of the cops says.

"Um," I start.

"If you want to schedule time to talk, you can reach out to my intern," Bettina responds.

They are not here for me. They are here for *her.*

Bettina snaps for Two, who steps forward while she reaches behind her to grab a bite of her breakfast sandwich, a bacon, egg, and cheese pressed between two scallion pancakes dripping with garlic chili crisp. The man with the mustache bristles.

"Ms. Drummle, your parents sent their lawyer over video call, but Ms. Brodsky will be in the room with you to offer emotional support."

Bettina's frustration is palpable for only a second. She masks it with an evil grin.

"I'll see you around," she whispers to me.

Two trails her as the cops escort her out the main doors. The whole room twists their necks back to me, the new girl left at the it-girl table. Back in the neighborhood, Bidi is the one everyone follows, but now two hundred eyes are on me, this stranger who appeared just before Bettina was escorted out by cops. The attention feels like a tiny drill in my skull. I look around for something to focus on to distract myself, but the pounding worsens when my eyes land on the figure in the windows of the cafeteria doors.

The same black hood that popped out of the van Estella drove off in that morning. The same black jacket that ran from the shop last night and left me that flower. My body moves before my brain as I abandon my feast on the table and run.

The hallway welcomes me with the faint echo of the hooded person's footsteps. I sprint to catch up, but they start to disappear. I've watched enough scary movies to know that this type of silence is never real, that there's a lurker lurking. They came to the shop; then they followed me here. I take a right, and the sound comes back. Louder, closer.

If they want to threaten me, they are going to need to do it with their whole chest.

"Hey!" I chase the echo of their feet around a corner of the school straight into a makeshift garden. Bouquets stretch from one side of the hall to the other, encircling what I assume is Estella's locker, which has been plastered over with an enlarged portrait of her face. Some of these arrangements must have cost hundreds of dollars. People would have been better off going to Trader Joe's for flowers. I can't resist. I pick them apart. My hands move so quickly that by the time I am in front of her locker, the rose stems are braided together, and the fully bloomed flowers accent the frame of the piece, bold and luscious. I place the masterpiece onto my head and face Estella's image. She may be the queen in this never-ending castle, and I may be just one of many subjects looking for her. But right now, *I'm* wearing the crown.

A flash of light from the window at the end of the hall catches something hanging out of Estella's locker door, which I see now is slightly ajar. I reach my pointer finger under the sharp corner of the locker and pull until a tear forms in the plastered photo of Estella's face and rips off her chin as I open the locker. A prick sears up my hand as the stem of the pink-and-gold peony pendant catches the skin under my thumb. I hold in a scream and pocket the necklace.

Whoever is in that hood has Estella, and they want me to know it. Footsteps echo once more, but in this cavernous building, I can't tell which direction they're coming from. I crouch, ready to get a good look. Whoever it is won't get away this time.

"Pippa?" Mo rounds the corner and freezes. Before I can silence him, another voice cuts through us.

"Mo? Pippa? What the hell?" Bidi shouts from the other end of the hallway.

CHAPTER 9

Bidi

Pippa stands before a garden in the middle of Beaumont Academy. She crosses her arms and pops out a hip at me, waiting for an explanation as to why I am here. Usually, I am where she is, asking for accountability for reckless behavior, but I can't deal with us until I've dealt with Mo.

"What are you doing, Mo? I told you that you needed to watch Caroline today!" I shout.

"I told you that I am busy—I have a life!"

"No! You have half a life. You took my room and my summer, so you now take half the workload," I clarify.

"Yeah! Plus, he stole my idea!" Pippa interjects.

She looks like she may bite Mo's neck open, but instead Pippa turns her wrath to me.

"Wait— Are you working with him?"

I can't tell if it's worse that I'm actually here betraying her all on my own.

"I wanted to make an informed decision." I whisper and hope that makes the truth hurt less when it lands.

"What the hell? You said we couldn't do this. You said it was a bad idea!" Pippa shouts, petulant.

"Shh! Can you both get it together and stop acting so extra?" Mo hisses. He spins around to make sure we haven't drawn an audience.

Pippa laughs, head back, mouth open.

"Everything about this place is extra! This whole school is endless! I spent most of the day uncovering hallways that didn't exist seconds before. Did you know they have an entire Tartine Bakery in the cafeteria?! I took two half loaves of bread."

Pippa opens her bag to reveal the oat-porridge bread and chunk of sourdough inside. They are still warm enough to smell the yeast. We breathe in a brief carb-loaded moment of peace before Pippa remembers she's mad at me and storms down the hallway. I turn and grab Mo by the top of his T-shirt.

"If you think being seen with us is going to ruin your life, you are not prepared for what my mother will do if she finds out you left Caroline at the Y unsupervised. I'm hella serious. If you want to keep this housing arrangement, you need to get out of here and pick her up by one-thirty."

The argument builds up in his chest, but he deflates. The risk is too high when he's living rent-free in our basement.

"Fine." He surrenders and leaves.

Mo may have grown to be three times my size, but I'm still the one in charge. I feel order restore itself. Now I need to find Pippa to have any chance in hell of maintaining it. Yes, I should have talked to her, but I also should be able to do something on my own, just for me. I should be able to dream—isn't that what Pippa said yesterday?

I race through the building and out the front door, where Beaumont's finest clutter the steps in a rainbow of designer outfits and bare collarbones. I spot Pippa and approach her, along with someone dressed in full-on neon orange. He steps right in Pippa's face and blocks her from moving. The frustrated stance is one I'm familiar with. She's already gotten under someone's skin.

"Keep your phone on you," he warns Pippa.

People in the crowd start to murmur and point to the street from the stairs. They move downward as a pack, and he disappears along with them. I grab Pippa's arm before she can follow him.

"Who was that?" I ask.

"Two," she says.

"I . . . don't understand."

"Two, second-in-command," she replies, as though that clears anything up.

Pippa wriggles out of my grip and stands on her toes, peeking over the masses with her neck stretched as much as humanly possible. My body goes along with her.

"That's Bettina." Pippa points to the girl on the corner who everyone watches walk toward Principal Pummel, followed by police.

In my research last night, I read all about Bettina. She and Estella met in middle school and had a real "enemies to lovers to enemies to besties to lovers to frenemies and back again" trajectory. Rarely in their history has Bettina come out on top with Estella, even with the myriad of nepo-baby-fueled accomplishments, like getting her mid photographs into genuine art exhibits because her mother is a famous art dealer. Somehow Bettina is always just a little behind Estella.

Well, one way to fix that is to make the competition disappear.

"Pippa, we should get out of here," I say.

When she doesn't respond, I turn to my left, where she was seconds ago, but now is gone.

CHAPTER 10

Pippa

Bermuda grass is also known as wire grass, scutch grass, or devil grass. Nearly impossible to kill, the weed emits a chemical that damages any plants whose path it grows in. In a matter of weeks, Bermuda grass can swell from meager sprout to the wingspan of a wandering albatross. Underground stems stretch into a map of complex roots, from which more are born, an ever-expanding, ever-reaching, endless beast. When asked how to control an infestation, gardeners typically laugh and simply say, "It controls us."

Seems like Beaumont needs to hire a gardener because the drama on campus is bountiful and blooming, spreading quicker than that grass ever could.

"Pummel looks weak."

"Of course he does. Bettina's dad donates millions to the school."

"I heard the Drummles aren't cooperating."

"I heard Bettina is the top suspect."

Pummel runs his hands through his hair, pit stains on display through his shirt as he and the police survey the students to find their next interviewee. Two rushes forward and ushers Bettina directly into a Lexus poised and waiting for her. The Beaumont students start to disperse after Bettina rolls out of the parking lot. They were only here for the show. Now that it's over, they have their lives to get back to. None of them actually care about Estella.

"Come on. We've got to regroup," Bidi instructs when she reappears beside me, back in boss mode.

Until today, I've always thought I needed Bidi to do most things. Maybe that's what she's always wanted me to believe. But here I am, one day solo on the job, and I've already got my number in Estella's ex's phone. I did that on my own. I start toward the bus.

"Where are you going? We need—" Bidi grabs my wrist.

She doesn't get to do that. Not right now.

"*We* aren't doing anything," I say. "You lied to me."

"Pippa! You go off on your wild ideas and then show up on my doorstep when the clock is ticking down on the explosive with a minute left and expect me to know which wire to cut." Bidi's neck vein bulges as she rants.

She isn't wrong. I am impulsive. I sneak into buildings and scare girls in graveyards, but this time I didn't *want* to just go off and do it on my own.

"I asked you to do this with me, and you said no! Multiple times! I can't believe you're investigating with Mo, of all people!" I shout.

Bidi maps out every minute of her life. She barely sleeps, but when she wakes up at four, it is to a meticulously planned day. When Bidi takes risks, they are carefully assessed. She didn't plan on me catching her in her own betrayal. Well, neither did I.

"I am not working with hi—" Bidi starts to mount her defense, but a voice shouts behind us and interrupts.

"She won't get away with this!"

Bidi and I crouch behind a bench—a temporary pause on our fight—to watch Principal Pummel's tantrum. He stops when Ms. Brodsky approaches and leans in close to whisper in his ear.

"Damn, they were hella cold to each other outside the gymnasium. It must have been an act," Bidi whispers.

They hop into a silver car together. In the front seat, a smile splits Pummel's face, and he reaches out to cup the guidance counselor's cheek. He pulls her toward his mouth. Bidi takes a few photos on her phone and tucks the secret affair into her back pocket.

CHAPTER 11
Bidi

Our bodies move through the awkwardness between us as we make our way to the bus stop without speaking. Pippa takes a seat toward the middle when the bus arrives, and I sit in the one beside her.

"Go on, then; get whatever you want to say over with," Pippa says.

"I'm sorry, Pippa. I need something to get me through this summer, something big. I know it was your idea, and I know I said no, but it's because I need this to work, and you tend to . . . do things without thinking."

"I'm a creative! I can't help that my brain comes up with innovative and brave ideas," she argues.

"Innovative" and "brave" are interesting synonyms for "reckless."

Pippa's justification proves my point better than I ever could, and yet I'm still going to give her another chance. That's just what best friends do, plus I haven't found an internship or job that hasn't already been filled. The investigation is a gamble, with terrible odds, but it's my best shot. The only way we find Estella is to lay everything out on the table.

"I will do this with you, Pippa, but you have to promise no secrets. No six steps deeper into hell before I've even uncovered the beginning of the mess you made."

Pippa's face turns purple, her hands fall to her pants pockets, and she closes her eyes. Whatever she's brewing inside, she doesn't seem sure if she wants it out of her or not. The bus turns the corner to our stop, where thick bold letters mark the awning of the shop.

"Um, Pippa?"

I point out the window, where Jo stands on a ladder, hanging a sign that reads CLOSING SOON while half the neighborhood stands around her.

CHAPTER 12

Pippa

We rush off the bus and over to the store, where the crowd stands whispering. But when I walk through, they make sure I can hear what they are saying. They grow louder with each step I take.

"Sellout."

"Let her go."

"I heard it'll be a real estate office."

"Thinks she's special."

"Snake."

"That girl probably sold the store from under her auntie's nose."

"Probably setting up deal with a contractor to get the whole block sold."

"Skin folk doesn't mean kinfolk."

"Rather be a sob story."

"Rather run away."

"Why are you doing this, Jo?"

We rush into the center of the madness to anchor the ladder; Jo is trapped at the top.

"Hey!" Bidi turns on the crowd.

A few people pause, but the group is now loud enough for it not to make a difference. I give Bidi the nod to grab the cover off the garbage bin beside us and upend the base to climb on top. Her hand balls up into a fist, and she punches the metal lid. The clang cuts through the chaos.

"Hey! I feel your frustration, but do you think they would be doing this if it were up to them? Consuela, you would take that money! Same with you, Jimmy, and you . . ." Bidi name-drops, and people's fists drop too.

Sometimes the truth hurts, but here she is speaking to the masses, and pain or not, the masses are enraptured. This is simply what Bidi was put on this earth to do: lead.

"When I launch my campaign for city councilwoman, I want to set out to change things. I want to make it possible for us to work and live comfortably. To invest in each other and feel security from our efforts. But I can't legally run for office until I'm eighteen, so until then, get on your socials. Call your reps, organize fundraisers, tag your local officials. Don't stand around here; go on! We need to show the corporate vultures we can't be bought."

Bidi glows from the roar she receives.

"Jo, can you come down?" I shout as the crowd disperses, energy redirected.

Jo throws her hands up to wave my concerns away while the ladder rattles and shakes with each step. She mutters to herself in Portuguese.

"What do you think you are doing?!" I ask her once she is safely on the ground.

"What am I doing? I am doing what you wanted! They come on Sunday with the paperwork. Once I sign, it's done," Jo spits.

"Wait, what! But Jo, it's Monday . . ." Bidi says. "There has to be something we can do."

Jo shakes her head solemnly.

Bidi steps away from the ladder, doing the same thing I am, calculating how on earth we can fix this before it's too late, but Jo has moved on. She has made her decision. The one I thought I wanted but that now sits heavy in my gut.

"We have until Sunday. Until then, you need to open up," Jo says. She turns and goes back upstairs to the apartment.

My heart burns from rising stomach acid. I have one week to find Estella. One week to untangle myself and my aunt from this financial mess. It's that, or I have one week to say goodbye to the family business. To home.

Bidi's fingers snap.

"Hello? Earth to Pippa? Did you hear what Jo said? Because I heard her say that selling is what you wanted. So when you begged me to help you find Estella to save this place, you were lying? But you think you can guilt-trip me for changing my mind and not telling you? This is what I am talking about! I hop into the burning building with you, but you are planning your escape out the back door without me."

I don't say "I love you" to anyone. I don't know how to say those words and mean them. They feel fake, but I do know love, and that is because of Bidi.

"Bidi, I thought selling was what I wanted, but I was wrong. I do want to live in other places too. I want to see the world. I want to be bigger than this. I want what I create to touch people everywhere. But that does not mean I will leave you."

"Of course you will! I see it happening over and over. Look at Mo. He went to Beaumont and never turned back. Leaving is leaving, especially if that is the world you are going to."

Bidi storms into the shop, and I follow. I don't have time to work through our issues because I need Bidi to help me solve this case. I still need that reward money.

My hand sweeps over my pocket; the necklace sits heavy. I didn't tell Bidi the whole story the first time around, and now I'm the liar with contraband and a stalker. If I don't tell her now, she will find out, and then I'll really be on my own.

"Bidi, you're right."

My words steal her breath. I shift my weight between my feet, toes pressing down on one foot and then the other. I never give in during our fights, not this early on anyway, but she claims she doesn't want secrets, so I hope she's ready.

"Say more," she says slowly, savoring the moment.

"What? You want groveling? Fine, okay. Bidi, you are right. I am not the type of friend you deserve. You have saved me since those kids tried to jump me in the library back in the third grade. Ever since then, I've known if I get myself into trouble, you'll be there. I like to live my life assuming the boat is just going to sink no matter what, but you always swim out to bring me a life jacket."

Bidi's hands are frozen in shock at my accountability, but I take them in mine. Instead of pulling her in for an embrace, I squeeze her wrists just enough to show I need her attention. I speak carefully, the way Instagram moms do.

"Okay, Bidi. Do you have what I just said committed to memory, or do you need me to do it again?"

She tugs her hands free. "What?"

"I was improvising, but I can give you the gist. It's just important for you to remember it—what I said, because we have a problem."

Every ounce of forgiveness Bidi had been emitting my way dissolves under her tongue. "What do you mean, 'a problem'?"

"Someone has been following me. The same person I saw with Estella that morning—well, I saw their black hood and jacket. And then I think they came to the shop and turned on the news so I would see she was missing. They left me the flower I wanted from the garden, and today, they followed me to Beaumont! I chased after them, but they got away—"

"So . . . you chased a phantom coat?" Bidi asks.

"The worst part is that's not the worst part. They led me to Estella's locker, and this was inside."

I take Bidi's hand and drag her deeper inside the store, then reach into my pocket to pull out a tight fist. The flash of gold falls forward. Estella's necklace dangles from my fingers and waves at the imprint it made in my palm. Bidi clamps both her hands over the contraband.

"This is bad. This is 'we're going to JAIL-jail' bad. You stole a custom diamond necklace from a missing person! And you've made me an accomplice."

Bidi drops to a squat, hands over her ears.

"I didn't steal it! I took it. There is a difference." I stand my ground.

Caught in her own doom spiral, Bidi begins to pace.

I lock the necklace away behind my panel and replace the crate in front of it. Bidi is the only person who knows about the hiding spot. When things get rough with Jo, Bidi puts notes in there reminding me to breathe and unclench my jaw and take a sip of water. From the vein bulging out the side of her neck, Bidi could stand to take her own advice, but I don't dare say a word.

I can see the brainstorm brewing on her forehead, so I grab the mop and get to work opening. When Bidi gets that look, it means we're going to be here for a while.

CHAPTER 13

Bidi

Hours have passed since Pippa came clean about the gold-and-pink-diamond-missing-person-evidence problem she has thrust on us both. The sun has started to set in the windows outside the shop, but we remain here, tangled in this conundrum she's led us into.

"What if we just throw the necklace into a pot and burn it in some gravy, then dump it all into the trash? If you don't have the necklace, there's nothing for whoever is under that hood to hold over you."

Pippa's head pokes out from an aisle. "We don't know what else they have! Somehow, they keep finding me wherever I go. I just can't stop thinking about Estella's mother in that house all alone, surrounded by that overgrown mess of a garden."

"How is the person you are concerned about in this moment the rich recluse woman?" I ask.

Pippa should be concerned about the fact that our fingerprints are all over this necklace, the only piece of evidence this crime has been linked to publicly, but that's not even the part that's getting to me. Pippa doesn't do feelings; she disappears into her head and shows up a week later with a skull molded from rotting roses. She broods, and she swallows emotion down. She buries her feelings and expects everyone else to do the same.

It's always been me and Pippa. And ever since elementary school, I have had this plan to stay in our neighborhood, to make sure kids coming up like my little sister have it better because we made it that way for them. To teach them how we hop into the water and swim over to the dock to save a stranger. We clank bones, we spit fire, we survive the journey.

We don't run away and attach ourselves to an outsider.

"Pippa. For real, what is all this about? Why do you want to find Estella so badly?" I pull myself up to sit on the counter. Pippa tries to ignore me as she busies herself tidying, but eventually, she has no other distractions to procrastinate with.

"Listen, this search is still about the reward and, yes, the potential for exposure for you. But when I saw Ms. Aubergine all broken and disoriented on the news, I felt like I was looking at a mirror of myself in twenty years. You don't know what it's like to lose someone with no explanation. If we figure this out and that helps her in the process . . . I don't know. Isn't helping people, like, your thing?"

We aren't all coming to the table equal; that's the point. The table needs to be splintered. We need to rebuild where we are because no one else will, not the rich heiresses or missing it girls.

"I like to help people who need help, which is why you convinced me to do this and leverage the attention for that purpose. So why don't *you* help me figure out what we should do now that you have a stalker, and the shop will be gone before we ever have a chance of finding Estella if we don't focus! Maybe you could try not making my life even harder than you already have, okay? In fact, Pippa, go get a piece of paper from the office. We need to make a list."

She obeys my orders and hands me a pen and an old inventory form that I flip over to the blank side. I narrate as I write.

"Estella walked out of her house and appeared to be waiting for something or someone per you, but she had a lot going on for herself: A *Teen Vogue* internship. Her online followers. Going into senior year as class copresident. A summer AP course. Why would she set all those things in motion to then disappear? Plus, you said the car drove recklessly and barely stopped before it drove off again? Something else could be going on."

I circle Estella's name and put a question mark.

"Bettina, her ex. They recently broke up and seem to love-hate each other. Crime of passion? Jealousy for motivation?" I add.

"The principal and the counselor, they're hiding their relationship. Maybe Estella found out their secret, and they had to shut her up?"

"Her mother: Amelia Aubergine?" I draw a big circle around her name as well.

"I really don't think—" Pippa starts, but I hold my hand out to stop her. Pippa may have empathy for her, but all I see is a potential suspect. "Nuh-uh, Pippa, no one is innocent until we prove them innocent."

Pippa starts to say something, then thinks better of it and returns to mopping.

I hop off the counter and walk toward the freezer to grab a double-chocolate-chip pint for my troubles. A few steps later, I am parallel to the front door and stop. My lips part to scream, but nothing comes out. Pippa storms past me—so in her head, she can't see what I see.

"Pippa!" I whisper.

"I get it, Bidi, okay? You have made it very clear you want to do things your way—"

"Pippa!" I force a hiss.

"What?"

My voice has claws now. "PIH-PUH!"

"Oh my God, WHAT!" She rushes over to me, and I turn her chin to a shadow splayed across the floor.

"Pippa," I whisper as she follows my fingers to the person cloaked in a black hood, waiting at the front door.

CHAPTER 14

Pippa

We can't see much. The outline of a person cut out by their all-black wardrobe. I walk forward and reach for the dead bolt.

"What are you doing?! What if this is the stalker?" Bidi whispers.

"It better be!" I shout.

Adrenaline surges me forward. I'm done with life throwing all sorts of mayhem at me. I'm reclaiming my time. The person outside steps in as soon as I unlock the door and pulls the hood down. Red hair spills out and relief floods me.

"It's okay, Bidi." I face the intruder. "What do you want, Two?" I ask.

"Who are you?" Two ignores me and interrogates Bidi.

"Why are you dressed like that?" Bidi snaps back.

Two looks around the space in disgust and pulls the hood back up, a shield. He doesn't want to be seen here, I realize.

"Bettina's not expecting you, so . . . go over there." Two points to the dark hallway around the corner of the counter with disgust.

"Excuse me?" Bidi starts.

"Just go." I nudge her arm. Bettina either knows something or did something. And right now she's giving us an in, even if that means putting up with this weasel.

Bidi relents but holds her glare on us both until she reaches aisle three.

Two pulls out an iPad and sets it onto the counter for a video call, then stands behind me, out of frame but nearby. The screen lights up to a white bright room, but Bettina is nowhere to be seen.

"Wow, your lighting is trash. What corner of hell are you in?" Bettina asks, off-screen.

I use my hands as a visor and step forward. "What is it, Bettina?"

Bettina steps into frame, wearing a lavender vinyl suit. The fit is perfect, but the color isn't right for her skin tone.

"I had some more thoughts, and you didn't answer your phone. I'm scheduling a lunch," she says.

"Oh . . . sorry, I've been dealing with some personal stuff." I pull my phone from my pocket and check. Sure enough, there are two missed calls from an unknown number. "How did you find me—"

Bettina's face scrunches up. "Did I say there would be time for questions? Hello?"

Two's face is as sour as a dough starter when he steps forward with forced professionalism. "Yes, Bettina, what can I do for you?"

"Get back here. I need your opinion on shoes and my schedule."

The call ends, and Two collects the iPad.

"You came all this way for *that*? I'd tell you how to unionize, but I can tell I don't like you," Bidi says, stepping out from her assigned hiding spot. She gives him the type of smile that lets him know she could wreck him if she wants to.

"When is this lunch happening?" Bidi follows up.

Two ignores her, and he looks to me. "You'll receive your instructions shortly. Pick up your phone when I call next time."

Bidi waits until he is gone to continue spiraling. "If you are going to be interacting with these people regularly, we need a plan."

I groan. "I think I have done quite well on my own so far. The universe is looking out for me."

"Yes, you have committed robbery. One of our top suspects has their minion making reservations for lunch. Oh! And someone is stalking you."

She can never just give me my flowers. If it's not done the Bidi way, it won't work. Well, I can be right sometimes, too, even though in our history, that's rarely been the case. Finding Estella was my idea; that has to count for something.

The bell on the door dings, and Malika marches in.

"Mommy?" Bidi asks, but Malika keeps moving my direction.

I brace for her wrath, but instead, she pulls me to her.

"I just heard about the shop. How's Jo doing?" She rubs her hand down the back of my head. With each stroke, a layer of my anguish peels away and is absorbed by her. In my lifetime, there have only been a few moments I have felt mothered, always by Malika.

"She's . . . out right now," I say, which is enough for Malika to understand. She pulls me into a hug and talks to Bidi over my head. "Mo said he had Caroline today."

Bidi holds her breath and waits for the bomb to drop that he sold her out as Malika continues. "He got her to eat a vegetable too. I know he wants to help out, but you know you are the only one I can trust with Caroline," Malika says to Bidi as she releases me.

Bidi nods. She really never gets a break.

"Wait, why are you in scrubs?" Bidi asks her mother.

"I have to go. I got booked for a private patient."

"Mommy! You promised you were going to be off this week in the evenings." Bidi's shoulders hunch. Every second of her life gets sucked out sooner than she can live it.

"The recruiting office made a mistake, Bidi. I have to take the job. They penalize if you back out the same day, and I can't risk these extra hours. I'll be back in the morning."

Malika's promise circles the room. She leans down to kiss our foreheads before she's gone. The fumes Bidi's always running on peter out, and she slinks over to the door.

"Where are you going? We haven't come up with a plan! You love plans," I say to lift her spirits.

"I've got to make dinner," she says, tired already.

"Wait!" I chase her to the door and hand her the Beaumont yearbook I got from the librarian. "I thought it might be a good place to find out more about her and her people."

Bidi wrinkles her nose.

"What? Is that silly? It's silly, never mind, I'll bring it back—" I backtrack.

"No, it's a good idea. All your ideas have been good," Bidi offers reluctantly. She takes the book from me and walks to the door, then turns back to me before she pulls it open. "Except for taking the necklace."

CHAPTER 15

Bidi

Estella Aubergine: class copresident, member of Gender and Sexuality Alliance and Black Student Union, trained as a peer sex educator, ACLU of Northern California volunteer. Debate team. Fashion editor for the monthly *Beaumontian*. Drag ball.

Bettina Drummle: president of the photography club, artistic director of the *Beaumontian*. Semester abroad in Lisbon, fluent in ASL and Portuguese.

On the walk home, I flip through the pages of the Beaumont yearbook, mentally noting every one of Estella's and Bettina's extracurricular activities. Then I come across a face I recognize all too well.

This sneaky, lying sack of muscles.

I barrel my way straight into the house and to Mo. My hand slams the top of his laptop down.

"Yo!" His shout doesn't hide the full-body tremble.

This is the Mo I remember, so shakable he might as well be a tectonic plate. I keep my glare. *Let him try me again.* This is a final warning.

"Wh-wh-what?" He shivers as an evil grin spreads across my cheeks.

"Mo, I don't have the oxygen to waste. I've got enough on my plate with Pippa, so you need to start being honest."

He sits up taller. "You know, I've been here two days, and you've already given Pippa one hundred chances. I just saved your ass with Auntie, I said it was my idea to watch Caroline, and you are ready to write me off? It's whack. So much for family." Mo crosses his arms, toddler tantrum–style.

"Pippa IS family, Mo. Just because you and I share blood doesn't mean I owe you!"

"Whatever." Mo opens his computer again, but I slam it shut a second time.

"Look, yes, part of this is about protecting my friend because she's about to lose everything, and she's got this one far-fetched chance to fix it. Helping her is what I do. Have you never had a friend who made you so completely livid but also laugh more than anyone else? Someone who you want to tell everything to? Someone who makes you feel seen and heard?"

He shifts uncomfortably. Enough said.

"When you find that person, Mo, you'll understand—"

"Maybe I did," he interrupts.

"What?" I ask.

"Maybe that person was you, Bidi. I got into Beaumont, and instead of being proud of me, you made me feel guilty for leaving. Maybe just because you think you're right about everything doesn't mean other people can't be right too. Maybe it was easier to walk away and pretend I wasn't losing something. Maybe *you* could have tried to check on me, Bidi."

The pain hits for me too. How was I supposed to know he was lonely? I can't go digging around through his feelings to find the source of his pain. I can't do the dance people expect you to do around their insecurities and fears. It's why I want to be in politics. I say the things everyone is thinking but doesn't want to hear out loud.

"Mo, you are probably going to disappear back into your bubble as soon as school starts. Let's be so for real. You chose the Beaumont world over us. You don't get it both ways."

Mo takes my hand where it rests on the top of his laptop and removes it.

"Bet. Well, you don't know what it's like at Beaumont, Bidi, okay? Yes, the school is fancy, and the cafeteria offers omakase lunch once a week, and they sponsor international trips and whatever. But the people? What do you think I had to talk to them about? They play credit card roulette at fine-dining restaurants and spend thousands of dollars on vacations."

So . . . he didn't stop calling because he was embarrassed of me. He was embarrassed of himself.

"I keep my head down. I study. I go to the gym. Bidi, these people have unlimited resources. It's like living on another planet. When I tell you that even if you knew what you were doing, there is no way you could uncover whatever they've hidden, I mean it."

"Maybe not, but you can."

I lay his truth in the center of us, undetonated, a threat, a surprise. A bomb can be anything until it explodes and kills everything in its vicinity. I slam the yearbook open to the page where his personal accolades are listed.

Maurice Walker—hackathon champion, annual twenty-four-hour true crime podcast champion, Berkeley public radio internship, Beaumont podcasting club president, coding club.

"You're, like, really good at this nerdy stuff, huh? I started thinking about how that would come in handy in a missing person investigation. Plus, you keep trying to convince me not to do it. What are you up to, cuz?"

He doesn't crack under the pressure; he savors it, then sits up taller.

"As you clearly figured out, I know what I'm good at. And I'm not trying to land myself in debt. That reward, it helps pay for college. Or maybe my tech skills find Estella and get me an offer at Google or Apple or some other tech firm so I can skip four more years of douchebags like the ones at Beaumont. Maybe it simply makes people at that school see me."

Pippa was right. He did steal her idea.

"So, you are telling me that you could help me, but you won't?"

Mo puts his computer to the side, and he smiles big. "Now, is that any way to ask?"

He's been waiting for this moment, for me to realize that he has something I need.

"What do you want, Mo?" I ask.

"I'll settle for the lead on the case, which means you have to do what I say. Oh, and I want a position on your campaign—to round out my résumé."

After that arrogance, he winks. He wants another chance. I can give him that. Mo glances out the window that faces the Bahia Padaria.

"She's not going to be happy," he says. A joy buffers the truth. Mo's going to love every second of Pippa's irritation.

“So you’ll help?” I ask.

“Yeah.” He nods, which is enough for me.

Someone else lifting a problem from my shoulders makes me buoyant. I could float.

He takes my hand but holds it firm. “Good, first things first. I can’t work on an empty stomach. As my assistant, you need to get me a snack. Salty and sweet, please.

Pippa isn’t the only one he is going to relish torturing.

CHAPTER 16

Pippa

The only thing that has ever made sense to me is flowers.

It started when Jo took me to the botanical gardens when I was ten. She pulled me down to bend over and smell the eucalyptus. We waved to the ice plants and studied the rhododendron. Chest forward, Jo guided us past the lilies, past the dogwoods and the cacti to the *Araucaria araucana*, the monkey puzzle trees.

I saw one of these the first time I set foot in Rio de Janeiro. It was the first time I saw a tree reaching for the sky. Your mother loved those trees. In Bahia, we had Brazilian rosewoods. Low to the ground, the branches sometimes reached all the way down to kiss the earth.

Jo's eyes climbed the trunk until the sun forced them back down to me. Maybe that was the moment when she realized we were tethered. She pulled me in, wrapped me up in her cocoon, where I could feel her heartbeat in Morse code.

Se você so ver o mundo do chão, você nunca vai saber o quão alto pode alcançar. Voa, e nunca olhe para trás.

If you only see the world from the ground, you will never know how high you can reach. Fly, and never look back.

I rise to the morning from the floor of my aunt's office, where I fell asleep slumped over scribbling designs for future statues. The hard metal pendant of Estella's necklace falls back down to my chest from where it dug into my chin. I put it on last night after Bidi left and I closed the shop up. I figured I should get the chance to wear something that is worth more than my whole life for a night.

I don't have anything of Mamãe's. Estella's mother should have this. I check my phone to see if Bidi sent any plans, but there are none. Every minute that passes is one we may not get back in this store if we don't save it. *No secrets,* she said. Since there is no plan, I am going to make one. I place the necklace carefully in my panel and get ready to go.

I text Bidi.

> Going to Aubergines', will be careful. Call you after.

Bidi has her suspicions about Ms. Aubergine, but there's only one way to get into Estella's world. Lucky for me, that way is through a garden.

Flowers in the back fridge waiting to be my next statue will work perfectly for a tiara, so I grab them and lock up. Forget-me-nots and violets form an ethereal crown. Halfway across the city, I twist the last stem, my latest masterpiece complete.

Out the window of the bus, I mark the moments of my life in street corners. El Farolito. Alamo Square. The skate park. Newer storefronts keep popping up behind the curbs, but that's the thing about growing up in a place like San Francisco—anyone saying this place is disappearing doesn't understand that the people are what this city is built on. We smooth the asphalt on the streets as we come up in them.

The smell of honeysuckles seeps into my nostrils as I arrive on the scene. I put my flower crown onto my head for courage and walk up to the Aubergine gate, but a car door creaks open behind me.

"Can I help you?" A cop rolls the window down from the patrol car stationed out front.

A door shuts, and I turn away from the cop to watch as Ms. Aubergine steps out of her front door. She wears a cardigan adorned in handsewn roses pink as the glow in the early evening, shining brighter than a brass monument coming to life. With each step, she sheds daffodils and camellias like the spring until I lose sight of her between the low-hanging willow branches, threatening to disappear.

"Ma'am?" the cop says to me sternly, but I ignore him.

"Ms. Aubergine!" I shout. Moments later the gate opens.

"Ms. Aubergine—" the cop starts, but Ms. Aubergine flicks him away. She walks like she is bulletproof, and he is nothing more than a poppy seed caught in her molar. The sight of my face makes her freeze.

"Hi, Ms. Aubergine. My name is Pippa."

She reaches out and pulls the flower crown from my head. She inspects my work, awestruck.

"Where did you get this?" Her hands shake as she brushes her fingertips over the flowers. She steps back a few feet away from me. The cop glowers and stands on his toes, ready to pounce.

"I made it, but you can have it. It's the least I can do," I say softly.

Ms. Aubergine buries her nose in the flowers, her eyes drenched in a pain that pierces through me. A deep sadness, the missing-someone kind. Guilt sears my skin where the imprint of Estella's necklace was an hour ago. I should tell her the truth.

"I think your garden could be the most beautiful place in this whole city" is what comes out of my mouth instead.

"Could be?" Ms. Aubergine's question pokes at my nerves.

"I am just really inspired by the space—" I clarify.

The world darkens around her as a man the size of a giant sequoia appears by her side. "Who are you?" he shouts at me.

"Jaggers, please!" she snaps to silence him and make room for me.

"I am here because of the garden," I explain, and hold out my phone to show her the photo carousel of my work. She gasps at the giant bee I made of daisies and black roses.

"Where did you learn how to do this?" Ms. Aubergine holds up the flower crown.

"I don't know. Flowers are so beautiful on their own. I like the challenge of making them into something more—"

Ms. Aubergine's eyes start to glaze over, though I can't tell if it's because I'm rambling or if she took something for her sadness. There is a familiar detachment in her face. One I see every day from people who come into the store when they are done feeling empty and are ready to be full.

I have so much I could offer her. The necklace, the hooded stalker, the last look on Estella's face before she disappeared. I could tell her everything, but if I do that, I forfeit the mission. Maybe it's cruel to use this family's misfortune to our advantage, but isn't that how the game is played? If I find Estella, Ms. Aubergine will benefit too. *Stick to the plan. Eyes on the prize,* I tell myself. Distraction is the easier choice to make in this situation, and I can offer that. More words bubble out of me.

"I have a thing with cemeteries. In the early morning, if you are in the right spot when the sun rises, there is a moment when the whole place is covered by oranges and pinks. So much color that you don't see the gray stone; you see the flowers. I know it's weird, but I like the quiet there. Sometimes I rearrange the bouquets to make them look nicer. Ms. Aubergine, I can't fix everything else, but I can help with your garden."

"Do you know my Estella?" Ms. Aubergine asks.

"Everyone knows her, don't we? She invites us into her world with her. I don't know her well, but I do know that Estella is built out of tiny pieces of a million different stories. She has already made such a mark on the world. Everyone in the city knows Estella. She's legendary," I say.

A tear drops from Ms. Aubergine's chin. She slides her open palm under to catch it. "I have had gardeners over the years. This garden just does what it wants to do," she says.

Stubbornness is my brand. "I'll give it my best shot."

"As your attorney, I have to say that I don't think that's a good id—" the Jaggers guy interrupts us again.

She silences him with her open palm held up a few inches

from his mouth, then she curls a finger, hooking the air between us to pull me with her as she turns and walks into the greenhouse I hadn't noticed, so distracted by the mess of the garden.

The nose of the spade plunges into the soil until it hits the ceramic planter below, digging holes for seeds. The thrash of Ms. Aubergine's arm as she brings the tool down would kill if it weren't preparing for a new life. Everyone paints gardeners as gentle and calm. But the whole point is that you get to dig the hole first, dredge things up, and root out all the bad stuff.

Her arms keep moving in circles, down into the earth, then back up again. I've been where she is, hurting the only thing I knew would come out looking better when the flowers bloomed. Ms. Aubergine stops to rub her palm with her thumb. Likely a cramp from inexperience.

"I don't really know what I'm doing out here," she admits.

"Here, let me." I take the tool from her hands.

"Thank you." She lifts herself onto a metal stool.

Ms. Aubergine watches as I work through punctured ground. I fill the holes with her sorrow, then gather compost to mix in. I set up the table where we will need to attach lights to grow the flowers. I photograph the blueprint of the garden we roll out to map the floral design.

Ms. Aubergine looks around. "Do you want to know a secret?"

I try to act casual when I nod. I want to know all the secrets that live in this mansion.

"I don't know where those honeysuckles came from. They started growing shortly after we bought the place. Estella was nine months old. It was just us in this big house. We built our lives from the inside out. One day, I noticed that the air tasted sweet. We followed the scent into the garden. The flowers felt like a welcome, a promise that Estella would wake up every day to a sweet life. They grew toward her window. I didn't plan on the honeysuckles taking on a life of their own."

Ms. Aubergine closes her eyes and opens her mouth to taste today's air.

Honeysuckles are a group of flowering shrubs. Many of their elements are edible or used for medicinal purposes. Some healers believe honeysuckle has antiviral properties. Certain varieties can live for twenty years when cared for properly. But there's no way anyone is tending to these with enough regularity. It makes no sense that they are alive. Then again, Jo did the bare minimum in her parenting, so you could say the same about me.

"Your mother must be so proud," Ms. Aubergine says.

"I don't have a mother." The words come out harsher than I intended, the way the truth can so often be.

"Everyone has a mother," Ms. Aubergine pushes.

"Not me. She left me with my aunt and didn't come back," I say quietly.

Tears start to fall down Ms. Aubergine's cheeks. I look away for her privacy and mine. I know how it feels when you realize a person you love may never come back. My whole life has been spent trying to avoid the gaping hole in my heart that my mother left. Pity pulls the truth closer to my teeth. *I was here*. The words start to form, but I force them back down. I close my eyes, and I dream up the garden.

"Ms. Aubergine, I want to gut this space. Dig up the entire garden and start fresh."

"Dig up the whole thing?" she whispers. Shooketh to her core.

"Not the honeysuckles!" I correct. I wouldn't take away the only thing she seems to love out here. The creases in her forehead soften.

"I can start right tomorrow, if you want—" I offer.

"Is there a rush?" she asks.

"Well, um, sort of," I admit. "I know you have so much going on, so this pales in comparison, but my aunt owns a store, and well, she's selling it at the end of the week. So I don't know where I'll be after that."

Bidi would tell me not to share anything about myself, but I know so much more than Ms. Aubergine; it's only right she knows something.

"What is the name of the store?" she asks, a follow-up I wasn't anticipating.

"Um, the Bahia Padaria," I say.

"Brazilian?"

"Yep, but I've never been." I always give this disclaimer—the lack of connection to my heritage makes me feel like a fraud.

"You should go. I did once, but that was a long time ago," Ms. Aubergine says, lost somewhere far away. "Anyway, yes, of course, you can start right away. It will be nice to have some new energy around here until Estella comes back. I'm thirsty. Let's have some tea, shall we?"

Ms. Aubergine walks toward the main property. Inside the house, our footsteps echo between the maple wood floors and the sixteen-foot ceilings. The dining room is a nice mix of modern and traditional. The long table is dark wood with thick legs and benches, with one emerald-colored velvet chair at each end. An open arched doorway leads into a bar with a lit glass wall of bottles and a ladder to reach the ones at the top. We take a left down a hallway where a line of photos of Estella and her mother walk alongside us and lead to some steps made of Spanish lacquered tiles and into a massive kitchen.

She opens a drawer and pulls out little bags of different dried ingredients. She pours the mixture of herbs and flowers into a stone mortar and pounds the pestle. Before they turn to powder, she mixes and measures and portions the homemade tea into baggies. When the cup reaches me, Ms. Aubergine's fingers are red, dyed from the pomegranate and star fruit with a hint of hibiscus. She takes the seat beside me.

"I think my Estella was going through something I had no clue she was going through."

Her hands shake as she sips from the matte-gray ceramic teacup.

We sit together, two phlox in a field of irises. Sets of feet march toward us from the hall where we entered initially. Jaggers walks into the room moments later, followed by the juiced-up cop I encountered outside. The necklace in the wall of the shop pierces my brain. I can see the place being torn apart as I sit here in this custom kitchen.

"What is it?" Ms. Aubergine asks, stress levels visibly rising.

"Can we speak with you in private?" The cop addresses Ms. Aubergine, and Jaggers moves to her left.

"Just tell me what is going on!" she shouts, agitated. A shade of maroon creeps up her neck.

"We need you to come with us, please." The police officer points to the front of the house.

A raw and terrible expression washes over her face; whatever they have to tell her can't be good. The investigation might already be over. Ms. Aubergine walks forward, head slumped between her shoulders.

"Don't move," Jaggers commands me before he follows her out of the room.

The second they are gone, I take my chance and climb the staircase beside the pantry. Stairs ascend under me as quickly as doors fly open as I rush down a hallway to closets and guest rooms, a library, and more bathrooms than necessary in a home with two people. The last room I come upon is the one I need. I can tell by the way the scent of the honeysuckles seeps under the door that this is *hers*.

Ms. Aubergine said the honeysuckles grew under Estella's window, but the room smells wrapped in the petals. Estella's world is smaller than I imagined. The space is huge, of course, the full size of Jo's apartment. Doechii and Billie Eilish sit among a wall of outfit selfies in her mirror, similar to what she posts on social media.

The image I have conjured of Estella ruling over her court and berating her minions is less plausible here in her sanctuary. Piles of books, some with bookmarks peeking out, stand in haphazard towers. Her vanity is covered in various skin products Bidi would die for. A sharp knock sends me to the ground, and I will my body to sink into the wood. The tap comes again, this time more clearly. A branch from the tree by the window.

The garden calling me out before I get caught doing something I regret.

I should leave now, not press my luck. I retrace my steps back to the front but hear loud voices and move toward them.

From the doorway, I see Ms. Aubergine standing nose to nose with Jaggers, the cop, and another man in a suit.

"Where were the stationed officers?" she questions.

"Unfortunately, ma'am, the incident happened during their brief lunch break. We are reviewing the security footage to see if we were able to capture anything," Suit Man explains.

"How is it that I am not feeling safer in my own home than I was before you got here?" Ms. Aubergine shrieks.

The man takes her heat. "Is there anyone who might have a problem with you or your daughter? A neighbor, maybe?"

"I make it a point not to know my neighbors. All they want is to start petty fights over who owns the best tableware."

Ms. Aubergine wrings her hands in sorrow. The type that's going to remind her that waking up is worse than having a bad dream. She looks up and sees me at the door. "Pippa?"

I rush to her side.

"Has she been questioned?" Suit Man sees me for the first time.

I freeze. They will search the store; they will find the necklace. They will find out I was here that morning.

"No!" Ms. Aubergine stomps her foot and assumes a protective stance. My heart swells, no one but Bidi has ever stood up for me. "You will not be harassing a minor, a young Black woman at that, in this house when my Estella is out there. No. She was inside when this note was dropped off. Now show me whatever it is, Detective."

Suit Man bristles. The uniformed cop steps forward. "It's ready. We've dusted and sampled. We can show you now."

Ms. Aubergine takes a second to compose herself, her spine straightens, and her neck untightens. The detective strides over and holds up his phone screen. "We've got the footage from the security up front."

Ms. Aubergine looks to her counsel for approval. Jaggers nods, and the cop plays the security video on his phone. The footage is black-and-white but not grainy. Clear as day, the top of a head covered with a black hoodie appears. They reach their arm through the slats of the gate, and we see the paper fall to the grass. My stomach drops along with it. If this is the same person who has been chasing me, I could have stopped this from happening. Before I can open my mouth to confess, the cop speaks again.

"This is what was found." He swipes to the next image, to a scrap of paper with three words written. Alberta sees you. Ms. Aubergine inspects the note carefully. A wave of concern flashes over her face.

"Mm-mm, no, I—I don't know what this means. Am I supposed to know what this is?" she asks, desperate to get the answer right.

"No, you're doing great," the cop coaches. "Unfortunately, in times like these, teens think it's funny to play pranks. We will continue to look into it, but it's likely this is just the result of a not-so-fully-formed frontal lobe."

Or it's a kidnapper who took Estella that morning, is chasing me, and might hurt Ms. Aubergine.

"Jaggers, I'm going to show Pippa out, and then I need to rest. Can you deal with this?" Ms. Aubergine tilts her chin to the police and links arms with me to walk toward the front.

"I'll tell you another secret. I almost died when I had Estella, but I promised to keep her alive no matter what. And I did. Things tend to appear just when I need them, even if I can't tell why at first. The honeysuckles. You. Dig it up, Pippa. Let's make this garden the grand welcome home Estella deserves."

She needs someone else to believe it as much as she wants to.

"You will come back soon, won't you?" she presses.

Not if I tell her the truth. She'll regret defending me and hand me right over to the police. I keep my mouth shut, though, and put my hand on Ms. Aubergine's, then she does the same. We hold the layers.

"I'll be back soon." I whisper my promise.

Eight o'clock is soon. Tomorrow is soon. I am going to be a legal adult soon. Mamãe said she would be back for me soon. "Soon" can be stretched like taffy. "Soon" is the thing you say when you don't have an answer. "Soon" is just as easy to drown in as a river. "Soon" is the place I can never quite reach.

I take my time walking through the garden. The lilies and azaleas are grown so haphazardly they stand intertwined, mid-kiss. When I turn back to the house, Ms. Aubergine stands in the window, just above a tangled mess of hydrangeas. There she is, needing a daughter, and here I am, waiting for a mother.

A puddle waits at my feet back on the street; the water ripples from the slam of the gate behind me. For a second, before I blink, Estella's gaze sits in the reflection and stares back at me like my own. Nose to the sky, I suck in the sweet air as long as I can before the truth turns hope rancid. Because I am not Estella Aubergine, no matter how much I wish I were.

Tires squeal, and a gray car pulls up on the curb in front of me. I have to jump back to avoid the splash from the puddle.

"Hey!" I shout, and pull out my phone to record whoever this jackass is, but the battery died while I was in the house.

The back door opens, and an arm reaches out and yanks me inside. Two's beady eyes stare into mine once the door is closed. I swallow the scream down my throat and wait for it to settle.

"What are you doing here?" I hiss at Two.

"Oh my God!" Bettina gasps. "You look like a rack just grew feet and walked out of a Kohl's!"

She turns to Two. "Check what we have in reserves."

Two slides himself out and opens the trunk, then slams it closed. When he climbs back into the car, he pushes a large shopping bag into my chest. Bettina moves over for him to sit in the back seat of the SUV with her.

"You can change when we get there," she instructs.

"Get where?" I ask.

They share a smirk, and the car drives off.

CHAPTER 17

Bidi

"Pippa, whatever you are doing, just stop. Step away from the rich lady. I am almost there. We may only get this one chance to meet face to face—anyway, stop what you are doing. Please. And answer me." I finish the voice note and send it to accompany the six similar messages I have sent this morning.

My phone buzzes, but Mo's name flashes on my screen, not Pippa's.

"What is it, Mo?"

"I think she left," he says.

"Why do you think that?" I ask.

"Because Bettina just posted a story, and Pippa is in her car."

She would somehow decide to do something reckless and then one-up that idea by doing it twice instead.

"You need to rein her in. Anyway, check out the videos I just sent you," he replies.

A few seconds pass before my inbox dings. I open the message and click the link. Apparently, the Beaumont security system has flimsy protections, and Mo broke into it to scrub any images of us in the building. I guess he also decided to snoop around and found something useful. Blurry videos slowly load from the footage Mo hacked.

"Are you watching?" His voice hops out from where the video call is hidden behind these newly opened files.

"Shh," I hiss.

The footage starts. I see Ms. Brodsky, the guidance counselor, opening her office door for Estella to walk inside. The next video is from the same day, ten minutes later based on the time stamp. The door opens again, and Estella walks out of frame. The third piece of footage is from a different day. Someone with their back to us and a sweatshirt pulled over their head pounds on the door until Brodsky opens up. They argue, but before the person storms off, they point inside the office. Seconds later, Pummel walks out and joins Brodsky in the doorway.

"Wait, Mo, we can't see their face—how do we know that is Estella?"

"Good catch. Zoom in; it's the same purse," he says.

I put my eyes right up to the screen. The footage is black-and-white and grainy, but he is right. The purse in all three videos is identical.

"When were those videos taken?" I ask.

"The first two are from the same day, a month ago. The third one, where they're fighting, happened . . ."

He stops. I hear keyboard clicks. "Oh, shit."

"Mo? What is it?"

I minimize the security footage to catch the look on his face.

"It happened the day before she disappeared. Bidi, forget about Aubergine, you need to go!" he shouts, excited.

"What? Where?"

"Back to Beaumont! You have to keep Brodsky away from the computer while I break into her digital files. The computer will be frozen for the ten minutes it takes to download. Also, figure out a way to grab her paper files—there may be notes from meetings, other documents they didn't digitize. She has walk-in hours every day until one p.m." Mo returns to his rigorous work, face down in the laptop again.

"Are you sure now is the right time?" I ask, unsure I can pull this off with my recent trend of bad luck.

"Yes. What did she say, by the way?" Mo asks.

"Who?"

"Pippa. About me helping, or, you know, basically running this whole operation," Mo clarifies.

She doesn't know yet. "Oh, she didn't say much," I answer.

It's not a lie.

"You should go. It's already eleven-forty-five. Call me when you get there!" he says, and then hangs up.

Then

The Middle Part

The first six months of Amelia and Missy's new life had been chasing adventures. Each morning, they dragged themselves from the beds they had crawled into a few hours prior and did their work. They spent the mornings taking care of the lobby for their rent, mopping the floors and emptying the garbage bins full of takeout and beer cans from the night before. Then they went to their second jobs, bouncing around between cafés and restaurants. In the early evenings, they came home to shower and sort through the sea of clothing that bobbed between their two mattresses; skirts and tops flew into the air until they both found themselves in unique combinations.

Missy had never indulged in living before this. She had never gnawed on the neck of impulse. Amelia gave Missy permission to be free because she wasn't alone. They were together, and for the first time, Missy understood how lonely she had been her whole life without a friend. Amelia felt the same, most of the time.

Occasionally, Amelia had to fight the overwhelming urge to run. Then she reminded herself that this had been her idea. She had proposed this life, she persuaded Missy to join her, and yet she had begun to feel smothered. On the other hand, just because this was her idea did not mean she had to like it. Not all things work out. That was the principle of life or something, wasn't it?

What she and Missy shared were the truths they ran away from and a loyalty to never looking back. But they didn't know each other when this all started, and now, Amelia would be lying if she said, at times, that Missy didn't grate her last nerve. The clinginess, the need for every second of Amelia's attention. Missy had begun to dress like Amelia, speak like her.

Knock, knock. The hand on the other side of the bathroom door interrupted the only time she had to herself. Amelia let the hot water pour over her face one more time. She took a deep breath as she stepped out of the shower.

"What do you want to do tonight? Go somewhere close? Are we dancing?"

Missy's voice came under the door and Amelia's body tensed with irritation. "I don't know. Let's just do something local. I'm not sure how long I'll last," Amelia called out.

She was fine; everything was fine, Amelia told herself. A good night's sleep would make her feel better. She stepped out of the bathroom and right into Missy.

"Jesus," Amelia muttered.

"Sorry, are you . . . okay?"

The concern on Missy's face made Amelia even more annoyed, which in turn made her feel guilty.

"I'm fine; I'm fine. Let me get dressed. I'll be ready in a few minutes."

The server at their local bar brought them their regular order of seltzer with lime. The friends sent the rum they hid inside apple juice bottles down their throats as a man walked up.

"Can I join you?"

Amelia choked on the liquid she was downing and spit it all over his face. The crooked smile, the scar that sewed its way through his left eyebrow. She recognized him; he had moved into the building a few doors down months ago. He was often outside, sitting in a chair and strumming his guitar.

"Sorry . . ." Amelia said. "Let me get you some napkins."

She stood up, and they locked eyes.

"I'm Felipe," he said, and placed his hand in her palm. "In case you were about to ask."

"I wasn't," Amelia said, and walked to the bar.

What she needed was a night out to talk to someone new, switch it up. Be worshipped in a different way.

Missy stared at the back of the man's head where he stood paralyzed by Amelia as she walked away. She hadn't even asked Missy if she wanted a drink. She hadn't said a word to her since they sat down. Missy coughed, and the man jumped. He turned to her. "Sorry, I didn't—"

"Yeah, yeah, you didn't see me." Missy stood to go.

"Oh no, you don't have to leave." In fact, he urged her to stay.

Probably panicked that his chance might already be over with Amelia if he offended her friend.

"It's fine. Tell her I wasn't feel well." Missy nodded in the direction of Amelia and walked out into the night.

Back in bed, Missy stared at the remote sitting on the other side of the coffee table, willing it to move closer to her. She had forgotten the tightness from the knot in her stomach. The ocean of loneliness she had spent her whole life floating in.

Amelia didn't return until the following afternoon. She walked in with her heels draped over her finger. There was a stained ring of lipstick that had been smeared around her mouth. Missy could see in her eyes that Amelia hadn't slept for a minute.

"Where were you?"

Missy wanted Amelia to explain herself and prove her wrong. She wanted Amelia to tell her that she wasn't pulling herself away, inch by inch, but her friend barely responded.

Amelia avoided Missy's eyes as she stomped across the room, unbuckled her belt, and climbed into her bed. Amelia had hoped a night out would cure her of the concerns she felt about Missy.

She had thought Felipe could remain a distraction, and yet, from the moment their eyes met, she cracked open like a snapdragon ready to bloom in the spring. She had never felt whole the way she had with him, but she couldn't say that to Missy. Amelia wanted last night all to herself. She wanted it for the rest of her life.

"I'm really tired," Amelia announced, and lay down.

There would be no more talking until she was awake again, but even then, Missy was never going to get what she wanted. Her friend, the person who had been by her side with almost no breaks for half a year, was gone.

As Amelia began to snore, it all crashed down onto Missy, how wrong her choice to stay with Amelia in the first place had been and how, if she wanted to get out, she would have to do it on her own.

Teen Pulse magazine

Forty-Eight Hours Without Estella: An Ex-Girlfriend's Journey Through Grief and the Unknown

When a person vanishes, the first fracture you think of is the family. Those closest in proximity. They are also the first to be suspected, judged. The first to crumble or to be changed, and the wounds do not stop there. Colleagues, classmates, crushes, the bus driver who tells them the same joke every morning, the neighbor whom they collect mail for, their best friend—everyone in their orbit feels the absence. Bettina Drummle grew up parallel to Estella Aubergine. Raised only blocks from one another, they came together when they were both accepted to Beaumont Academy. We sat down with Bettina, one of Estella's closest confidants and her ex-girlfriend, to check in.

TP: Bettina, thank you for being here.

Bettina: Thank you for having me.

TP: It must be difficult to live this nightmare and then be asked to talk about it in such an open and public manner. I know this is a loaded question, but how are you doing?

Bettina: Every day is different. Some days, I am so sad and stressed. Like, how do you focus on your future when someone you love is missing? It's hard not to get sucked down the rabbit hole of the online conspiracy theories and Reddit deep dives. Sometimes I get mad. Like, this was our year! A bunch of us were planning to go to Yacht Week in Croatia this summer. Now if we go, we're going to be seen as spoiled, insensitive rich kids. Why did she get to take that away from me? From my grade? Herself? But sometimes, the sun comes out, and I sit outside, and someone says something funny, and I forget.

TP: Yes, grief has so many stages. I know school is not fully in session for summer, but what is the mood like in the Beaumont community?

Bettina: It's pretty weird. She has a big presence here, so things are off. I'm sure she's loving that.

TP: You sound pretty sure that she is still out there.

Bettina: She has to be. This world doesn't make sense without her in it.

TP: What do you think it is about Estella that makes her so beloved?

Bettina: She's magnetic and dynamic—it's hard to be both enticing and surprising. With Estella, you never know what you are going to get; you just know that you want some of whatever it is.

TP: Is Estella a partyer?

Bettina: We are all quite social.

TP: Were you worried about her?

Bettina: We had broken up, but I do know she was seeing the school counselor. It doesn't really seem she got the help she needed . . .

TP: Do you think she needed help?

Bettina: Maybe. Like I said, we used to tell each other everything, and then that changed.

TP: If you could tell her anything right now, what would it be?

Bettina: That I am not going to let this bring us down. High school, summer vacations—they're supposed to be the best times of our lives, I want that for all of us.

TP: In her honor, you mean?

Bettina: Sure.

TP: Thank you so much, Bettina.

Teen Pulse has reached out to Beaumont Academy regarding any concerns the administration might have had about Estella before her disappearance, but they have yet to comment.

Now

CHAPTER 18

Bidi

I wait for the security guard to wave me in after Mo explains on Facetime that I'm family and I need to pick something up from his locker. As soon as I'm in, he sends me instructions.

Mo:

Keep your phone on. Send a text as soon as you're inside and the computer is clear. I'll need ten minutes.

My feet swallow the light streaming out from under Ms. Brodsky's door. I knock and wait.

"Come in!" her voice sings. I turn the knob and stick my head inside.

"Hi, you have walk-in hours now, right?"

Ms. Brodsky waves me in. Her room is airy and highly oxygenated, with plants in every corner. The wall of wooden drawers stands in the sunlight behind her desk. There's barely anything on top of it, just a photo of an expensive-looking dog, a computer monitor, a tiny black vinyl Chanel purse with a gold chain handle, a desk phone, and a black appointment book.

"Take a seat . . ." She waits for me to fill in the blank.

"Elizabeth."

Ms. Brodsky settles herself into the comfy chair across from me but raises an eyebrow at my phone. I push send on the text I had ready for Mo with one word, "go," and sit at the edge of the couch.

"Sorry, setting it to silent," I explain.

"So tell me, Elizabeth, what's going on?" Ms. Brodsky asks.

The amount of things ready to monsoon out my mouth make it hard to come up with anything remotely reasonable to share with her.

"I imagine it can't be easy being here right now, hmm?" She tries to help me out, and I nod.

"Mm-hmm," I concur. *Sure, let's go with that.*

"Any feeling is normal in this type of situation—worry, fear, jealousy—"

"Jealousy?" Seems like an odd reaction to a missing person.

"Oh, sure, the attention. The fanfare. All feelings are valid, Elizabeth."

"Well, I guess I just don't understand how this happened." I push.

A phone buzzes on her desk, and Ms. Brodsky sits a bit taller. "Yes, confusion and shock are completely normal in situations like these. Are you close to Estella or her family?"

"Mmm, no," I reply as the buzzing on her desk intensifies.

"What grade did you say you were in?" Ms. Brodsky starts to lift herself up, probably to look my name up in the student directory on the computer I am supposed to keep her away from. I begin to unravel.

"If something so terrible could happen to Estella Aubergine, it sort of made me realize something terrible can happen to anyone! Like, how can I trust people?"

She picks up a pad and takes some notes, locked in again.

"I can understand that concern. I assure you, though, that you can trust me. Can you tell me more about your relationship with Estella?"

"I mean, hello? She is missing! We all failed her! I did, you did!" I lean into the melodrama.

"We can't blame ourselves. We don't even know what happened." Ms. Brodsky coughs. Her phone buzzes for a third time.

"You think she was taken, don't you? There could be someone snatching beautiful rich people up at any second. Plucking us like grapes in Sonoma!" I shout.

My phone begins to vibrate as well, over and over. I sit back and cover it with my hand and take a deep breath while Brodsky tries to unpack my fabricated panic. I don't give her much time.

"When stories start this way, they rarely end well, ya know?"

Ms. Brodsky's phone buzzes again, and this time, she rises. I jump up to stop her. I don't know how long it's been, but I can't risk her catching Mo's hack job.

"No! I mean . . . don't go. I'm feeling so vulnerable!" I beg.

"One second." Ms. Brodsky ignores my plea and walks over to the desk but doesn't even glance at her computer. She grabs her phone right as mine buzzes again in my bag beside me. I take a peek while she does the same.

> Google News push alert: **BREAKING**—Influencer Estella Aubergine's ex Bettina Drummle gives exclusive interview. Claims signs of struggling prior to disappearance. Hints at mental health troubles. Did the Beaumont therapist drop the ball?

The headline leaps from my screen. I shove my phone back into my bag before Brodsky notices. She grabs a sweater that rests on her chair and rushes to the door.

"Sorry, Elizabeth, there's been a bit of an emergency. Let's schedule a follow-up?"

Ms. Brodsky storms to her office door and ushers me out, then walks down the hall and out of sight. She leaves so quickly, she doesn't realize there is no click of the lock on her door, because I catch the knob before it closes and slip back inside.

I pull out my phone and dial. There's only one ring before Mo answers.

"Did you see the news?" I ask.

"Yeah, the headline is clickbait. But *Teen Pulse* wouldn't have posted the article without running it by the police. So I checked their records and they don't have the videos of Brodsky and Estella in their evidence. Then I went back into the Beaumont footage and found that someone had tampered with it, scrubbed those moments. We are the only ones who know the truth. Us and Estella. That means we have a real shot at catching them. I couldn't get into any other files remotely, so I've gotta do it in person. What else did you find out?"

"Nothing. She just ran out of here!" I shout at him. This whole "not getting things right the first time" is not a muscle I want to keep flexing.

"Bidi! Are you telling me you are in her office alone?" Mo shouts.

Silhouettes darken the door's frosted pane, and the knob jiggles. "I have to go!" I whisper, and hang up.

I barely make it under the desk before the door opens. Two people storm in.

"You need to calm down," Pummel says.

"They are eviscerating me, Ruben. I'm all over the internet. I don't need any more attention on me right now." Brodsky's voice is frantic.

"You? This could ruin my livelihood!" Pummel shouts. Stress emanates out of them both, more pungent than whatever body spray Principal Pummel is doused in.

"We gave her a chance. If this is how she is going to behave, then she's going to pay." His voice is grave.

"Oh, Ruben—"

There is spice behind Brodsky's tone, a jarring shift in their conversation. Something ignites. A thud on the front of the desk and then the sound of kissing penetrates the wood I am hiding beneath. My stomach turns at what might come next.

"Take me to lunch, somewhere expensive," Brodsky coos.

Her feet come toward the chair I am hiding behind. I hold my knees tight, prepared to be spotted and pulled out, but the chair doesn't move. Instead, the chain on her purse drags across the top of the desk.

"Of course, I've got the company card—omakase at Akikos?" Ruben Pummel asks.

"Yes! That milk bread–gold caviar situation is exactly what I need."

"You encrypted the files, right?" He double-checks.

"Mm-hmm," she says.

"And the paper files?"

"Yes," she hisses. "Locked up safe in this room."

"Good girl."

I wince at the sloppy mouth sounds of another kiss. The real mystery here is how Pummel convinced a woman to fall for him and do his bidding.

They follow one another out the door. I wait a few minutes to move, then rush to the wall of cabinets and rip open the drawers. My fingers dance over the tabs with student names, but Estella's is missing, a gap in the filing. Not even a medical form remains. I pull out my phone and send a text to Pippa.

Where the hell are you? We have a problem.

CHAPTER 19
Pippa

Bettina's and Two's phones started blowing up ten minutes into the ride. I sit in silence and try to listen to Bettina's sharp whispers. Without a charger, I have no clue what's going on.

"I told them what would happen if they didn't give me what I wanted." Bettina throws her arms up in irritation.

If Bettina did make Estella disappear, I am not interested in being next. The car stops.

"Get dressed. We'll wait outside," Bettina tells me.

Bettina exits first and waits outside in front of signage. The Bay Area Social Club makes Soho House look like a Starbucks. The exclusive high-society club rotates locations, chefs, ambience. Entry is more competitive than an Ivy League college. Two follows her, but I stop him.

"But what if these clothes don't fit?" I plead.

Two shrugs with his whole body, his expression giving, "That's never seemed to bother you before!" He slams the door shut, so me and my raggedy underwear have privacy.

Unfortunately for Two, the indigo top and matching high-waisted skirt fit me almost perfectly. His scoff when I step out of the car confirms that I look as good as I feel.

"Your table is ready," Two informs Bettina before he gets back into the car we just exited.

"Why isn't Two coming with us?" I ask.

Bettina's face morphs, confused, amused.

"I can't eat with my intern. That would totally mess with the power dynamic, obviously. Come on, the girls are upstairs."

The lobby of this building is narrow and twisty. The walls are plastered with collages of vintage movie magazines, but the ode to Hollywood turns into a black metal wall behind a young woman with maroon hair. She sits up at the sight of Bettina and picks up the receiver of an old rotary phone.

"Ms. Drummle," she announces into the landline.

The black wall behind her slides open to reveal a loft space converted into a fine dining restaurant. There are no decorations, just power-washed walls in a stark cement room with massive round booths placed haphazardly with twenty feet between them. On the other side of the room, a DJ vibes to diffuse the sounds of ice clanking and champagne corks popping beside a bar made of brass and acrylic.

We walk past a table surrounded by servers, who reach out over the patrons' heads with huge saucers mildly sunken in the center. The dishes touch down in front of each guest at the exact same time, and the servers vanish along with any empty glasses. The precision is unmatched.

Bettina stops at the back of a round blue velvet booth and waits as a life-size lazy Susan built into the floor activates. The table turns slowly to reveal the rest of Estella and Bettina's crew.

"Finally, you heaux! We're starving," one of them snarks.

"This is Pippa," Bettina introduces me. "Pippa, this is Prue, Essence, and Patina."

No one offers so much as a fake smile. They are not amused to make the acquaintance.

Bettina scoots in and reaches for a clipboard with the menu attached to it. I sit down on the edge of the booth, but she kicks me out moments later to step onto the main floor. Multiple servers rush forward.

"I need to speak to the somm. This champagne selection is vile," Bettina declares.

"Sit back down," Essence says, offering me an invitation once Bettina has been ushered to the bar.

I slide into the booth and settle where Bettina was. Smiles crack across her friends' faces, one mouth at a time, until they are all one big leopard licking their lips. Prue pulls out her phone, the others do the same.

"Oh my God! She never got over Estella. Never," Essence whispers.

"It's so cringe. I'm shocked she showed after that interview," Patina snarks.

Prue turns to me. "Was she mortified in the car?"

"I think so? I don't actually know what happened. My phone died." I pull the device from my bra strap, where I stuck it after changing, and show them the proof of the black screen.

"That *Teen Pulse* reporter did her no favors," Prue whispers with delight.

"It's so embarrassing considering Estella was at *Teen Vogue*," Essence adds.

"The story did *not* come off well. It seems like she's on the brink of a menty b? Evaporating like a pile of coke at a bonfire on Muir Beach?" Patina smirks.

They just lost Estella, and are already hungry for anything to take down Bettina.

"I got the last branzino!" Bettina reappears, and I slide out of the booth so she can return to the center seat. I fit myself back in, relegated to the end.

"Queen."

"Love that for you. Love that for us."

The girls all gush, gears switched back to adoring her. They wash Bettina up and down with compliments like they weren't just imagining slipping the shoes off her corpse. A server with no food walks up once Bettina is settled. She nods her approval for him to speak.

"The fry tasting menu," he says.

His announcement triggers the plate drop: Three baskets, each with a duo of dips, are presented before us, along with a bucket of champagne. The shoestring fries are dusted with a yuzu-and-garlic salt. The white-pepper buttermilk ranch is a perfect complement to the crispy outside and smooth, creamy center. Bettina reaches for the crinkled purple yam paired with wasabi aioli and nước chấm.

"So is this just a regular lunch, or is this a strategy meeting?" Essence asks.

The head server interrupts again to announce another dish before Bettina can answer.

"The salad."

A huge metal bowl the size of a steel drum lands in the center of our table while a server climbs a ladder to hang over us with clown-sized tongs to toss and dress. They portion servings into bowls and then vanish.

Bettina's friends' eyes look at each other in a silent language. Finally, Essence clears her throat. "We saw your interview."

"And?" Bettina dares them to defy her.

"We just . . . didn't know you were doing that," Prue says quickly.

"Well, neither did I! They came to me. I couldn't say no to *Teen Pulse*, could I? Plus, I'm vulnerable. I mean, hello? I'm experiencing trauma in real time. I need support, not for you to make me feel worse," Bettina scolds. "They say you really know who your people are when times get tough."

Bettina pulls an expensive camera out from her purse. She scans her minions and takes a photo of each of them, then turns to me and snaps a few photos as well, as if her lens sees through to our truths.

"Well, if you want your people, then who is she?" Essence points at me.

Fair question.

"I told you; that's Pippa." Bettina chews and talks at the same time. The friends check me out again.

"We haven't heard of her," Prue says, as if I can't hear her.

"Of course you haven't. I recently discovered her," Bettina snaps.

"What does she do?" Essence asks.

"I haven't figured that out yet. But . . . okay, so there is another reason why you are here. I want to have a party," Bettina announces.

Silence falls.

"Do you really think you should be having a party right now?" Prue asks.

Another server appears with the rest of our lunch before Bettina can respond. Plates rain down. Crispy sushi rice with spicy salmon on top and little gold flecks. A pizza with a perfectly fried egg and freshly shaved truffles. A burrata bowl with a whole baguette to dip. Wagyu sliders. Seared asparagus.

When the servers finish and depart, Bettina reaches across the table and grabs a slider, training her eyes on Prue.

"You were saying, Prue?" Her words are simple, but we all hear the threat on her tongue.

"No, I just, well, I don't want you to overexert yourself with everything that's going on . . ." Prue stammers.

"What? Estella disappears, and now we don't get to enjoy the summer before senior year?" Bettina responds.

"That's not what I mean," Prue says.

"Then what did you mean? This whole thing is just Estella doing what she always does: anything for attention."

Bettina isn't experiencing trauma. She's not even worried. She's pissed.

"If she did leave, that means she might come back . . ." Prue reminds Bettina.

"Are you scared of Estella, Prue?"

Prue takes Bettina's jab head-on. She's practiced. A pecking order cracks through their flawless contouring.

"We need to have an event, so everyone can see that we don't need Estella Aubergine!" Bettina rattles off.

All of us flinch at the same time, but Bettina is too deep into her speech to notice.

"Everyone knows she is a heinous witch. The only thing she is better at than making you feel seen is letting you know you aren't anything at all."

Her friends shrink behind their glasses and food to avoid the tirade.

"Why did you date her for so long, then?" I ask.

A pause hits.

"You can't help who you love. But she doesn't get to ruin my life anymore," Bettina snaps.

Patina notices something, then reaches across the table to the electric-blue purse between me and Bettina.

"Oh my God, *the* Balenciaga? Weren't there only four made in that color?"

Bettina's wrath shifts to Patina as she holds the designer clutch close to her chest. "I can't believe I let Estella borrow it when we were together. She kept 'forgetting' to return it, just messing with me, like she always does. Thank God I got it back before all of this went down."

Yes, the purse that can barely hold your cell phone is more important than your ex-girlfriend's well-being.

"So what sort of party are you going to have?" I pivot again and try to save face.

Bettina drops a lychee from a plate of fresh tropical fruit into her empty champagne flute and then fills it to the brim. The bubbles fizz over the top.

"An epic 'moving on' moment. We just need a theme."

Her friends start to spitball. They shout out ideas from every direction. It's pitch after pitch, like *Shark Tank* on 2x speed meets the *SNL* writers' room.

"Wellness, spas, and self-care: microneedling and macro partying," Essence says.

"You need to go deeper. Vulnerability. Like that show where people are dropped in the middle of nature and have to stay alive. It's like a metaphor for resilience. We are going to survive this, ya know? Naked and NOT afraid vibes?" Patina's pitch comes with an earnest conviction that balances a completely unhinged idea.

"I think you go full vitamin D, beach, and high-concept frozen beverages," Prue adds to end the pitch fest, short and sweet.

They wait for Bettina to respond or critique or give the nod. Instead, she snaps her fingers above her head and the guy who summoned the food reappears at the table.

"We need all of this packed and brought down to my intern. He's downstairs. Make sure to use extra dry ice."

He accepts her commands, and the servers descend, this time to collect our food. Essence is midbite when they remove the plate from under her chin. Bettina rises. I see the other girls' eyes talk back and forth, unsure how to respond. Prue begins to get up and follow, but Bettina shakes her head. "You aren't coming."

"Bettina, we always go to Marlowe after lunch," Patina says, confused.

"Oh, I'm still going to Marlowe. You all need to take a moment and decide which side of history you want to be on. Those ideas were pathetic. Come on, Pippa; we're going shopping."

Bettina doesn't even ask to see the bill. She holds her credit card out to be scanned, then scooches me out of the booth.

The San Francisco weather has shifted brisk in the hour we were gone, as it likes to do midday. Two stands at attention, now covered in a thick moss-green knit scarf like the north side of an oak tree, waiting for us to return. The procession of servers carrying the leftovers covered with bags of dry ice is straight out of District 1 in *The Hunger Games*. Bettina walks past Two and steps into the back seat.

"All right, get in," Bettina calls to me while Two collects the food. He piles it all into the trunk, then jumps in quickly so as not to impact the customized temperature.

Bettina relives the luncheon to Two, historical fiction at its finest—she plays the victim so well, she deserves a prize. Well, Two would probably give her a Pulitzer for waking up in the morning. When she finishes, she picks up her phone to scroll and ignores him.

Two puts in his ear pods, then turns his music loud enough that I can feel the bass.

"Bettina, you don't really think Estella would pretend to get taken, do you? Why would she do that to her mother?" I ask when it's clear Two isn't paying attention.

"I think Estella is gone, and that's all that matters," she snaps.

The car stops, and Two opens the door for her.

"Come on, they closed the store for us." Gleeful for the first time since meeting, Bettina pulls me into the boutique.

Shopping with Bettina is the same as eating with Bettina, expensive and overabundant. Shopping has never been a pastime of mine, but when I go, I head straight to the sale rack. Bettina shops in stores that don't even have sale racks. The clothes aren't even marked with prices. She stands while the staff buzz around her. They gather clothes by the armful from the racks and shelves.

"No stripes."

"Grab every scarf on the premises."

"What do you have from last season?"

An employee steps out from the back, and I rush to her before Bettina can issue another instruction.

"Do you have a charger?" I ask the sales rep.

She inspects my Android with deep confusion, like she's never seen a non-Apple product.

"I just need a USB-C cord. You must have one somewhere. I'm a guest of Bettina."

She takes the phone from me and walks across the shop to the front desk. After rooting through some drawers, she pulls out the cord I need and holds it up for me to see. I give her the thumbs-up and watch her plug it in.

"Ahem."

The manager of the shop circles me like a buzzard, hitting every angle available. She and Bettina shoot Pinterest board themes back and forth over my head: vintage but not gimmicky, retro but not too specific, don't want to get caught up in one era. Bettina sends me behind the curtain with a rack of outfits.

"Why were you there?" Bettina asks me once I step out of the dressing room in a red strappy dress.

"Where?" I ask.

"At her house," Bettina presses.

Her eyes burn a jealousy as green as a jade geode.

"I'm helping with the garden. Flowers are sort of my thing. I, uh, I was getting inspiration at the school yesterday. You know, walking in her shoes."

Bettina eyes me, but relief betrays her venomous glare. The reason why she's taken such interest in me becomes clear. She thought I was dating Estella. Her competition.

Bettina flips her wrist and swats me back with displeasure. She opens the door to make an announcement.

"Let's go with the next color palette, everyone!"

Metal racks and flat shoes shuffle around the shop at her command.

"I've literally never seen you at . . . anything," Bettina says to me.

Of course she hasn't.

"I work a lot," I explain.

"You have your twenties to work. You should enjoy this now."

"Enjoy what now?" I ask.

Bettina holds up a silk baby-pink slip dress against my skin. She wrinkles her nose and flings it onto a bench behind her.

"High school! This whole city is still ours for the taking. Especially now, with Estella gone. There's enough for all of us."

The vibes aren't particularly giving "not guilty."

"You think she would walk away from the chance to try to show you up at every event of the year?" I ask.

Bettina's face knots as she begins to sort through outfits, sliding hangers down the rack more and more violently.

"If she really was taken, a lot of people think it could be you," I add.

She stops. "I have no more energy to spend on Estella Aubergine, let alone disappearing her. But don't get me wrong; I could. My father has clearances you don't even know exist."

The note that the cops came to talk to Ms. Aubergine about floats across my memory. A knock on the door prevents me from digging in further. The staff stream in with new outfits for her to approve. Once she is satisfied, they ask my shoe size. All I've ever known is cotton stuffed in the toe, buying two sizes too big so there's more room to grow.

I reach down to my foot to try to read the number on the bottom of my worn-down sole. Bettina snatches it from me and throws my shoe into the trash.

"Who has the measuring tape?" She dissects me in centimeters. Bettina pokes and prods with each option, shaping me into what she needs. A distraction, but one that's not so loud that she will be overcome by my presence, just enough to tolerate me in her line of view. The same way I bet she built up her minions.

"What happened with you two? This time, I mean," I ask.

Bettina touches the points of her fingernails against the pads of her thumbs as she talks.

"It was just time," Bettina says.

That's code for she got dumped. She must hate that she didn't get a say in their breakup.

"I need to go charge my phone. Put the blue look on; I think that's your color," Bettina commands, then walks out of the changing room.

The blue-and-green-bejeweled two-toned shorts with a white shirt, socks, and clogs wait for me on the wall. The ensemble gives peacock, but I don't hate it. I pull it on just as the door flies back open.

Bettina holds my phone above her head. I expect there to be a text from Bidi revealing our investigation, but all I see is my screen saver. A collage of my flower creations. My best work.

"You made these?" she questions.

"Yes. I told you I do flow—" She holds her finger up to silence me and types furiously on her phone.

"How have you not gone viral?" She searches my name on Instagram but my main grid is empty.

"Because I'm not giving my work up for free," I shoot back.

I use a finsta to lurk and snoop, but I don't post my sculptures.

Bettina's whole face smiles. She jumps up and down and shrieks, "TWO, TWO!"

Two comes bounding in like the white Labrador he is.

"I literally DID discover her. I was just talking shit before to keep those idiots in check. Wow, my instincts are so good."

It's not every day you get colonized on a shopping spree. The gift of relevance Bettina believes she is offering me sets her ablaze.

"Are you . . . okay?" I ask.

"I'm more than okay! The theme. The party. Flowers. Rebirth. Growth. YOU are going to make me a flower crown for my party, and I am going to introduce you to the world. Make you a star."

Bettina beams; the ego inflation is palpable. I take a few steps back to make room for the extra space she takes up. Bettina dangles her fingers at me, a handshake deal.

"I, um—"

I feel myself begin to splinter. The offer is what I have been dying for, an entryway. The way Bettina moves, she could really help me . . . But if I let Bettina Drummle become my publicity pimp, she will have total control. I will owe her forever, be *owned* by her like Two is, which I imagine is exactly how she likes all her relationships. Plus, Bidi would never forgive me for selling out.

"The vibes are very philanthropic. This is going to be *epic*. Two, write this down!" Bettina ignores my hesitation, lost in whatever dopamine boost comes with saviorism. Two pulls out his iPad, ready to type.

"Umm—can we pause? I need to think," I say, unsure if I want to sign over my fate to someone I still think could be involved in a kidnapping.

Bettina moves toward me, and with each step, she doubles in size.

"Pippa, maybe you aren't understanding. Do you even have a clue what I can do? I could snap my fingers, and you would have Chappell Roan's people contacting you to art direct a music video. I could post a picture and in days there would be seven people out there re-creating your style, probably better than you. Have you been living under a rock so long that you think you haven't been drenched in my influence for years? You think Estella would be who she is if it weren't for me? I don't put my signature on everything I create, because you'd see my name so much it would be tacky."

The weight of her starts to build pressure in my head. Lips curled in both directions. Bettina leans in. "Don't you want to be rich?"

Laid bare, the question stares back at me in the mirror. *Of course I do. Who doesn't?* But right now, I would settle for knowing I'm not getting kicked out of my home at the end of the week.

The personal shoppers return, all six hands filled with hangers. Bettina ushers them in to hang the outfits up around us, covering the walls with a new wardrobe. Bettina collects her things, then looks me up and down.

"Keep what works. Consider that your payment for the crown." Bettina points to the clothing strewn across the room.

"What? No. Bettina, I can't; you can't." I never agreed to create anything; this is happening too fast.

"The correct response is 'thank you.' I'll be in touch."

Bettina throws her sunglasses on and walks out. Alone, I check my phone now that it has charge.

Estella Aubergine's Troubled Secrets Bubbling to the Surface

Estella's Darkness Before the Disappearance

School Denies Any Contact Between Aubergine and Beaumont Counselor

Clickbait headlines pop up one after the other about the interview Bettina gave.

The last notification I open is a text.

Bidi:

We have a problem.

Of course, we have a problem. Our lives are just years of problems we never could afford to fix. Instead, we stuffed them into our thrifted jean pockets and too-big shoes. We pass them on to whoever's next to receive the hand-me-down.

I pick up a skirt from the wall with a bright floral pattern. The petals overlap, crowded, until dahlias burst out, overshadowing the rest. I throw it over my arm and take a few more things from the wall. The shopper who helped me with my phone earlier knocks and enters. She reaches for the clothes in my hands. "Is that all you want?"

I scan the room. I'm never going to be able to afford clothes like this, but accepting them means binding myself to Bettina forever.

"No. I'll take everything." I make my decision.

She collects all the clothing, then hands me a tote bag. Inside are the clothes I put on this morning. Ill-fitting and washed out compared to the deep turquoises and blues I wear now.

"That guy with Bettina said to give these to you," the shopper explains, then leads me out.

Smoke-rimmed cooler bags of dry ice with the leftovers from the lunch sit by the staff members who hold two garment bags nearly as tall as me with my new wardrobe. The manager catches my gaze and swoops in to explain.

"Ms. Drummle said something about these bags making her car smell like a Whole Foods hot bar. Whenever you are ready, you can order your Uber. It comes with her membership, so I'm sure she won't mind."

Money is the secret code to another universe.

He grabs an iPad out of the stand in front of him to hand to me. I am binding myself to her whim, but she could also catapult me out of this stratosphere. A montage of my ascension plays in my head. Pop-up flower crown shops throughout the Bay, my sculptures appearing overnight on a corner, people hoping to catch me in the act. I could be the Banksy of flowers. The Bouquet Basquiat.

I enter the address for Bidi's house.

When a car arrives, the staff stream out carrying the excess of clothes and food as though this is normal. They load the trunk while I get into the back seat to respond to Bidi.

> We have so many problems, you have no idea. Meet me outside your house, I'm on the way.

CHAPTER 20
Bidi

A giant black SUV pulls up. The back door opens, and a garment bag flies out of the back seat and into my arms. Pippa steps out of the car with an identical bundle. The driver unloads more onto the curb.

"Pippa? What is this? And should you even be touching those?" I nod to the white smoke swirling around the bags she attempts to gather.

"It's fine." Pippa manages to lift all three bags, but I drop the one she handed to me. I don't move. I have to tell her that I've been working with Mo on our case, even after he pretended not to remember her and then stole her idea.

"They aren't bombs, Bidi; these are the leftovers."

"Why didn't you text me?" I hiss. I may not be a fan of capitalism, but food is a universal right, which I deserve to partake in.

"My phone died," she explains.

"What happened to 'no recklessness'? What happened to communication?" I stand up and storm into the house. Pippa drags the bags and follows me. When she gets inside, she talks one thousand miles a minute.

"I offered to help Ms. Aubergine with her garden so I could get inside their house, and it worked! She hired me to fix it all up, which means I'll be there all the time. Bettina must have followed me because she was there when I left, and she took me to brunch and shopping. She is having this deranged 'yay Estella is gone' party and she hired me to make her a flower crown. Two jobs in one day, not bad. Plus, that means we get insider access to her. I mean, we basically solved this thing," Pippa boasts.

Of course, Pippa gets kidnapped to brunch while I was hiding under a desk trying not to hear elder-millennial face sucking. She lifts the dry ice out of the bags and starts unloading the Tupperware, which covers the whole counter in two rows of food, all labeled. Each has its own vibe. The hamachi tartare with microgreens and avocado is my first stop. The accompanying wonton chips were expertly packed into a mesh bag to preserve their crispiness. Pippa grabs a container I haven't gotten to yet, and she pulls the top off some extremely gooey mac and cheese.

The bathroom door swings open, and Mo emerges through steam thicker than the dry ice's. Shirtless with a towel wrapped around his waist, he walks through the apartment silently, straight up to Pippa. Eyes locked, they share a glare for a moment, one of mutual hate and respect. Finally, he breaks and turns to the food.

"Yo, what is all of this?" He hovers over the containers.

"Just pick something," I say, and wave his ass out of the way. He can't be the one to drop the news about our joint investigation.

The garlic mashed yucca and seared duck breast calls his name, and he nabs the last mini shortbread tartlet with sweet potato mousse. He sits at the table and stuffs his face.

Pippa looks at Mo. "You are dismissed." She tries to shoo him away.

Mo rolls his eyes. "You don't own this kitchen."

"Fine. Come on, Bidi."

I let her pull me down the stairs.

"Okay, continue. What is going on? And remember: no secrets," I hiss, and swallow my hypocrisy with a big gulp of bone broth consommé.

"I forgot the biggest thing!"

Alarm bells ring in my brain.

"Bidi, this is a for-real secret. Big-time."

"Okay . . ."

"Someone left a note for Ms. Aubergine. It didn't make any sense. It said, 'Alberta sees you.' The cops say they think it's just a prank, but they caught someone in a black hoodie dropping it off on the security tape—"

The same person stalking Pippa . . . they're getting bolder. There's no time for feelings or reason. We need to put everything on the table.

"Sorry, Pippa, hold on. Mo! Get down here!"

"What? No! I just said you can't tell anyone!" Pippa shouts.

"Listen, he's already been helpful! He has been keeping tabs on the police investigation. He is giving us access to Beaumont. If you want the money, then we can't get got like Estella did. That means Mo has to be in, all right?"

"I can't believe you!" Pippa shouts once she's heard the truth. "You ARE working with Mo?! Behind my back? You lied to me?"

Mo hops down the stairs, still eating. Pippa's neck twists like a Snapple cap once he reaches the bottom.

"No, I mean, yes, but not the whole time—he knows what he's doing," I explain to her.

"Fine. If you get to make decisions, so do I. And I say Ms. Aubergine is no longer a suspect," she pushes back.

"This isn't about her—" I say.

"She's alone. You don't know what that's like."

Pippa's right. I've never known peace, and I never will if we get so caught up in this that we can't pull ourselves out. All the butter and truffle oil I consumed starts to make waves in my stomach.

"Right now, we need to focus on getting Mo into the counselor's office without her knowing so he can open the restricted file about Estella because the paper copy is missing. While you were off being wined and dined, I was in the trenches, and Estella wants something in her file that the administration is not giving her," I say.

Stubborn, Pippa crosses her arms across her chest.

"If you want to help Estella's mother, then help her, Pippa, by finding out if someone took Estella. I am telling you that Ms. Brodsky has something to do with it, and we need Mo to prove it."

"If she doesn't want to help, she shouldn't. She's clearly already too emotionally invested in the investigation, which makes her a liability," Mo interjects.

Pippa storms over and snatches the remainder of the hamachi from his hands. "Fine," she says.

"Fine?" I ask.

"Yes, I will get you into the school counselor's office. We share what you find, then we go our separate ways. You focus on your investigation, and I will focus on mine."

Mo snorts.

"Laugh all you want," Pippa says. "But I know how to get back into that office."

"How?" Mo wears his disbelief as rudely as possible. I elbow him.

"You have to do everything I say," Pippa tells him. In other words, she's going to make this hell.

"If you know how to do this, why wouldn't you just do it on your own?" I question.

"Because she needs us," Mo croons.

"I do," Pippa admits. "But like I said—after this, we're done."

CHAPTER 21

Pippa

The garment bags drag along the gravel and leave a trail of my disdain from Bidi's place to mine. I can't believe she took that traitor's side.

"Hey!"

I stop and turn to Mo, who jogs toward me.

"What is it, Mo?"

His eyes jump around, from my shoes to my hair, but they never make direct contact. He thinks he's better than me.

"I want to know what your issue is!" he says. "You've changed."

I stand before him, this guy who's doubled in size since the last time I knew him. A guy who now knows how to shape-shift to navigate these worlds.

"I am not the one who has changed, *Maurice*. You left. That's my issue, and now you come barging back in pretending like you don't even know who I am. Then you try to get in the middle of me and my best friend? I get that you go to school with rich celebrity kids and you think we need you to find Estella, but you know what I realized? All of this mess started happening when you came around. Maybe you should worry about me switching my focus to you. I'm keeping a list, my dude." I glare him down bad.

Mo's face hardens.

"You think you are different from Bidi, Pippa? You do exactly what you want and expect other people to fall in line. You deserve each other, honestly—"

Mo storms back to the house.

It takes all my strength to get the clothes across the street. After the bell chimes as the door of the shop swings open, I collapse onto the garment bounty. Jo's fingers snap in my face.

"You're blocking the door. Come on!" Jo says.

Crowds march to the counter, where a big yellow sign with black letters is taped.

EVERYTHING MUST GO.

Bettina's name flashes on my phone. I've learned my lesson about missing her calls.

"I've got to take this." I shove past everyone and rush to Jo's office, pulling the garment bags inside with me.

Bettina enters from the left of the screen and stops to check out her profile in a short, deep blue, sequined dress, then disappears behind the nearest dressing curtain. She reemerges in a new look, this time a fairy purple. The draped gown moves in waves.

"I decided I want you to make four of your crowns. One for me and one for each of the girls," she says. A bribe to keep them on her side.

"Um, four custom pieces?" I clarify.

I can hear Bidi in my head. *Tell her no. Don't sell out. Stand your ground.*

"Yes, and I want you to really go for it. Performance pieces."

Bettina disappears again behind the changing curtain. The purple look flies out onto the floor. She reappears seconds later in fabric that looks like liquid silver. It cascades from her chest into a one-arm waterfall.

"I hope you have been paying attention. You should design the crowns for these outfits," Bettina clarifies.

"Blue, purple, silver. That's three," I remind her.

"Yes, those are for the girls. I haven't picked my outfit yet, but even when I do, no one can see it. I can't risk it getting leaked, so you better make mine flexible and fierce."

She wants a coronation headpiece. "When exactly is this party?" I ask.

"You'll get notice." The call ends.

When I step out into the shop, Bahia Padaria is popping. Customers pull the snacks and napkins off the shelves. The cat food goes five cans at a time. Shoppers come to the counter, arms full of tissue boxes and tampons and chips, and they lay down their offerings in condolence. I guess the neighborhood isn't too mad about us closing as long as they get a deal out of it. We watch the hours pass on the clock on the wall. Each one marks another empty shelf.

Jo stares from her perch at the devastation after the last customer walks out. There won't be a need to pack if there's nothing left. When night falls, I start to clean and organize as Jo sips ginger ale.

She's drying out, but I'm not getting my hopes up. We've been here before; it never lasts long.

I finish my duties and walk out of the store. Instinct makes me grab my phone to text Bidi and let her know I am heading to the cemetery, but I stop myself. I need to learn to do life by myself now.

Leaning up against a gravestone, I take out the blueprint of the garden that Ms. Aubergine gave me and begin to draw. I mark which colors and flowers will go where. Space fillers, like the thoughts I can't keep from floating up to the forefront of my brain.

I wonder about Mamãe, if she's really coming back and not just hovering above in the morning fog to tempt me out of sanity. Dissipating before I ever get the chance to know her outside of my imagination. I wonder if she will prove me wrong and release me from the night terror I've been trapped in since she left and never looked back.

I wonder about Estella, if she's tied up somewhere starved of light or lying face down in a canal, or if she's been going in every direction but ours, thinking about everyone but us. I wonder what Estella is doing while her mother's heart hangs so heavy it could shatter the peony pendant in my panel. The one I have started to wear every night.

I draw and work so long the early-morning mourners stream into the cemetery, grieving mothers who remain unaware that I picked apart their well wishes and condolences to make something new. I walk through the same door that opened into Estella's disaster just a few days ago. On the street, I see a massive shadow stalk through the garden across the way. My signature move to dive behind the nearest bush sends me into the neighbor's front lawn. I watch as Ms. Aubergine's lawyer, Jaggers, stops under Estella's window, then doubles back to get a better look. *Creep.* I wait for him to go back inside the house before I step out. From here, it should take only twenty minutes to get to the school.

I text Bidi.

Meet me at beaumont.

My phone buzzes.

Bidi:

leaving now

Beaumont is empty as the heavy door clicks shut behind me.

"Mr. Maurice's guest, right?" the security guard asks, squinting. I nod.

The air-conditioning feels good against the layer of sweat on my skin when I walk deeper inside.

Ms. Magwitch adjusts her eye patch as she comes out of the office behind the front desk of the library. Her keys lie strewn halfway out of her purse next to her badge.

"Oh!" She jumps when she sees me. "Pippa?"

"Ms. Magwitch, I think I need your help."

She rushes to the other side of the front desk. "Pippa, what is it?"

I turn to her wide eyes. "My aunt's store. We're losing it. We probably will be moving by the end of the week."

"What? Where?" she asks, aghast. When I first met her, she seemed desperate to be helpful. I tugged on the right heart-string.

"I don't know, but we can't afford to stay. And I didn't know where else to go."

"I'm so sorry, Pippa."

Ms. Magwitch pulls me in for a hug. She smells like rosemary and lemon.

"Well, there's only one thing to do in a situation like this," she says.

"What?" I ask.

She grabs her keys. "Come with me."

We take the stairs and then turn a few corners and land inside the cafeteria. She shuffles the keys and pulls one to unlock the door of the walk-in fridge.

"I worked in restaurants for years, from high school all the way through my MFA program. One thing I know about fancy places like this is if you get in good with the kitchen staff, you are set."

The cold is powerful when we first enter the walk-in. Pristine steel stretches in every direction and makes the kitchen feel like people are brought back here and sliced open from head to toe and then hung out to dry. Magwitch grabs half a loaf of bread and takes a hunk of cheese from a nearby shelf. I admire the rack of ramps and quail eggs, then grab a few items before we head out to the empty cafeteria.

"Cornichon, pickled beets, mortadella. Ricotta. A foodie, huh?"

"I've worked at the Padaria my whole life—almost anything can be a sandwich," I say, shrugging off her words.

Ms. Magwitch tears a chunk from the loaf of bread and starts to dress it. I follow suit, and scoop the middle out just enough to make a divot, then stack the meat thinly slice by slice before marinating it with the various condiments, like oil and vinegar and sweet plum mustard. A layer of ricotta smothers the other half of the bread. My phone screen saver activates when I knock it with my elbow; images of my sculptures shift every few seconds. They catch her eye.

"I make these big flower crowns and sculptures," I explain.

"These are wonderful, Pippa! You could sell them!"

"I do. Well, I did, at the store—though I guess I have private clients now, too . . . Bettina Drummle hired me. Ms. Aubergine did too."

"You've been spending time with her? Estella's mother?" Magwitch asks.

"Mm-hmm, yeah. She needs the company, and the garden needs my help."

She thinks intently. "Pippa, you should be careful . . . with all of this."

She gestures at the larger space.

Ah. She means this world and whatever I am trying to do in it. The awkward librarian I have met twice thinks she knows me enough to give life advice, which means I have her exactly where I want her.

"Listen. I'm still new, but this whole situation with the Aubergines sounds messy." She adds, "People like us, we don't get the upper hand in these situations—"

I shove my food into my mouth and start to clear up. Her plate is still half full, but she rises as well.

"No, don't get up. You aren't done eating." I grab the keys lying on the table and shake them. "Trust me. I get the shop sorted in thirty minutes, and it's way bigger than this."

I grab all the food we picked out and return each item to its rightful spot; all the labels are centered and facing forward by the time I get back to the table. Ms. Magwitch gathers her belongings.

"Don't forget these!" I say, and drop the keys into her bag.

Magwitch studies me back out in the hallway. "Pippa, let's go upstairs. We can look into loans, I can help you with the paperwork—"

"Oh, thank you, Ms. Magwitch, but I don't think there is time. You were right, though, I do feel better," I say.

"Well, if you change your mind, you know where to find me," she says, and walks away. I wait for her to disappear down the hall to head to the next stop.

A voice ricochets from the direction of Ms. Brodsky's door. I stop a few feet away and watch Mo pull out a bobby pin. He jabs it at the keyhole.

"Aren't you supposed to be good at this?" Bidi juts her chin out in judgment, like she knows how to pick a lock.

"No, Bidi. I'm not a robber. I am a sleuth. One's an art; the other's a crime."

"Well, you and your art suck—"

They flap their arms and lips at each other in slow motion, while I sit in the glory of what I am about to do.

"Need some help?" I speak before they see me. Bidi's and Mo's backs arch. They whip around, startled.

"Where the hell have you been?" Bidi asks.

"Having lunch." I smirk.

"Um, this was *your* plan, so . . . now what do we do?"

Bidi points to the locked door. I let them squirm a bit before I hold my hand out to reveal the massive piece of metal in my palm.

"This is the skeleton key. It opens all the doors in the building. Ms. Brodsky is off today; I called earlier. Sounds like her car got towed, super unfortunate." I wink and wait for them to gather that I was the one who made the call to have the car towed. They are going to wish they didn't burn me when I crush this investigation.

"Text me when you are done." I unlock the counselor's office door for them.

On the way back to the library, I bask in the pride that for once, I came up with the plan, made it work, and saved the day. The room is still, so I tiptoe in and will the universe to stay on my side. The door to Ms. Magwitch's office is open, and from the other side of the counter I can see it is empty. Her bag rests just at the edge of the desk.

"Ms. Magwitch?" I speak loud enough that if she were close, she would hear, but there is no answer, so I rush into the office and rummage through her purse in search of the massive key chain.

"Pippa?"

I jump and turn to Ms. Magwitch in the doorway, where she holds the key chain in her hand. Her eyes land on the giant skeleton key I removed earlier in the cafeteria.

Crap.

"I—I—"

Plants cry for help when a pathogen invades. The leaves call out to their roots to secrete an acid that brings good bacteria to fight off the bad. If they held their sobs inside, they would die, but why would they? When they cry for help, help comes.

"Pippa, you need to tell me what is going on right now."

"We're just trying to help!" I word vomit.

Ms. Magwitch starts to shake with rage. "What did you do?"

"I, um—the counselor's office," I whisper. Magwitch runs, so I follow.

CHAPTER 22

Bidi

Mo sits down at the computer, and the monitor lights up his face like he just found the Holy Grail. He bypasses the desktop login with no problem, but the computer beeps loudly when he searches for Estella's name and is denied entry to the files.

"Okay, but this is the thing you *are* supposed to be so good at," I push after a few beats.

"Shh." Mo rushes over to his bag and pulls out a device with a cord, then attaches it to the computer.

"What are you doing?"

"I can't do this here. We don't have time. The school security system is shit, but the encryption they added is something that will take more time; these files are way harder to crack into. Once I download her desktop, I'll work on it at home. I just need ten minutes to get it all."

I decide to use the time to snoop. We know the file cabinets are useless, but I open Ms. Brodsky's desk drawer and find a Halloween candy stash. I take a dark-chocolate Milky Way, then try the drawer underneath to see if she separates the salty snacks from the sweet, but it doesn't open.

It's safe in this room.

Ms. Brodksy's voice from the last time I was in here replays in my head. I assumed she meant the main cabinet. I drop down to the keyhole, which isn't as ornate as the one on the door. Maybe the bobby pin trick does work sometimes. I pull one out of my pocket and jiggle it. Nothing. I twist it upward and back again and the drawer clicks and opens. Estella's name stares back from the file inside.

"Done! Bidi, what is that?" Mo says from the computer chair beside me. He reaches out and snatches the file.

"Hey!" I snatch it back. He doesn't get all the glory here. I open the file quickly before he starts another round of tug-of-war, but no papers fall out. It's completely empty.

"So much for that," I say, dejected. I just need a win.

"We'll get it from the virtual files," Mo reminds me.

I return the empty folder to Ms. Brodsky's desk before we head for the door, but the knob turns before I reach it. It swings open to reveal Pippa and a woman with an eye patch blocking our way.

"I'm sorry, Ms. Magwitch. We only wanted to help. You've been so nice to me. I am sorry I lied—" Pippa steps in front of me and Mo. The librarian opens her mouth and closes it a couple of times, unsure what she wants to say or do.

"I've gotten to know Ms. Aubergine, and she's just so broken. I want to do whatever I can to help." Pippa tries to patch up the mistakes she made in real time. I'm usually so busy cleaning up after her, she's never had to feel the burn. The silence makes room for Magwitch's tongue as it clicks against her teeth.

"Pippa, I know you think you can handle this, but there are good people, and there are people who want to seem good. I don't want you to confuse one for the other," the librarian says.

"Yeah? And which are you?" Pippa spits.

I may be mad at the girl, but my hand throws itself up into the air and gives two snaps for the clapback, the international "go on, girl" for Black women everywhere.

"Pippa, I am trying to help you." Ms. Magwitch speaks the way Mommy does. With authority because she really cares.

"I can help myself," Pippa says, but this time, she looks straight at me. "I always have."

Ms. Magwitch turns to Mo. "What did you take? We can put it back now. I'll give you a pass as long as you promise to stop what you're doing," she says, then holds her hand out.

Mo and Bidi share a look. "We don't have anything. There was nothing to find," Bidi says. She opens her backpack to prove it's empty beyond her personal belongings. Mo does the same.

Ms. Magwitch eyes us. "I've seen you, haven't I? You come work in the library to do the editing, right? Podcasts?" Mo freezes, a stone statue. This is what he was afraid of, putting his scholarship in jeopardy.

Voices out in the hallway get louder. We all join in a chorus of silent panic, frantically finding places to hide. On instinct, I grab Pippa's hand and drag us both under the desk just as the door opens.

"Ms. Magwitch?" we hear Pummel say. "Maurice?"

Pippa tries to get up, but I hold her in place. We can't all get caught; that won't help anyone.

"Why are you in here?" Ms. Brodsky shouts.

"Um, um, um," Mo sputters. Magwitch coughs before she speaks.

"This is my fault. I want the reward money, so I'm looking for Estella—"

Pummel interrupts; he clears his throat. "You both need to come to the office, immediately."

"No!" Magwitch shouts. "He did nothing wrong! I, um, well, I hired him to help me, but he turned out to be useless—"

"Hey!" Mo and his ego snap at the burn.

"Enough," Pummel says. "Darlene?"

"Yeah?" Ms. Brodsky replies.

"Call the lawyer and the detective. Seems like there's a new suspect to add to the list."

Mo clears his throat. "Oh, so they know about your affair?"

Pippa and I tighten our clutched hands as Mo exposes the administrators' secret. The silence is thick and harsh.

"Come. With. Me." Pummel lays down the command. They shuffle out, and we wait for the door to click before we move.

"We have to go!" I pull Pippa toward the office, but she digs her feet in. "What are you doing, Pippa? We have to help Mo!"

Guilt flashes over her face, quickly replaced by indignance.

"It was always a risk. I helped you like I said I would. So, we good?"

She doesn't mean, "What's next?" or "Are we all right?" She means "goodbye."

Panic starts at the back of my tongue. The only thing I don't know how to navigate is truly losing Pippa. But this isn't Pippa, all stone-cold, walking away from me toward the graveyard and that other world with Ms. Aubergine.

"We're good," I answer.

CHAPTER 23

Pippa

I feel Bidi's eyes on me from one of the last rows on the bus. She's going to have to live with the fact that she chose the wrong team. Bidi clomps behind me as we get off at our stop.

"Oi!" Jo waves her arm over her head. She stands outside the store, eyes so large they take up half her face, even from across the street.

"There's a man here for you," Jo says when I reach her.

"A man?"

"He's big," she adds.

"How big?"

"Big, big. Like if Bruno from down the block ate Jimmy and then came in here for a sandwich after," she says.

Jaggers.

My heart pumps hard against my ribs. The necklace is in there, he's in there, and we're out here. Bidi steps up beside me.

"What did she do now, Bidi?" Jo asks my former best friend.

For a moment, I can see the thread that ties them together

stretched so thin it's just a glimmer. Jo told me once she always saw herself in Bidi, the way she dreams and goes for it. The way she soldiers through her responsibilities as they mount before her. Bidi may end up broken, too, if she isn't careful. People raise children that aren't theirs to keep the world turning, but that wasn't Jo's dream, and it isn't Bidi's. That doesn't mean those of us who get stuck being raised by reluctant guardians don't suffer from that hard truth as well.

"Nothing. I didn't do anything, Jo! Just wait here; I'll be right back," I shout.

"You think I'm letting you go in there alone with him?" Jo's nerves fly around the ragged Bay Area summer breeze. She opens the door, and we step in.

"Finally," Jaggers grumbles.

He moves closer, filling the only gap in the space he hadn't already consumed. His hand reaches forward, and I brace for whatever it is he needs to deliver, but I am met with an envelope, not a fist clasped around me ready to haul me off to jail.

"What is this?" I ask, but he leaves without another word.

Jo grabs the envelope from me. She pulls open the flap and unfolds the paper inside. After a few seconds, the bell on the door rings, and Bidi enters from where she has been watching on the street.

"Ahhh!" Jo's scream ricochets off the glass jars still left on the shelves. We all jump and duck but Jo is steeped in joy when she hands the letter to me. I try to read the words, but they bounce around the page. It is almost impossible to focus when they all come at me so fast.

To the Attention of Miss Philippa Santos,

Pursuant to the request of the party hereby known as "the benefactor," a gift of $250,000 is to be relinquished to the recipient of said benefaction, hereby known as Philippa Santos. Recipient will collect funds from Jaggers, Esq., once account information has been transferred. The gift will become available immediately with no expectation of repayment to the benefactor.

The benefactor has chosen to remain anonymous at this time.

Sincerely,
Jaggers, Esq., and Associates

I hand it back to Jo, who reaches out for the lifeline that just fell into our laps.

"We're going to stay!" Jo announces.

"What? What? What?" The word comes out of Bidi's mouth a different type of confused each time. The paper is damp from the river of relief that's been flowing from Jo's eyes when Bidi takes it.

"Ms. Aubergine, she sent enough money to save everything. Like, enough for us to be good. We don't have to move," I say.

"Ms. Who?" Jo asks.

"I'm helping her with her garden," I explain. The less Jo knows the better.

Bidi hands the paper back to Jo and walks to the street. I follow. Outside, Bidi paces from the door of the store to the curb and back.

"You can't accept this," Bidi says, mind racing.

"What do you mean?" I ask.

"She's buying your silence, your loyalty. She's going to hold it over you. Ms. Aubergine could be protecting herself! Like, she makes this big, amazing gesture, so no one would ever think that such a generous person could disappear their kid . . ." The tin-hat theories shoot out of her. Bidi says I am the one obsessed with Ms. Aubergine, but jealousy sprouts and grows from her veins.

"Bidi, what are you talking about? Ms. Aubergine is doing this anonymously. She isn't posting or using it for performative allyship. You have to get past your wild conspiracy. She didn't make her own daughter disappear! I'm not even supposed to know she gave me the money; the letter is anonymous!"

"But you know she's the one who did, and she knew you would know by sending Jaggers. Don't you see? It's manipulative," Bidi pushes.

"Isn't this what you wanted? We aren't selling!" I shout.

The fading sunlight hits the silver clasps in Bidi's braids. Tiny halos to remind me that her words are gospel.

"Why would I want this, Pippa? You kept the store, but you sold its soul. You owe her forever, and you are the only one who can't see that!" Bidi shouts. Another bus pulls up and Mo steps off.

Bidi rushes toward him.

He throws me a harsh glare, then sends the same look her way. I watch her chase him to the house, doing her best to battle his silent treatment.

I check my phone. The screen is filled with notifications.

Google News push alert: **BREAKING**—Bloody shirt found in the San Francisco Bay. Initial lab results unable to confirm DNA. Further testing required to rule out connection to missing person Estella Aubergine.

Dread sinks through my body. For Ms. Aubergine, for me, for Estella. Any chance of getting a happy ending rolls off the rocks and back into the sea. Except Bidi is right. I *am* tied to Ms. Aubergine's story now. Maybe the universe brought us together. Maybe the point is sometimes people get lost and sometimes they get found. I rush up to my room to change. Once I throw on a clean tank and black jeans, I run to the bus.

Jaggers's shadow crawls up the street between the cop cars. It swallows me as I approach the gate.

"You really cannot take a hint." He bristles just as Ms. Aubergine walks into the garden. All I see is a piece of hope and not the heavy kind. This is winged and slippery at the same time. So light, it curls around itself if I try to balance it on my palm. Bidi can't take this opportunity at a fresh start from me. Jo can't, and Jaggers won't either. I don't need to worry about the investigation now that the store is saved. Jo gets a second chance, and I have Bettina's party to showcase my work. I have Ms. Aubergine and a chance to rebuild her garden.

"Ms. Aubergine! Amelia!" I shout, and wave my arms.

"Pippa?!" She runs over, as do the lingering cops.

The gate almost slices the tip of Jaggers's nose when she opens it. Ms. Aubergine takes my hand in hers, and she leads me into the house as though she can't wait to have me to herself. She sets tea before me, just brewed, as if she was expecting company. Candied orange and allspice and honeysuckle.

"I wasn't expecting you," Ms. Aubergine says.

"I just saw the news. I wanted to check on you. Are you okay?"

Her eyes are open wide, probably still in shock. Of course she's not okay. But she straightens and lifts her chin.

"They don't even know if the blood is hers yet. Until they show me her body, I am going to keep looking for her."

I wish I could explain to her that a missing person being alive makes it worse if they don't come back.

"Estella's lucky to have you . . . and so am I. Thank you, Ms. Aubergine," I say.

"Thank . . . me?" Ms. Aubergine asks.

I didn't plan on doing this, but I can't ignore her generosity, not when she got the worst news of her life today.

"I know I'm not supposed to know it was you who saved the shop, but your support means so much. We don't have to sell now. We can pay the debts. We can pay off the mortgage. We can stay. You don't have to say anything, I know the letter said it was anonymous, but I just . . . I had to thank you."

Ms. Aubergine drinks her tea. I do the same.

"I see something in you, Pippa, something your mother clearly didn't."

The words hurt because they are true. Ms. Aubergine sees me. That's what I wish Bidi could understand.

"My best friend thinks I'm a liability. She thinks I'm selfish."

Ms. Aubergine's hand covers mine. "That's not a friend, then, Pippa. Jealousy does terrible things to people. Women are always expected to give, to nurture, to oblige. It's been that way since the beginning of time, but not for Estella. I raised her to be strong and to prepare for everyone to take from her with no expectation of giving back—"

She starts to crumble into tears, but she catches herself.

"There is one thing you can do for me. I want you to stop feeling sorry for yourself. Stop letting your mother win. Stop that this instant. If I can believe Estella is still somewhere out there, you can believe in yourself. We are the makers, but we can also be the destroyers. Don't you ever forget that, Pippa."

"We?" I ask.

"Of course! We are both women navigating a troubled world," Ms. Aubergine says, as if that one simple fact makes us the same. Footsteps precede his mountainous frame as Jaggers storms into the room, ready to lead Ms. Aubergine away from me.

"Can I work a little in the garden, Ms. Aubergine? I need to rake the soil. Plot out the separate sections—" I plead, desperate to stay close.

"Of course you can. Oh, and Pippa?" She reaches out. Her hands are cold and powder soft when she takes mine. "You're welcome."

Then

More of the Middle

Missy paced the perimeter of the apartment. Amelia had been back only to collect clothes over the course of the past few months. No meals or overnights. This week, she hadn't returned at all. But her paycheck from the café had arrived. Missy spent all day practicing what she was going to say to Amelia to effectively communicate the termination of their friendship.

The thing about having never had a friend before was she had no context on how to end it. Missy had not been prepared for the pain that comes from this kind of love or loss. All the movies and books talked about heartache from a failed romance. Had she known what she'd been spared from in the name of some loneliness, she'd have gladly abstained from relationships of any kind, but Amelia had dragged Missy to this place—she had persuaded her to stay, and then she had decided to leave.

Rage climbed atop the self-preservation resting on Missy's back. She'd done nothing wrong. She trusted someone whose actions she should have seen as red flags. Amelia was impulsive and irresponsible. She thought everything should look and feel like a coming-of-age novel. Everything was a show, an extreme. Missy was standing up for herself, she reminded herself. But when the key turned in the lock and the front door opened, Missy was drained of everything but the dread that she'd been suffering.

Recently, their interactions had been cold and distant, but Amelia's energy now was jumpy; perhaps she sensed the tides preparing to change. Before Missy could start her speech, Amelia darted into the bathroom and shut the door. Missy walked over and pressed herself against the door. A sob came through the thin wood. Despite her best efforts to ignore Amelia's strife, she couldn't help but worry for her friend.

"I'm coming in, Amelia," Missy yelled, and then followed through.

"Get out!" Amelia waved an arm while bent over the toilet retching. Missy turned to give her privacy.

The moment was not ideal for Amelia, but Missy needed to take advantage of her weakness. It was the only way she would get the words out.

"You have to move out," Missy said and turned back to face her.

Amelia's face was green as she vomited bile into the toilet.

"I'm sorry you're sick, but you—you just left me, and you don't even help me clean the lobby anymore. So, you know, you can just keep staying wherever you have been staying, effective immediately." Missy stomped her foot to punctuate her point.

Amelia lifted herself and washed her hands, then rinsed her mouth out with water from the sink.

"Can I stay here, just for a little bit? I need to figure some things out," Amelia whispered, and flushed her despondence down with the rest of what she had let out.

"Why?" Missy asked, curiosity overpowering the hurt.

Amelia sighed as she stepped out into the apartment, then gently lowered herself to her mattress and explained. She had been with Felipe, the man from the bar. They had lived in his bed. When they had to shower, that became the bed. His love had been the only thing she needed to survive.

Until her period stopped.

Amelia explained that she waited for a test to confirm, but the second she saw the blue positive, there was no way to hide it from him, and she wasn't ready to tell him. Missy read between the lines. Amelia was coming home.

"I'm sorry. I wasn't fair to you." Amelia offered the apology to her friend, and she meant it. As much as she had filled her heart up with Felipe, the space Missy had kept before remained untouched. The distance had rekindled her fondness for Missy; she was willing to admit that. But every time she came back to the apartment, Missy ran away or ignored her. Amelia had accepted that this was what she deserved for mistreating her friend, but now she needed Missy. Amelia wasn't sure how Felipe would react to the news that she was pregnant, considering they had known each other only a few months. She wasn't sure what she wanted herself.

The reality of motherhood alone sat like bricks in her belly. The nausea swirled back up at the prospect of this new life with Felipe. She had derailed her old one for this different version of love, even though the love of a true friend had always been here waiting for her.

"Please, Missy, can I stay? Just until I figure out what to do."

Amelia rushed to the bathroom and folded herself over the toilet again; her body bounced as she retched. Missy felt the rejection climb up her throat, but she swallowed it back down. Despite the fact that she had waited for this moment to make Amelia feel as small as she had felt all these months, Missy couldn't suppress the love she still had for her best friend. Her rage shifted from Amelia to Felipe. He had been the one to steal their lives from them.

Friends fight, she told herself. Friends make mistakes.

Friends get tricked and taken advantage of, but Amelia was back. They could still be a family.

"Stay," Missy said after a long while. "We'll figure it out together."

Now

Press Conference, Estella Aubergine Transcript

Police Chief Arthur Broome: I'm here to give an update on the missing person case of Estella Aubergine.

In the past seventy-two hours, we have received thousands of tips claiming she has been spotted as close as within a five-mile radius from her home and as far as multiple countries abroad. People have been chased and filmed without their permission by bystanders who believe they might be Estella. While we appreciate the attention and enthusiasm the country has found to help locate this promising young woman, we ask that everyone let us do our jobs and to contact the hotline only with viable information. While this case will remain open, given the length of time since the disappearance, we do have to shift from a missing person case to the search for a body. We will now take questions. Yes, you with the yellow shirt.

Reporter with the yellow shirt: What about her mother?

Police chief: Based on cell phone towers and sleep-tracking devices, Ms. Aubergine has an alibi. She has also been fully cooperative with the investigation and is not being treated as a suspect at this time. You, with the glasses.

Reporter with the glasses: Can you tell us—has there ever been an official suspect?

Police chief: Not an official one, no. You, with the red pen.

Reporter with the red pen: Do we know why Estella was seeing the school counselor?

Police chief: We have no documentation that proves she was seeing the school counselor.

Reporter with the red pen: What about Estella's ex-girlfriend Bettina Drummle?

Police chief: She is a minor. Next question. You, with the jeans; no, not you, you. Yeah.

Reporter with the jeans: Have you noticed the criticisms coming from community activists about the disproportionately high coverage Estella's receiving over other missing persons with less affluent families, specifically Black and Brown youths?

Police chief: I have.

Reporter with the jeans: Do you have any comment?

Police chief: Sounds like a budget issue with the mayor's office to me. That's it for questions.

CHAPTER 24

Bidi

Elizabeth Jones, the voice of the kids.
Elizabeth Jones, born and raised, Bay all day.
Elizabeth Jones, fighting for us all.

The AI search engine spits out the potential campaign slogans, each one worse than the last. Whoever decided this was the way of the future needs to go all the way home, lie down, and stay there. I close my computer and face the bathroom sink, where my personal face-rejuvenation routine is laid out.

I start with the oil cleanse, a custom blend of avocado and coconut oils that I rub deep into my face until it starts to thicken, emulsifying with the stress that's been flowing from my pores in excess. Then I wash that off with a CeraVe face cleanser and sea salt exfoliant, then apply moisturizer. After that, I pull out the knock-off gua sha roller I got at the Oakland flea market by Lake Merritt.

The door swings open without a knock. Mo stands in the doorway of the bathroom, balancing his computer on his arm.

One week has passed since Mo boxed me out of our investigation and his life. One week since Pippa decided to focus on Ms. Aubergine's garden and stop speaking to me as well. A week ago, Estella was basically declared dead. A lot can happen in a week. 168 hours. 10,080 minutes. 604,800 seconds. Most colds last a week. Sliced ham can keep in the fridge for a week . . . but it should probably be smelled toward the end. My period lasts a week. The life expectancy of a luna moth is seven days. There was a guy in Wisconsin I read about who fell off a ladder and spent a week in a coma before he woke up speaking German and using a different name, his true self eventually breaking through the haze. You can lose everything in a week. But apparently, you can also get a whole new life.

Pippa certainly has. I watch out the window as she walks to the bus stop to go to Ms. Aubergine's house every day. From the bounce in her step, she seems to be settling into this new world of hers just fine. Mo has too. He spends all day hunched over his computer, working the investigation we are supposed to be on together. When he isn't typing furiously, he is whispering into his phone, avoiding me at all costs.

"I need to use the bathroom," he says.

Ms. Magwitch resigned under the condition that Mo's scholarship remain in place. But they will be watching him next year, waiting for the chance to expel him the second he messes up. Since all that happened, he's barely looked in my direction, but I've got him now.

"Mo! If we prove they are involved in this, they can't hold anything against you! Come on, you have to forgive me!"

Mo rolls his eyes. "Bidi, if you think I'm going to make the same mistake and work with you again, you really need to get a neuro evaluation. Focus on your campaign. I saved you there, too, didn't I?"

He did, but that's not the point. If he won't forgive me, I can be stubborn too.

"There is a bathroom upstairs," I say, and close the door in his face.

I should just give up the investigation, but I know things he doesn't. The stalker. The necklace. All Pippa's secrets I never told him because even in a fight, I'm loyal to a fault.

I open Instagram on my phone and prop it up against the mirror for research while I resume my skin care. One hundred forty new notifications wait for me. Mo really did come through with ideas for the campaign before our falling-out. I pull up what is now my only post after he scrubbed my profile. The picture is the black silhouette of a young woman against a white background. Swipe to the next photo and a list appears, with the header *The Girls.*

 **ElizabethJonesforSFCityCouncil** • • •

Francesca Brown, 17

Days before her disappearance, Francesca, known as Franny to those who loved her, reported an ex for stalking and sending her threatening messages. Case is ongoing, no traditional media coverage.

Latisha Darby, 19

Last seen December 23, five years ago, leaving a holiday party three blocks from her home. Case was closed citing inconclusive evidence she was a missing person. No traditional media coverage.

Lena Martin, 16

Was placed with a foster family with multiple warnings on their record. Social worker reported her as missing to the authorities after she didn't show up to their meetings for a week. Social worker never heard back. No traditional media coverage.

Selena Ruiz, 16

Had never been late picking up her little brother from school but never showed up on April 17 five years ago. When reported to the police, they said, "Teenagers will be teenagers." Case has remained open. No traditional media coverage.

Deborah Tompkins, 17; Marshai Williams, 15; Adriana Diaz, 18

All disappeared from the same bus stop coming home from school within two weeks in May, six years ago. All three parents reported their children missing within twenty-four hours of their disappearance. With the help of volunteer internet sleuths and community members, the girls were discovered to have been kidnapped and trafficked. Deborah's and Adriana's bodies were found in Arizona and New Mexico, respectively. The search for Marshai is ongoing. Local media coverage, less than fifteen minutes in total.

Estella Aubergine, 17

Popular socialite with hundreds of thousands of followers and an impressive extracurricular and academic résumé. Estella's mother paid for private investigators. The local and national news has picked up her story, and multiple avenues have been used in the attempt to find her.

FIND THEM ALL.

Local activist groups reposted me, which means I need to follow through. If I don't, the post will just look like what it is at the moment, an attention grab.

I use my free hand to scroll through Bettina's grid. Estella is all over the page, their love saga makes my belly burn. I don't know the girl, but recently, I've spent more time thinking about Estella than my own life.

I scroll past the more abstract pieces Bettina has posted and stop at a selfie posted the day before Estella was taken.

A small electric-blue purse sits in the palms of Bettina's hands. Her lips are poised to give it a kiss with her eyes pinched shut. I zoom in to check out the details, then pull up the Beaumont security footage to compare. Even in black-and-white, I can tell it is the same bag.

If she had this purse on that day, it wasn't Estella fighting with Pummel and Brodsky the day before her disappearance. It was Bettina.

CHAPTER 25

Pippa

The patch of honeysuckles, now trimmed into a manageable clump, is the only color in the space. Until today the garden was just a pit of soil, but now the grass buds have begun to sprout, filling some of the gaps around the various shapes of soil that will soon form a rainbow from the ground up.

Ms. Aubergine looks around at the dirt pit I have created. A symbol of the mess her life has become.

Considering Estella's probable death last week, things have been not terrible. Ms. Aubergine has not yet acknowledged that the police no longer believe Estella is alive. The squad cars only do sweeps rather than standing guard. Every day I listen to Jaggers' updates from his private investigation as I plant and sow and rake: Bettina's phone records cleared her. Pummel and Brodsky have also been ruled out as suspects. Whoever is in that black hood remains a mystery. Maybe it's better for everyone that they stay that way, at least now that they seem to have left me alone as well. Ms. Aubergine and I have found a rhythm together. Like this is how we were always meant to be.

Ms. Aubergine holds the gardening shears to chop off excess branches while I poke holes in the freshly mixed soil for seeds.

"Should we have some tea?" she asks, and rises, blank and winded. She turns to the door, and we step back out into the garden. Above is a purple sky. Even in a glass building, I hadn't noticed the retreat of the sun. We pull off our gardening coveralls and take turns rinsing the dirt from our hands and faces. Clean and refreshed, I perch on my stool in the kitchen and watch Ms. Aubergine create the tea bags, different herbs and spices, always dried fruit and flowers.

Once they are drowning in boiling water, she brings over the tray with our cups and sits.

"Here you go. I don't think you'll need honey. This one is pretty sweet on its own."

Ms. Aubergine picks up her mug and bends her face over the wide-rimmed Heath ceramic. I do the same.

"Sprigs of maple, dried orange, honeycomb," I say when I pull my face back.

She nods, impressed. "Pippa, would you do something for me?"

"Um, of course," I reply, unsure what I am agreeing to.

Ms. Aubergine waits for me to drink and then discard my mug on the counter. She guides me, and we walk up the stairs, through the house. Past her office and into her bedroom, which is light and airy. The faint smell of jasmine oil is the only distinguishing feature. Otherwise, it is just white and pillowy. She walks through the bedroom and primary bathroom, and into a dressing room, adorned with a cushioned vanity.

"Have a seat," she says, and pulls out the chair.

I sit and face the mirror framed by white bulbs. The stark light makes my fluorescent-beige skin almost see-through. I look away from myself and to Ms. Aubergine. Her eyes inspect my hair. They try to make sense of the pineapple of curls at the top of my head.

"Can I?" She nods to the mess I wrapped haphazardly in an elastic three times.

"Um, sure?"

She gently untangles and frees the curls, one by one, then brushes away any remaining debris from the garden. Ms. Aubergine works meticulously. She sections my hair, then sprays it with a detangling serum until it's thoroughly damp before she combs it with a moisturizing conditioner. After that, she starts to braid.

Jo never did my hair; she didn't understand how. The best Jo can get out of her thick straight hair is loose waves and the only way to do that is to shellac them into place, rock hard and crunchy. I didn't get Mamãe's melanin, but I did get her hair. Wild and thick. Once Bidi realized I had no clue what I was doing, she taught me how to care for my curls, but I so rarely follow the proper protocol. I'm lucky if I remember to wear a bonnet at night.

Ms. Aubergine's hair is straight. She wouldn't have learned how to do this for herself. She learned for Estella. She's doing for me what she always does for her daughter.

Ms. Aubergine makes one tight braid, then moves on to the other side.

"So what's your big secret?" she asks.

All I can see is the necklace, cold and burning against my skin every time I put it around my neck. The secret is making it hard to stand upright for long. The truth curdles on my tongue.

"Wh-what?" I ask.

"The way you work out there, it's like you are possessed."

Ms. Aubergine's tongue drags as she speaks. In the mirror, her gaze is lopsided and too comfortable. Her fingers fumble a few times as she works through the second braid, a snag at the roots sends a pain down my neck. She must have taken something to numb herself. To make it until tomorrow. She won't remember anything I tell her tonight. She's flying high. So I let a piece of the truth slip and release some of my burden.

"I—I don't really have any secrets, but I have a secret place. There is a panel in the back of the store. No one knows it is there."

"Mmm." Ms. Aubergine's pupils are huge; whatever she took is hitting her hard.

"You don't have to keep coming, you know. I don't know why you do—" Her head bobs.

"What? No!" I push. This has become the only place I want to be.

"I have Jaggers. He's loyal to me. Not like the rest—"

She ties off the other braid, but she doesn't let go. She grips and tugs it down, hard enough to pull my head back. Her eyes are dark in the mirror as I try to lift my head free and upright. She pulls it harder.

"Ms. Aubergine!" I cry, and reach back to wrench her hands away. She didn't mean to hurt me. Her eyes are practically closed, like she's almost asleep standing up.

"Sheee tried tew take'er fromme."

Her syllables start to melt together, slurry thick enough to turn a soup into a stew.

"Who? Who took who? Estella?" I ask.

"She's mine." Ms. Aubergine sobs in her hands, unaware that moments ago she was ripping my hair out.

"Come with me. You just need to get some rest," I whisper.

I help her out of her shoes and guide her to the bed, a mountain of white pillows.

"It's her. She's the one," Ms. Aubergine says, though her eyes are already practically closed.

"Who?" I ask.

"Missy," she whispers.

Ms. Aubergine turns in the bed; her legs curl up and into herself, forehead so creased she may give herself a strain headache.

In the hallway outside Ms. Aubergine's room, I look around. The way I came sits to my left, but the rest of her world is to the right. I step into each bathroom, soak in the theme and her vision. Ms. Aubergine may not know how to garden, but she designed every inch of this house to perfection so she'd never feel the need to leave. What happened to her out there that she never went back out? The next door I open is her office. Maroon velvet curtains and a black shag rug. I pad in and let my fingers run over the books on the shelves. I sit down in the chair behind her desk, place my hands on the wood.

Feet pound just outside, and I leap into a closet behind the desk just as the door to the room cracks open. Jaggers's shallow breathing overtakes the darkness.

"That girl was here. She's always here; she's making things more difficult. You need to—"

Jaggers stops talking and moves toward the far wall. He pulls one of the curtains open for the early evening light to spill in and spins to make sure he's alone. I cover my mouth with both hands and will my lungs to freeze.

"Fine," he says gruffly to whoever is on the other line, and marches out of the room. I count to five before I follow.

At the bottom of the stairs, I hear the echo of the front door. *Loyal, my ass.*

Through the window, I check the garden before I step outside, but Jaggers is gone. I make it to the gate door and onto the dark sidewalk where it is still and quiet, until the headlights of a black SUV blast on, straight into my eyes.

Before I can think, I run and they follow. The blaring whiteness hits like a hammer so hard in my skull it fills these dark streets, a beacon for my sneakers on the pavement. The wheels catch up to me in seconds, so I stop short and let the car zoom past down the narrow one-way street. I double back to the house, but my breath tightens when I see the warning of a fresh pink peony lying on the ground.

The screech of tires makes me jump. I turn to run again, but a different car than the one I just escaped cuts me off. The door swings open.

"Get in," Two says from the back seat of the car.

Somehow, despite the fact that I've just been chased by a psychotic stalker, Two's face is more disturbing.

"This is getting weird!" I snap as I step inside.

Fritillaria delavayi grows on the side of the Hengduan Mountains and is believed to have medicinal properties that protect the lungs. Recently, harvesters' daily crop weights have plummeted.

Lack of resources, experts said. They claimed the herb was dying out. Eventually, they discovered it had evolved, camouflaging itself to its surroundings. To protect itself, the plant learned to disappear. I'd like to be invisible, too, rather than trapped here with Bettina and Two in the back seat of this car.

"What do you want, Bettina?"

Bettina Drummle winces at the sound of her name in my mouth. "Check your phone," she commands.

Unknown Number:

This is your official SUMMER REFRESH invitation. Private party hosted by Bettina Drummle. A car will be waiting to pick you up at 9 p.m. this Wednesday.

"Can you be ready in two days? I wouldn't want the free press I'm offering to be negative."

Bettina wants me to remember how lucky I am to know her.

"Speaking of which, I'd like to see the designs to make sure we are on the same page," she adds.

I have no designs.

Stop feeling sorry for yourself, Ms. Aubergine said.

"Well, you can't. That's not how I work . . . Plus, we haven't discussed payment." I push back.

Bettina's pupils rage purple.

"I gave you those clothes, you scammer." Bettina yips in her seat. She's worried, maybe even afraid. She needs to deliver with this event to keep everyone drooling over her without Estella, and to do that, she needs me, her new discovery. The next star she's launching to prove she's the kingmaker, and maybe, finally, the king herself.

We are the makers, but we can also be the destroyers. I didn't know what Ms. Aubergine meant when she said that to me. Bettina wants me to know she's the boss. Meanwhile here she is, waiting for me while I hang out in her ex's house.

"You paid me when the agreement was for one crown, or do you not remember?"

I can feel the blood pooling out of the gaping hole where her heart was before it burst into flames. My smile widens, so sweet my cheeks hurt.

"Pippa," she says through clenched teeth.

"Listen, sis, we're friends, right?"

Disgust projects right off Two's face straight onto Bettina's, but I'm not finished. I may have given up the investigation, but I'm not convinced Bettina is innocent.

"I just feel like I wouldn't be keeping it real if I didn't tell you that you sort of look . . . I don't know . . . tired? The whole point of this event is revival, right? You can't be showing up so haggard. Is something weighing on you?" I ask, but don't let her get a syllable in. "About payment, let's start with the flower budget—"

Bettina recovers from her shock and cuts me off.

"Give her the petty," she tells Two.

"All of it?"

"Yeah, we can use the card tonight," she says, already behind her phone, tapping.

"Don't talk; just listen," Two commands. He rummages through his bag and pulls out an envelope with cash inside.

“This is three thousand to buy your little flowers. You will not keep the change; you will return it with a receipt.”

When Two finishes his speech, Bettina nods to the door. He leans over and opens it for me to exit.

“You are dismissed,” Bettina says. “And don’t buy anything cheap,” she threatens. “I want luxury.”

CHAPTER 26

Bidi

After a day of self care, I finally exit the bathroom.

"I have to go," Mo whispers harshly into his phone, and hangs up. "I'm going to take Caroline to get ice cream."

Mo stands and hops up the stairs. Moments later, I hear the front door slam, leaving me in the house alone with his computer that is sitting open at a 140-degree angle.

Well, since everyone else is looking out for themselves, I'm doing the same. I open his laptop wider to reveal the folder titled "Encrypted File."

I push the cursor down and the folder opens. My first stop is the tab labeled "Psych." But the folder is empty.

Even if it was Bettina arguing with her in that last video, Estella still went to the school counselor for something. I saw the footage before the school hid it.

I click the Medical tab. There's nothing of note, just records of vaccines and doctors' visits for PMS symptoms. Next is another tab titled "Family History."

Inside are two files for birth certificates. One is labeled "New," the other "Old." The old one is completely blacked out but the new one is standard. Estella and Amelia Aubergine's names are printed neatly. Beside "father," the word "deceased" is printed instead of a name. Maybe Ms. Aubergine does not want Estella to know her who her father is. Maybe Pummel and Brodsky figured out Aubergine's secret and are holding Estella hostage as collateral to make her mommy pay up.

The front door slams upstairs. Caroline's footsteps race across the floor above me. I reposition the computer exactly where it was and leap into my recliner just before Mo descends the stairs, ready to ignore me some more.

CHAPTER 27
Pippa

“You want to come with me to the supermarket?” Jo asks when I walk into the store after a traffic-heavy ride on the bus.

“We have food here—” I start to walk away, but she grabs my shoulder.

“No, I’m cooking, come on. You’re never around anymore.”

Bonsai trees need to be pruned regularly and trimmed to maintain their shape. To encourage their healthy branches to grow. To do away with the ones rotting or stunting or knotting. Jo is pruning too.

We walk the few blocks to the market in silence. Let the city noises fill in the gaps for us until the supermarket doors slide open and we walk inside. It’s been a while since we didn’t shop our own aisles. Jo heads to the produce section first. She scratches a lime to smell its essence, and squeezes a tomato with her eyes closed, so as not to be swayed by its unscarred skin. I follow her to the canned aisle, for coconut milk with the right label. We head to the fish section next, where despite the monger’s look of disgust, Jo leans over the seafood and smells it for freshness. She’s not here for pleasantries. We need peppers and palm oil. We're here for the ingredients to make Brazilian fish stew. We are here for moqueca.

In the line for the register, she searches her pockets, an old habit formed of a long-term situation, a gamble every time you make it to the front. The cashier smacks her gum as she counts our pile of small bills and coins, handing back one quarter.

Her eyes drop to my hands, where she expects to see the reusable bag I forgot. She pulls the quarter from where it rests on Jo's palm and hands us a paper bag to take home.

The kitchen in our apartment waits as Jo unpacks the ingredients; then she cleans and preps them to cook.

"This was the meal my mamãe would make for us on our birthday. We didn't do much celebrating, but this was what we wanted, and she made it every year. We were eighteen when we left home, my sister and I, and we never spoke to my mother again." Jo pauses, as if the reality just hit her.

"Did you ever try to call her?" I ask. She shakes her head.

"No. But if I had called her, she would have told me the first time I made this recipe, I forgot the lime. The lime marries the tomato to the coconut milk. Without it, the dish is bland."

At the stove, she stirs a pot, shaking and tapping her foot to stay grounded. She reminds me of a rose of Jericho, one that almost died but is miraculously growing back. She never talks about before, the life she left for the one she was forced to live because of me.

"The second time, I forgot to add the palm oil, and the dish was missing a ruby-red color. The palm oil gives it that earthiness."

The grouper slides from her fingers into the broth, its final body of liquid. "The third time I got a different fish, frozen tilapia, what I could afford. Wrong consistency. The fish gets tough and sinks to the bottom rather than becoming something together with the rest of the ingredients."

She tosses in the shrimp and turns off the burner. It's hot enough to cook them through and keep them supple. Jo takes a spoonful directly from the steaming pot to her mouth.

"A little too much salt, but it's almost done. It takes a lifetime to get some things right, Pippa. It's only over if you give up."

Jo stands before me as she has in the past, clear-eyed, hopeful, desperate for forgiveness, but her sad story doesn't change the lonely truth of mine.

"Your mother always wanted noise and laughter and flowers around. We left Bahia together, but she didn't go as far. She wanted me to stay with her in Rio, but I had a dream to come to America and go to school to become a businesswoman, so we went our separate ways. We spoke when we could, and she told me she had nothing, and that was all she needed. She made friends everywhere she went." Jo's disdain flows, but all I hear is magic.

"She sounds fearless and fun." I close my eyes and imagine Mamãe's hair reaching out in every direction. Static from the amount of energy she produced.

Jo shakes her head. "She was impulsive and reckless. She had no fear because things just always worked out for her. Your mother, she lived her life however she felt she should at that moment."

The story I have always asked for pours out before me. My frustration leaks, as deadly as carbon monoxide, and our alarms are on the fritz. Jo has continued to dry out, for the most part. I have seen her slip: a sip here, a glass there, but it's progress. Now that she has decided to get her life together, I have to deal with the wreckage of everything that came before. Jo's never gotten to this stage of the process—she's making amends.

Jo stuffs food into her mouth and concentrates hard as she chews. After a few bites, she looks up. "My sister hadn't told me she was pregnant. I didn't know about you until she showed up at my door. She was beaten down and breathless. She made no sense. She wouldn't explain anything to me, not who your father was or how long she planned to stay or why she came all this way from Brazil in the first place. She just kept repeating the same sentence over and over: 'I need to find her.' "

"Find who?" I ask.

" 'Her.' That was all she said, over and over."

Jo puts down her bowl. Her hands lift up to cover her ears and close her eyes. A nightmare floods her body. Their twin connection punishes her from the inside out.

"One day, you were screaming. But your mother just kept walking back and forth, repeating the same words, 'I need to find her,' and—"

Jo stops again. She adjusts her jaw to make space for the truth.

"You weren't a good sleeper, Pippa. She was confused and tired. Her hormones were all over the place. But I didn't know anything about that; no one did. I was a kid too! It was too much for me," Jo pleads. The pain she has been trying to quiet and quell, the feeling Jo drank and spent and yelled away. What she stirs into tumblers with ice—*that* pain spills out. We face each other covered, heart to heel.

"'I need to find her. I need to find her.' That's all she said over and over, so I grabbed her shoulders and I said, 'go find her, then.'" Jo pauses; she collects herself. "You stopped crying after she walked out the door. I never saw her again."

"You are telling me that despite the fact that my mother, your sister, had brought a newborn all the way from Brazil and seemed to be having a nervous breakdown, you told her to leave?" I scream.

After years of being a Band-Aid to the gaping hole she carries, I push Jo's excuses out the window. I will not rest until my cracks have been patched, until everything stops seeping out of me and I am full. Everything up until now hasn't mattered. The good months and the bad years. None of them amounted to anything, because this is the piece of the puzzle I needed, the moment to wipe the slate clean.

"Pippa, I was overwhelmed. I was tired. It wasn't the life I had worked for. I didn't ask to be a parent."

She sings a song I know all too well.

"I didn't ask to be born. I didn't ask to be raised by you," I shout.

Jo's mouth keeps opening and closing like the last gasps of a salmon lying out on a rocky beach.

"I didn't expect her to listen! She never had before. You don't understand; this is what sisters do. This is how we behave. We take everything out on each other. We speak our own language and fix it our way. I didn't think she would do it, Pippa. I didn't actually expect her to leave you behind. I can't fix the past, but I can try now that we've been saved."

I jump from my seat. "*I* saved you. Consider it payment."

"Payment?" Jo whispers.

"I will be eighteen in two months. I asked you so many times what happened and why she left. And you just kept this from me, that you told her to go? You let me believe this whole time that it was my fault."

"I'm sorry, Pippa, that's—"

"No!" I cut her off.

My bedroom door slams so hard some of the Polaroids of my sculptures fall. I walk over to pick them up. But instead, my hand reaches up to pull more down. I destroy everything I've managed to create. I scatter the past, then sink down onto it and call the only person who will know what to do.

CHAPTER 28

Bidi

Mo hasn't looked up from his computer since he got back hours ago, though to be fair, I haven't either. I decided to look into Darlene Brodsky, and what led her into Pummel's whack-ass spell. What I found, though, tells an interesting story. She has worked at a bunch of prestigious schools all over the country, but it seems odd that Darlene has bounced around every year between elite institutions. She's worked in at least six schools over the past seven years. Counselors aren't supposed to move that often. The cops cleared Beaumont as soon as they hid the evidence. No one did their due diligence; they never do with nice white ladies.

A white light flashes onto the wall from the window, interrupting my thoughts. It pulses a few more times. Pippa's bat call, the one she does when she and Jo get into it. I sit up, alert.

"Answer it," Mo says.

"What?" I ask.

"I know Pippa only does that if something really bad happened. Plus, you are both backstabbers who deserve each other.

Mostly, I could use some space without having to look at you, so go!"

It's true, Pippa only uses the flashlight if things are really bad.

"I'm not doing this for you," I clarify before I walk out and up the stairs.

I knock a couple times before the doorknob to Pippa's apartment twists and the door opens. Jo's face is red and puffy.

"Hey, Jo," I say cautiously, unsure of what I am walking into.

"She's in her room," Jo says.

She sits down at the table, face in her hands.

"Listen, why don't you go over to my place? Mommy made lasagna and banana pudding."

"Thank you, Bidi. But I'm going to go lie down. I'm tired."

Jo trudges past me toward her bedroom, which is also the living room, and sets up the pullout. The mattress and metal coils sag underneath Jo's body just before I step into Pippa's room.

"Scooch," I say to Pippa.

She shuffles her body a few inches over on the ground to make room for me to lie down beside her.

"I like the renovation," I say, and nod my chin to the torn-up wallpaper of photos she spent her whole life creating.

"Spontaneity is the spice of life." Pippa fights off tears with sarcasm.

"What happened, Pippa?"

"Jo said when my mom showed up here with me, she was having a meltdown, but she didn't help her! She told her to leave. And she did, without me."

I always take Pippa's side, but deep down, I hold space for Jo too. Because right now, with my whole future ahead of me, I am Jo before life won. I am all the chances she never got to take.

"Jo said sisters are mean to each other. She said that's just how it is. In the past, she and Mamãe would have made up. But they didn't get to because she never came back, and now they never will."

Her hand finds mine and squeezes.

"I don't want to be mean sisters, Bidi. I don't want to not make up."

I squeeze her back. After a few minutes, I clear the silence.

"Well, you may think you have problems, but perhaps we can get a little perspective here on the scope of what I am currently going through. Mo talks in his sleep all night long in a podcaster voice."

Pippa laughs and squeezes herself closer to my arm.

"Bidi, are you still looking for her?"

"Estella? Yeah," I say.

Pippa sits up so I can see the fear on her face. "Good. Because the stalker is back. They were outside the estate waiting for me in the black car and chased me. I got away, but they left me a peony just like the necklace."

I resist the urge to tell her about the birth certificate and files. "You should get some rest, Pippa. I'll stay here until you fall asleep."

"Okay." She nods. "Thanks for coming, Bidi."

She snuggles into my shoulder while I listen to her breathing steady and slow and strategize how to deal with Darlene Brodsky. When Pippa begins to snore, I roll her to her side and rush home to gather what I need. Because while I lay there listening to her, I came up with a plan.

The security guard smiles and waves me through when I flash Mo's badge. I weave through the Beaumont halls—past the blue lockers and hype myself up.

I am just going to go in there and convince these grown-ass people to admit to me whatever it is they did and why and, oh yeah, also where Estella is . . .

There was this TikTok I saw where men were asked whether they thought they could land an airplane in an emergency with no prior experience or practice, and nine times out of ten, they said yes. I take a deep breath and try to tap into some of that delulu energy.

At a hallway intersection, I pause and pull my phone out to dial the main office number for the school, about to pull a Pippa.

"Yes, hi. Are you in apartment 5R at 256 Maiden Lane? Mm-hmm, yes, there seems to be a leak from the apartment above yours. Well, the problem is the apartment upstairs was remodeled recently, and their bathroom is above your kitchen. Right—"

A nearby door slams open to heavy footsteps and panicked breaths. I peek around the corner to watch Pummel's assistant rush down the stairs. Once he is gone, I walk through the open door of the main office, then adjust the microphone I'm wearing, which is hooked up to the radio I placed outside Brodsky's door before I came here. All tools I borrowed from Mo without his permission, but that's what he gets for holding a grudge. My hand raps against the double doors to the principal's office, and after a few seconds, I hear feet pad toward me.

"Barry?!" Pummel shouts as he opens the door.

"Oh, are you looking for that guy who was just out here? He got a call. I heard him say 'landlord' and 'leak.' He had to rush out."

"What!?" Pummel shouts.

I walk in before he can protest.

"Where should I set up, sir?" I ask.

"I'm sorry, but are you a student here?" Pummel follows me to his office.

"No. We confirmed this interview days ago with your assistant. You only get one shot to defend yourself." I push the lie with full conviction.

"Defend myself? What do you mean? Who are you?" Pummel turns and asks.

"Mr. Pummel, I'm Elizabeth. I'm a junior reporter interning with *Teen Pulse*. They wanted to proceed without reaching out, but I felt like you deserved a chance to tell your side of the story. You must know by now that all theories about Estella Aubergine's whereabouts point back here," I explain.

"The board will sue for slander. It's summer; school isn't even in session."

Pummel flails around, too perturbed to question the validity of my claims.

"The allegations aren't about the school, though, sir. They are about you." My lie fills the room. "Since you're the only one who knows your truth, we'd love to give you a fair shake. To do that, though, you've got to sign a release," I add, holding up the form.

"Well, I'd need to consult the legal—" Pummel is gruff.

"That's not what Darlene Brodsky did. I spoke to her earlier. If I were you, I'd get my message out there."

This move is risky. I went back through Pummel's LiveJournal. He seems to fall hard for women who realize very quickly they can make him do what they want. I'm willing to bet he still hasn't learned his lesson. If I'm right, Pummel ain't the brains of this operation, but I need him to prove that.

"Give it to me," Pummel says. The pen scratches against the release.

"Let's just start with your full name," I say.

Pummel loosens the phlegm in his throat. He croaks, "Ruben Pummel, principal of Beaumont Academy and tied for fifteenth place for best hatchet thrower on the West Coast."

This guy is such a clown.

"All right, Ruben. Can I call you Ruben? As you know, the police have kept a tight lid on the investigation into Estella's disappearance in the hopes of bringing her home safely, but that is also leaving room for the internet to unleash their theories in abundance."

I put on my best podcaster voice. Joy Reid meets *Las Culturistas.*

"Well, the internet will do what the internet will do," Pummel grumbles.

"Absolutely. Have you heard any of the theories?"

Pummel scoffs. "Me? No, I don't spend much time on the internet."

"Really? Our researchers found you seem to have a pretty

robust social media presence. You have a personal account, an account for your cats . . . Thackery and Binx, is it? I saw you also posted a few times to Estella's memorial page."

Ruben shifts in his seat.

"Yes, of course. I post in solidarity for the morale of the students. We are all in this together. Top down, through and through." Pummel chuckles with pride. I pause for another few seconds to make him squirm.

"We obtained security footage from the day before Estella's disappearance that wasn't released to the media. Was that your decision to withhold details? The police don't seem to be aware of it." I throw the first grenade.

"No—no, no, that's not—" Pummel tries to reject my words, but his fear is like a key to the truth.

"The tape is just the beginning, Principal Pummel," I goad, and hope he follows with the rest.

"You've got it wrong." Pummel starts to tremble. "I have nothing to do with her disappearance. Nothing!"

"Then what happened?" I lean closer to make sure he speaks into my hidden mic. "Because this doesn't look great for you."

Pummel inhales. "Estella wanted her birth certificate, but she can't gain access without parental approval until she is eighteen, and her mother wouldn't allow us to release it," Pummel says.

If Brodsky got my package and is listening, my guess is phase two of my plan has just been activated. The only thing to do now is keep him talking and hope.

"What do you mean?" I prompt.

"I mean, Ms. Aubergine told us in no uncertain terms that we were not permitted to give it to her daughter. Darlene, I mean Ms. Brodsky, wanted to have a meeting, a face-to-face, to discuss the secrecy, but Ms. Aubergine refused. And Estella kept pushing." Pummel stops himself. "I think I need my lawyer."

"You signed the release. What you have already said here is mine," I remind him.

My ears reach for any sound out in the hallway. She should be in here by now.

Meanwhile, Pummel is spiraling, dropping all sorts of information in random spurts that doesn't match. "We never took anyone. The truth is that this was all Darlene's idea. She manipulated me. She said we'd be safe. It was her idea to use the file to blackmail—"

"But if the certificate is blacked out, how could you betray Ms. Aubergine? It seems like her secret is already kept," I interrupt.

"When Estella started at the lower school, Ms. Aubergine tried to get out of submitting the certificate. She said it was a matter of safety, but rules are rules, and for any other family, we would have just declined the admission. But she offered the type of money a school won't pass up. The lawyers finally agreed that we would take the birth certificate, review it, and then black it out," Pummel explains.

"But?" I lead.

"I was assistant to the director at the time. I made a copy. I figured in the future, I could use it as . . . leverage," Pummel admits.

That's how he got the job. He said he would reveal their secret and blow up the largest new addition to the endowment in decades.

Brodsky slams open the door, a temper tantrum brewing so big, she could rival Drake after a Kendrick diss track.

"What are you doing?!" Ms. Brodsky charges and Principal Pummel leaps out of the way.

"Darlene, you have to believe me. She forced me to say that—" Pummel crouches behind his desk.

"You conniving idiot." Brodsky stalks him with every ounce of lunacy a midweek ABC daytime drama confrontation deserves. "If you think I won't sell you out, you sorely misjudged the type of woman I am. And *that* means you never really loved me in the first place, because you can't love someone if you don't know them."

Brodsky's venom injects itself directly into Pummel's veins. While they go at each other, I launch phase three: the 911 text.

"I was *this close* to getting the money from that girl. She was ready to give it up! And then she vanished." Brodsky rampages. I move closer to try to get as much on the recording as possible.

"How did you know what to do?" I ask.

Her eyes narrow.

This is why she bounces from elite school to elite school. She blackmails the rich and then moves on once she gets what she wants.

"You've done this before, haven't you?" I call her out. "At Oakwood Prep in Missouri, Harrington in San Diego, Brinewood Hall in Connecticut. You are telling me that if we call the admin at those places for comment, they won't tell us that you left on bad terms?"

Brodsky scoffs. "You'll find that we signed NDAs. They won't say a word. You think I want to be a school counselor?" She turns to me with the same wrath she just spat at Ruben.

"What she means is—" Pummel tries to talk over her, but Darlene's expression is one I know well. She has had enough of this man.

"I can speak for myself, Ruben," Ms. Brodsky snarls. "Everything was set; we had a deal with Estella."

The pieces put themselves together.

"But then Estella disappeared, and you would have had to go directly to Ms. Aubergine and threaten to out the files yourself?" I turn to Pummel. "But you didn't know that the hard copies were gone, and you had no more leverage."

I follow the trail straight down their plan and see the way it unraveled.

"Estella was going to figure it out one way or the other. She turns eighteen in two months. She would have marched in here, and I would have no power to prevent her from getting what she wanted. All I did was ask for compensation for keeping my mouth shut and expediting the process!" Brodsky is manic now.

Heavy footsteps get louder until they stop at the door.

"What did Bettina have to do with all of this? Did she take the hard copies? Is that why she showed up the day before Estella disappeared? Were you trying to make a deal with her?" I ask just as the door opens and a horde of cops storms in.

"I don't know what you are talking about." Brodsky clamps her mouth shut. She finally has something I want, and I don't have the upper hand.

The police perp-walk Brodsky and Pummel through the halls, and I follow. We walk past the few people here for summer school and senior projects and AP courses, who now line the lockers.

Giant cameras flash once when the door swings open. Camera shutter clicks bite at the sky all the way down the stairs to the street.

The birth certificate could be the reason Estella ran away, or it forced Ms. Aubergine to intervene and shut her up. Either way, I don't care what Pippa says.

All's not well at that estate.

CHAPTER 29

Pippa

The garden is beginning to bloom under my care, the patches of flowers spread like a quilt. A color block that grows in order of its shades. I tend to the soil and work on replanting some budding flowers I needed at a specific height, moving them from the greenhouse into the garden flower bed.

Ms. Aubergine is not talkative, but her mood seems to shift lighter as the day moves on. Maybe she just needed more time to come out of whatever fog she drugged herself into. I take the moment to tell her about Jaggers. She needs to know who she can trust: me.

"Ms. Aubergine, there's something about Jaggers—"

"What do you mean?" Ms. Aubergine sits up.

"He gives me a bad feeling. He's always . . . around—"

"That's where I pay him to be, Pippa."

"I know, but I mean, I've caught him . . . lurking in your office and in the garden early in the morning."

Her eyes squint. "Darling, if you caught him in those places, doesn't that mean you were there too?" She pats my hand. Pity before the correction. "I know when I'm being betrayed, Pippa. I always do. I learned that lesson a long time ago—" Ms. Aubergine's eyes go violet, the color of a lily of the Nile, petunia. Purple is the color of someone who takes what they want, not what they need.

Maybe this is the moment I come clean about everything—the necklace, my original motive for being here, beside her.

"Come, Pippa. Let's have some tea," she says.

We take our shoes off in the mudroom and march through the halls. In the kitchen, Ms. Aubergine puts the pot to boil and pulls dried flowers haphazardly from the drawer to fill the netted satchels. The she drops them into mugs and drowns them in the hot water.

We slurp our tea and wait for the heat to cool on our tongues. "How is your aunt doing? Still making a mess of things?" Ms. Aubergine asks. I can't help but notice a delight behind her words.

Jo's confession of betrayal still rests dark and heavy on my heart, but she is doing better. I can't deny that.

"She's trying, I think." I offer Jo grace out of her earshot.

Ms. Aubergine places her mug down with a sharp click.

"Oh, Pippa. You sound just like your mother."

This is the first time I've ever heard those words. I never expected them to sound so much like a curse.

"But you don't know my mother," I sputter.

Ms. Aubergine bridles. "Of course I don't. But I have heard enough from you to know the type. Look, Pippa. I've been where you are, starting over, and trust me: The only thing you can control is yourself."

"Ahem."

Jaggers interrupts, and for the first time, I'm grateful for him. "Ms. Aubergine?"

She rises to his call. As soon as she's out of the room, I take out my phone to check the millions of notifications stacked up on the screen. I click the first one, a video shared with me on TikTok. Crowds stand outside Beaumont, more packed than videos from the floor of the *Cowboy Carter* tour.

"Lock them up! Lock them up!"

The masses chant as the heavy doors crack open, and the phone stills and zooms in to the front stairs, where two police officers in full gear escort Brodsky and Principal Pummel out and into a cop car. Bidi steps out of the school doors behind their procession and looks around at the crowd. The person filming runs toward her with one of those tiny microphones, clearly an amateur TikTok journalist, interviewing on the fly.

May I ask your name?

Elizabeth Jones.

Tell me, Elizabeth, are you a student here?

No, but my cousin is. I just wanted to help find Estella. I didn't expect to stumble onto a blackmailing scheme by Beaumont's principal and guidance counselor.

So that means, even with the arrest of those two, Estella's case has not been solved?

Not yet, but we're not giving up.

Students are already buzzing over the arrest of two vital members of Beaumont's administration for blackmailing Estella and her mother. The controversy may be at the root of her disappearance. The details are still unknown. We'll keep you posted.

Bidi can't help but stand smug on the screen. Ms. Aubergine rushes back into the room to peer out the windows, where cars have started to double-park and camerapeople are poised at the gate.

"I'm so sorry, Ms. Aubergine—Bidi didn't mean for this—She's only trying to help—" I speak without thinking as panic rises up her cheeks.

"Who? This clout chaser? You know her?" Her face falls into a look of disappointment.

"Um—" I stop short on the edge of an impossible cliff. The necklace burns bright back at the store, but I can't tell her, not now, not with this most recent news coming to the light.

Jaggers storms in, and she turns her attention to him.

"What do you want me to do, miss?"

"Send them away." Her eyes meet mine. "Everyone."

She dismisses us both with a wave of her hand. The rejection sears.

"Come," Jaggers commands.

We walk in silence through the house. For someone as staggeringly tall as he is, I would have never known Jaggers was there if he wasn't standing two feet in front of me. He's light on his feet. Stealth is a good quality to have if people around you also need to disappear. He stops before the gate and blocks it.

"There are only two reasons why people show up at times like these. Either you think you are going to solve this case and claim the reward, or you've got something to do with whatever happened to the girl. Regardless, you're going to get yourself hurt if you keep this up," he says. His breathing is heavy, not winded. It carries a weight, a bludgeon waiting to come down.

"Is that supposed to scare me?" I ask.

"Depends. Which one of those people are you?" he bites back.

Both, sort of.

Jaggers opens the front door. I wait in the garden for him to clear the cameras before I exit onto the street.

My phone buzzes.

Alert: Flower Pickup in Two Hours

The crowns need to be assembled tomorrow for Bettina's party.

My Uber driver rushes to place three bags full of flowers onto the corner of my street as I open the passenger door. I lug them through the busy store and open the door to a decluttered office. Jo must've cleaned up. She steers clear of me as I move in and out of the store.

I start to pull the flowers out and organize them the best I can. There were so many options at the flower shop, and the money Estella gave me was enough to take everything. The doorknob turns after a knock on the door, and Bidi walks in.

"You know, you could have given me a heads-up about your whole reveal today," I say, not hiding my irritation.

"I know you think Ms. Aubergine is innocent, but she wouldn't let her child see her own birth certificate, and you don't think that's sus?" Bidi snaps back. When she says it like that, of course it doesn't sound great. I'm sure Ms. Aubergine has an explanation, but I can't think about her right now. I need to think about flower crowns.

"Look, I need to get started if I'm going to finish in time," I say.

"In time for what? What is all this?" she asks.

"Bettina's party is tomorrow. I have to build the crowns."

"You are still doing that?" Bidi pushes.

"Why wouldn't I?"

"Because you got what you wanted," Bidi shoots back.

It's unclear if she means Ms. Aubergine or the store, but I don't ask her to clarify. I have to focus, and the flowers strewn across the floor read mayhem.

Bidi stomps to the office door. "I'll make some coffee."

"What—wait—no—wait, what are you doing? I can't hang out right now. I have to get this done."

Scattered flowers taunt me. I lift a couple to sort.

"Pippa, if the party is tomorrow, you are not going to be prepared. And . . ." Bidi begins.

"And what?" I ask.

"Bettina has something to do with this! I am just missing what ties it all together. So do you want to help Ms. Aubergine or not?"

"Yes, I want to help her!" I say for the hundredth time. *Even though she doesn't want my help after today.*

"Then I'll help you get ready while you work. I've researched everyone relevant to the case. I've got flash cards!" Bidi exclaims, very on brand.

I look down at the sprawl of flowers. The lack of color coding is offensive. The shades do not ascend properly. The flower types are mismatched. I would have never laid them out this way if I hadn't been distracted. The more I stare, the more transfixed I become. I begin to make piles, haphazardly sorted, uneven in color. Bidi got me out of my head. Somehow, she always does.

CHAPTER 30

Bidi

People always talk about my drive and dedication. Mentors and teachers love to praise the way I sort my different responsibilities into neat piles with labels and instructions on how to keep clean as I go. *It's commendable,* they say, how much I seem to manage. Some people[1] like to refer to my mere existence as "inspiring." But the way Pippa works with flowers, it is performance art. She sheds her skin. She talks to herself, silent, bobbing her head as she angles her line of view to somewhere only she can see. Her hands working to perfect the image she's envisioned. A secret to the rest of us until she is done.

When people tell me they think I'm amazing, I swallow the compliment whole and hope it seeps in because I have seen amazing. I'm staring at it right now as she sits on the ground, weaving stems and shaping petals.

I read the next name aloud. "'Ron Barlow.'"

---

1 You know which people.

"Mmm, rich grandpa?" Pippa says through the bunch of string between her teeth.

"Pippa, they all have rich grandpas! You have to be able to fit in with these people. That's the only way they will talk to you."

Pippa has been working long enough for me to run through all Beaumont's top players twice, and she still barely remembers a single person's name.

"Are you sure you can handle this party?"

Pippa's eyes pop up for the first time in hours at the challenge.

She really wants to be one of them, I think. This life, our life here, isn't enough.

"Go again," Pippa suggests. I pull up a photo of a student. Pippa gets up to stretch her body, and her neck rolls from one side to the other while her uneven curls swish back and forth. She rolls her shoulders and then her wrists.

"Geri Mumford. Transplant from the UK, father known to have extramarital affairs. They are loaded from going all in on a huge gamble in the early days of Silicon Valley. Geri spends half the year at an international school in London, no real tie to Estella other than general popularity." Pippa pauses to clock my satisfaction. "Next."

I show her another photo. She shoots off the answer in under a second.

"Adeha Harper, rumored to have had a few flings with Estella over the course of her Bettina years, and as a result, Bettina and Adeha always had tension, but she has a solid alibi for the morning Estella disappeared. She was at a Pilates retreat to waive her senior year PE credits all in one extremely expensive week."

Pippa keeps getting them right. As she recites their bios, she lifts a Styrofoam mannequin head and places onto it a crown made almost entirely of yellow daisies except for one cluster of black roses. Pippa puts on an N95 mask. I do the same. She shakes a hair spray can and sprays the piece for so long the cloud of fumes turns into an orb. Pippa chokes on the air when she removes her mask to inspect the final product, her brain operating on that creative wave, half here and half straddling some other state of being. She kneels back down to start constructing the next piece as I walk to the door. The clock reads six a.m. We pulled an all-nighter.

"Where are you going?" she stops to ask.

"To bed. You're ready," I say to her with a smile.

"Pickup is at nine tomorrow," Pippa says.

"Pickup?" I ask.

"Yeah, come with me. You are better at the people part, and that way you can find out what you need to find out," Pippa says.

The Pippa translation is *I don't want to go by myself.*

"Fine, but I'm going through those clothes and taking what I want."

"Deal," she says.

Outside, exhaustion drags my feet forward. I open the door to my house.

"Bidi?"

I launch myself onto the floor for cover. I wasn't expecting Mo to be up.

"What is wrong with you?" I whisper shout.

"What is wrong with YOU? You go pull that stunt at my school?!"

Mo's rage sits on his surface. He seethes.

"I'm sorry, did you mispronounce 'thank you'? I just got rid of your problem. You are a scholarship student—you think they want the bad press of kicking you out because those ding-dongs said to?"

Mo considers what I said. Clearly, he hadn't thought of it that way.

"Well, you didn't have to go and show me up." He pouts.

For once, I am finding my groove in this investigation, and he wants to make it about him.

"I'm not thinking about you. I'm thinking about me, and the way I'm going to win that election after I get to the bottom of this."

I storm back out of the house and wait for the bus to huff around the corner.

I'll never tell Pippa, but the graveyard isn't as creepy as I thought it would be. I wait and watch for that Jaggers guy to march out of the estate to make my move because I'm still unconvinced of Ms. Aubergine's innocence.

I walk onto the empty street where Pippa's work in the garden stuns. Periwinkle blue coats a whole section of the ground like a body of water. She trimmed plants into cones, dotted perfectly with orange flowers to grow evenly around each other. The bush of magenta flowers fits like the corner piece in *Tetris*. The whole garden is mesmerizing, and only a fraction of the flowers have begun to bloom.

"Hello?"

I jump back from the gate of the estate to see Ms. Aubergine standing just a few feet away in the garden.

"Uh, hi, sorry I was just—" I start to come up with an excuse, but the creak of the gate cuts me off as she opens it for me.

"I recognize you from the news. Elizabeth, right? Come in. I was just about to make some tea," she says.

The chance to step inside the world Pippa has been building presents itself to me, and I take it. We walk along the path toward the main house.

"You'll have to excuse the state of the garden. It's a work in progress, but you know that, don't you? Pippa mentioned she knew you when we saw your detective work in action yesterday."

Pippa's betrayal stings. *Way to sell me out.*

Ms. Aubergine opens the door to the house.

She shuts the door and turns the lock with a click. Ms. Aubergine stares into my eyes and softens.

"Thank you, by the way, for your help. Seems like you were able to get farther than the entire SFPD and my personal investigator."

She takes my hand to squeeze it. I fix my face to hide the shock.

"Um, oh, you're welcome . . ."

She weaves us through the home to a kitchen Mommy would die for. The counter space alone would change her life. I take a seat on a stool as Ms. Aubergine begins to boil water and assemble the tea.

"Because of you, the police found that Ms. Brodsky pulled the same stunt with six other schools. Unfortunately, they don't see any ties to my Stella's disappearance. Brodsky and Pummel have sound alibis for the morning Estella was last seen. So, tell me. Are you one of those what do they call them? Sleuths?" Ms. Aubergine joins me at the island with turquoise mugs.

"No, I'm a high school student. I'm actually running for city council in the fall, when I turn eighteen. I'm planning to be the youngest person elected in this city. But one of my campaign fixtures is the imbalance in resources offered when lower-income Black and Brown girls go missing."

I wait for the pinched face of defense most white women have when I speak truths like these in front of them, but Ms. Aubergine only smiles.

"Very admirable. Ambitious, like my Stella."

"Yes, well, her disappearance helped me realize how important this cause is. I really want to help people, Estella included, of course." I turn on my charm.

"Pippa could stand to learn that from you. She's got so little confidence—it's such a shame. You're a great role model for her, I can tell."

Up close, she does give off a warmth I wasn't expecting, but I am not letting her shift the narrative. "You know, the reason Brodsky targeted Estella is because of an issue with her birth certificate."

Her eyes widen, then fall to my cup. "Don't you want your tea? I blend the spice mix myself. This is one of Pippa's favorites."

I look to hers, untouched, then bring my mouth to the lip of the mug and pause. Still a little too hot.

"Come." She stands and brings the mug with her. Ms. Aubergine takes a sip as we walk back the way we came and into the garden.

"You seem to have a good head on your shoulders, so I'll tell you what I've never told anyone, but first, you must understand, I just wanted to protect her," Ms. Aubergine says.

I don't respond. From where I am standing, it doesn't look like she's done a great job of it.

"I knew one day she would ask about her father, so I told her the truth, that he wasn't alive anymore. But she wanted to know who he had been. I couldn't risk her searching and finding out. So I took his name off the birth certificate," Ms. Aubergine said.

"Finding out what?" I ask.

"That he was a terrible, horrible man. He made me fall in love with him, he promised me the world and then, when I got pregnant, he said he wanted nothing to do with us and vanished. He tried to ruin our family." Apoplectic, Ms. Aubergine watches the tree branches until the siren of a police car sends the mug in her hands shattering on the stone path beneath her.

The lights pull up outside. Jaggers emerges, a cop follows, and Ms. Aubergine rushes to the gate.

"What is it? Is it her? Did you find her? Is she okay?"

If this is a performance, it is captivating. Pippa's insistence that Ms. Aubergine had nothing to do with Estella disappearing is beginning to ring true. Jaggers comes through the gate beside a detective in plain clothes. The gun holstered into his suit pants flashes on his side.

"Ma'am—we need to go inside," the man says.

The urgency in his voice hits sharp. The fear grows in Ms. Aubergine's eyes, and Jaggers goes to her side. I watch them enter the house; then I rush out onto the street and close the gate. Seconds later, her shriek cuts through the pavement. It's over. Estella must be gone. I have to get to Pippa and tell her before she sees something on the news.

My phone buzzes as soon as I turn the corner. Mo's name flashes. I guess he's forgiven me.

"What is it?" I answer.

"I'm sorry, Bidi," he says. *I wasn't expecting that.*

"For what?" I milk the apology.

Tires behind me screech to a stop, and I turn toward a large black SUV. A door swings open.

"It will all make sense soon, okay?" he says.

"What— Mo, what is going on?" I ask as someone in a long black hooded coat steps out.

"Elizabeth," they say, and pull me inside the car before I can even scream.

CHAPTER 31

Pippa

The weight of the gold peony on my breastbone wakes me, pressing against my heart. I check my phone: 5:03 p.m. I stayed up all night and then slept through the day. The shock jolts me up. I can't deal with anything, not Ms. Aubergine, who probably hates me, or Jo and the way she keeps looking at me, begging me with her eyes to start fresh and release her from her sins.

I have bigger problems I need to handle, like figuring out how to dress for a party filled with people I don't trust. How do I pick an outfit loud enough to make them take notice and muted enough to make it easy to underestimate me, so they spill their guts? This is a job for Bidi. Plus, she has to pick her outfit too. I rush across the street.

The door to Bidi's house swings open after one knock. Mo wrinkles his face when he sees me.

"What are you doing here?"

"I need Bidi's help," I say.

"She's not here."

Mo takes a thin shoelace and uses it as a headband to pull his hair back away from his face.

"Well, where is she?" I ask.

He shrugs.

We stand beside one another, me in a silent spiral and him watching it from the outside, debating whether to take cover in case I explode. I have only four hours until the party. I still have to get ready and finish my own flower piece to wear. Bidi must have a good reason to be gone, one more important than me, so now I have to do what I do best and improvise.

"We need to get ready," I tell him.

"What do you mean, 'we'?" Mo asks.

"You go to Beaumont, which means you know how to deal with these people. I'm switching teams. If you want to solve this case and find out what Bettina knows, get dressed and meet me at the shop at eight-forty-five," I say, then rush back home.

After trying every iteration of every outfit, a white corset top with the high-low poofy skirt covered in a pattern of bright flamingo pink and nectarine is the one that feels best. I balloon out the door, the skirt first and then me. I shove my feet into white leather booties.

"Look at you." Jo's eyes beam.

She steps forward with intention; her thumbs wrestle each other when she speaks.

"When she left, she didn't just leave you. I had to raise you and keep us alive, and no one told me how to do any of it. I had to figure out how to let her go, but I couldn't handle doing that for you too."

Leave it to Jo to have a moment of clarity before I go to my first rich-kid party.

"You know, I've been thinking about how we have this chance to update the Padaria, and I have ideas. We should hire someone to give you some time off and focus more on school. Maybe we can get that flower fridge that you've always wished for and I could never afford. Open a little stand out there on the corner."

Jo says all the things I have always wanted her to say. Her eyes sweep over me one more time, a full head-to-toe glance. "Wait, I have something for you."

She hurries to the closet and returns with vintage gold earrings. They clamp over my earlobes, clams chasing their jewel. Jo's shoulders tense up to her ears. She softens her eyes.

"Think about what I said about the flower stand, okay?" she asks.

"Yes, okay." I accept.

So many words live in the crooks of our teeth. They cling to the sides of our tongues, afraid they might come out wrong. Jo takes my hands and looks me in the eye.

"You look just like her." She says the only words that she knew would be perfect: "Go on, grab your stuff. I closed the shop for a little while. I'll reopen when you're gone."

Jo smiles at the door like she's tasted the beginning of joy and isn't going to let go.

Downstairs, I sit in front of my panel and take out the peony pendant. I squeeze it into my palm to burn the mold into my skin.

I will return it to Ms. Aubergine tomorrow. I will tell her everything. I will come clean, and I will walk away.

The emptiness of the Bahia Padaria is a blessing. Weeks ago, we thought we were going to be thrown out and now, well, maybe now we really will be okay. The gratitude is swallowed by the body I feel behind me, moving closer. I slide the panel back into place over the gold-and-diamond pendant and pick up my crate to swing in one swift motion of self-defense.

"Pippa!" Mo jumps back, narrowly avoiding my weapon.

"What are you doing?" I put the crate down and walk past him to turn on the light.

"You told me to meet you here . . . Wow," he says, looking me up and down.

He's never seen me dressed like this. I haven't either. I could say the same about him, but the word coming out of my mouth about his look would have a very different meaning. He stands before me in Adidas joggers, a blazer, and a button-down.

"What are you wearing?"

He glances down. "Clothes?"

There is no way that Bettina will allow anyone dressed like this into her event.

"Run, do not walk, to your house, and put on dark jeans and your shirt with the big satin duck on it."

"You remember my shirts?" he asks.

The fit made his cheekbones pop, that's all.

"Don't flatter yourself; you normally look and smell like a mole person. The only reason I remember is because it's the only fashion-adjacent thing you have. Go!" I shout.

"Hello?"

A man's voice jumps over our backs. We both turn the door.

"I'm here for the crowns," a man in his fifties says, looking around like he is quite sure he is in the very wrong place. Mo runs past him to follow my instructions.

"Right, okay, come with me." I walk the courier to the back and carry each sculpture myself to secure in the temperature-controlled van. When he drives off, I return one last time to the store for the large cake box, where my own custom piece waits for me.

Spray-painted gold roses glued to the top of weaved ribbon form a shrug that covers only my shoulders and neck. In the front, the ribbon is sliced into narrow fingers, hands clasped just under my chin. I didn't know what I was going to be wearing when I made this, but it fits perfectly. Mo waits outside dressed in the outfit I styled. I won't tell him how good I knew he would look, so I avert my eyes to keep from staring. The car Bettina sent pulls up in front, and Mo opens the door for me to walk through. The tinted windows make it impossible to see where we are headed, so I settle into the mystery. I wonder if I will ever get used to trusting that the universe will be kind enough not to knock me onto my ass the way it has so many times before. Beside me, Mo's knee bounces so hard, it overtakes the thrum of the engine.

The driver takes a turn that makes me slide into Mo in the back seat. His body heat takes away the slight chill dancing down my neck and arms.

"We'll be there in five minutes," the driver says.

Mo's energy shifts. I can see the short, small breaths, the ones he used to let out when he was struggling to get through a day of his cousins torturing him and needed to take a break. I used to sit with him until they passed. Now is not the time for short breaths.

"Look, I need you to get it together!" I whisper.

He holds his hand out in front of him; it shakes. "I'm not going to be much help. I don't go to parties."

"What do you mean?" From the look on his face, the mere mention of a high school party has him morphing back to his boyhood before my eyes.

"I don't socialize. They play; I work."

"Mo, you are supposed to be helpful, not make me feel bad for you! Bidi would give me a pep talk, one that's uplifting but firm." I give him his orders.

"Um, I don't know . . ." He wavers.

"Do it," I command. After a few seconds, he starts to talk.

"Okay, listen. You are the only one who can get more out of Bettina. You don't need Bidi tonight."

Mo stops, eyes glued to mine. He leans toward me. My chest begins to constrict.

"We're here!" The driver pulls to a stop and we fall back, away from one another.

Mo looks away first and opens the door. I slide out after him.

The line of Ubers outside the building snakes down Front Street. The downtown financial district is home mostly to corporate high-rises that have rapidly become vacant as the draw of remote work and higher rent prices have started pushing companies out. Looks like Bettina swooped one up for herself tonight. Mo and I follow the line of people entering the glass building and head to the thirty-fifth floor.

I've never been to one of Bettina's parties, but I have been to parties in my neighborhood. Street parties. Smoke parties. Starry-eyed, fists over our heads, fists on our hearts, fists around beers and burritos, tears and spit, sweat on the crown of your lips parties. An evolution in real time from the corner to the backyard. Parties that started because we found ourselves together and that is cause enough for a celebration—those rare moments when we are all we need.

This party is not like those parties.

Muted as the white brick encasing this room, a cold breeze blows off the ice block the server pours tequila through into a frozen glass. Skyscraper pillars hold tight to the ceiling. We wait while security checks us for paraphernalia and weapons. Once satisfied, they wave us through to the former office space now converted into a warehouse of adventure.

"You should go in and start investigating," I say to Mo, eyes peeled for Bettina.

"What? We should probably stick together at first, don't you think?" he asks, scratching the back of his neck.

He's scared. It's kind of cute.

"The point is to get Bettina to talk as much as possible. She won't do that if you are around."

Mo starts to argue but freezes, mouth parted, as another voice interjects.

"You made it."

Bettina stands before us in a cream jumpsuit with a cape. She wears the lace fabric like skin.

If Bettina Drummle were a plant, she would be an ivy. Waxy. Abundant. She is skilled at wrapping herself around you so gently, you don't realize she's covered all your air holes until it's too late. Bettina drags me to the corner lounge. I look back to see if Mo is trailing us, but he must have hidden before she could notice him. She pulls me into a space tented in scarves, layers on layers, fallen leaves on an autumn street. A cocoon for "the pharmacy," as she calls it, because it dispenses whatever you need.

"This is Pete. He's barely a junior at Berkeley and already running an empire."

Bettina introduces us, then turns to Pete. "I've got to make an appearance with the masses. Just a gummy for now, something light and fun."

He pulls a cube-shaped gummy from a tin on the counter. She opens her mouth, and he places it onto her tongue. Then she turns and leaves. Pete pushes a leather-bound menu toward me. I stare at the selection, unsure how to proceed.

"If you are worried about safety, I want you to know we run a no-risk operation. No one takes anything I didn't approve. Every item has been tested for fentanyl. We've also got the strips for anyone to stop and test anything at any time for assurance. There are cases of Narcan easily accessible just to be extra cautious."

He hands me a few white strips and an origami folded paper shaped like a swan with their instructions. "So what can I get you?"

I bite my bottom lip. I've never ventured past a few hits off a joint and booze.

"Sorry . . . um, yes, I was wondering if you could just, like . . . explain it to me?"

"Explain what?"

"All of it."

Pete takes the menu and faces it out to me.

"The tiny yellow pills are like the last bite of a lemon-curd doughnut, electric on your tongue before a swarm of sadness that it's over. Take an edible to keep it from dipping too much, but you'll probably clock out early. To keep the pace, take half a white, give it at least an hour before the rest, and try to stay seated until you get your footing. It throws people, the way your stomach turns to fireflies on the long slide at the water park. This purple one makes you land in a cloud and hang up there before plummeting to the ground. It's a wild ride and not for the faint of heart, definitely not for a newbie. For you, I'd recommend a green—it's a starter, a baseline. You feel the beat for a while and figure out if you want to turn it up a notch."

"Pippa!"

Mo's lips almost touch my ear, his warm breath sends shivers down my spine.

"Excuse us one second," Mo says to Pete. He wraps his hand around my upper arm and pulls me to the opening of the scarves.

"What are you doing?" he asks once we have reached the entrance of the tent.

"I'm doing what everyone else here is doing! I'm blending in."

"We have to keep it together." He sounds like Bidi, if Bidi hadn't abandoned us.

"Keeping it together is not really my brand," I say before lowering my voice. "I wasn't actually going to take anything; I was just going to keep it under my tongue and then put it in my pocket. Relax."

"Pippa, you killed it!"

Bettina's horde of pigeons descends on us in the tent, swallowing Mo and spitting him out. They hold up their phones to show me the streams of love and comments they are receiving on the stories they have already posted with my creations. People love my art as much as I do. But I can't enjoy the recognition until I deal with these crowns all placed on their heads incorrectly.

"You should have let me put them on," I say under my breath.

I pull Patina down to me and take the mass of daisies with the hole of black flowers off her head. I turn it and pin it behind her ear, so the black section encases her eye. The black covers her brows and camouflages her top lashes. She becomes part of the piece. Prue bends her head for me to adjust hers as well, which should be worn off-kilter like a fascinator rather than a perfectly centered top hat made of a range of wildflowers. I adjust the brim that starts orange and gets darker until it turns as red as a fatal wound, a bent saucer, a visor on steroids.

Essence is giving Erykah Badu in a triple-sized hat made of marigolds with a fringe of lilies of the valley hanging like bells.

"You're good," I tell her after I give it a quick centering tug.

"Tending to everyone else before the host?" Bettina asks, reappearing.

Two holds her crown on a pillow. Her hair is shellacked flat to her skull, so when I lower the bright shell down onto her head, it takes over. There is nothing else but the massive helmet of magenta flowers, chic and unavoidable. No matter what else is in the room, Bettina is all you will be staring at.

"Let's go." She puts her hands on my shoulders to position me toward a crowd of cameras. I oblige. Their lights flash for what feels like minutes.

"We need to talk, Bettina." I speak out of the corner of my mouth.

Bettina looks around. She bobs her head for the cameras. Once we get past the step-and-repeat, she turns to me, face to face.

"I mean it, Bettina. I have some questions."

Bettina smiles, and she leans in so our nose tips touch. "I'm sure you do, honey, but it's going to have to wait."

"Why? Bettina— Oh."

She places a purple pill onto my tongue that dissolves instantly, no time to spit it out. She takes one too.

"Bettina, I know you had something to do with Pummel and the counselor—"

The floor wobbles beneath me, and the room starts to melt. Not like fire, like chocolate.

Not burning, just liquefying. A beach ball launched out to bobble in a warm velvet sea.

"All you know is you are about to reach cloud nine," Bettina says, before she takes my hand and runs.

CHAPTER 32
Pippa (and the Purple Pill)

Bettina pulls me around the room, my pupils as big as saucers, as dark as the ocean at midnight, drowning me until the buzz kicks in throughout my body. A sense of calm and vibrancy meet under my skin for the first time. I can see why people chase this feeling, how it consumes, blasting holes through their reverie. The way my brain just floats between thoughts—there are no doors, only halls, like this party.

Every room comes at a different frequency, a new pharmacy, another crowd. There's a hum like a built-in white noise machine. An air conditioner blasting in my ear.

I think I've heard it's not your mother's heartbeat that lulls you to sleep in her womb; it's her blood gushing around you.

People walk around with floating trays, and I grab the tiny morsels of food as they pass. Eating is better this way, like I can taste colors. I can taste the air, bright blue powder pressed into the sky as the sun greets the magic hour. Maroon is layered; all chefs should use maroon. Orange blankets my tongue, first salt, then cream. I get why people disappear into themselves rather than face the music.

Here the music is inside, and it's not for disappearing—it's for bursting out.

There is a room so pink you would think that you never knew what pink really was. In the pink room, you can dance on the outline of flamingo walls, bubble-gum balls, and the syrup that collects at the bottom of strawberry milk. The music blasts pink, too, as we dance, as we jump. It is nice, all the guests being united by pink. United by the lack of Estella. We dance pink to forget her.

To declare she may be gone, but we are still here, we are still here. So we dance, we twirl the layers of a champagne pink rosé. We dance until we dry out, browning petals, drained of our pink worries. Free and pink, we raise the tight fists to relish that this is the most beautiful we've ever felt. Here, right now, it's just about cotton candy and grapefruit. The sweet and bitter. The essence of pink kissing our taste buds before clamping down with its teeth.

The music is loud enough for me to scream a pink so deep and dark, so full, it is almost blood. Bettina tries to get my attention, and so does Mo, but I'm here for me. Because it's always them. Always Mamãe chasing the trail she left. Always Jo and the mess she made. Always Bidi, sure she knows better than me.

Always Ms. Aubergine's sad eyes begging me to take her pain.

Always Estella.

Always Estella.

It is always Estella.

Voices curl around my neck, barbed wire lacquered in self-interest.

"She's wasted."

"Artists are always so messy."

"I heard she's been hanging out at Estella's house; it's bad karma."

"I heard she's a charity case."

"Bettina discovered her."

"I heard she showed up right after Estella disappeared."

"Sounds like a stalker."

I don't know what I expected coming here. Everyone is playing their part with not so much as a hiccup. It's only me and Estella breaking script—

"Pippa? Come on, you need to eat."

A hand pulls me out into the white room, frozen and utterly devoid of pink.

CHAPTER 33

Pippa

Mo drapes a blanket around my shoulders while I take huge bites of a cheeseburger over a plate in my lap.

"This is delicious."

"It's In-N-Out. Of course it's delicious." He holds out a napkin to catch some melty cheese before it drips onto my shirt.

"Where is there an In-N-Out around here?"

Mo smiles with his diamond teeth. The sparkle is so bright, it's hard to follow the words once they burst through.

"There isn't; they built one for the party. You've been in that room the whole time. I kept checking in every twenty minutes."

"You checked on me?" My heart beats so hard I can see my flower shrug bouncing from underneath. I try to slow my breath.

"Yes, because you're a liability. Drink some water." He hands me a glass to me. "You must be tired after your self-exploration moment."

Mo gets up and starts imitating me, slow sweeping movements with his arms, very modern. He pauses, holding a position and then lunges in the other direction.

"She drugged me," I explain, and take another bite of my Double-Double Animal Style.

"Well, get it together. We should try to get to Bettina again—"

The warm buzz in my brain starts to get soaked up by the grease in my stomach, adrenaline from the pill or the music or being this close to Mo. I shake my head.

"No, come with me. I have a better idea."

Two stands in the entry checking people in, coordinating coat check, and facilitating outfit changes. Mo stands back, but not too far in case I need him to swoop in. Two shifts his weight in the four-inch clear Lucite platforms he wears. As I approach him, someone enters the party and chucks their purse at him. Two dodges it just before it slams into my head.

He laughs and wheezes so hard he turns purple and coughs. Two bends to collect the bag from where it landed. "That was what I needed, thanks," he says.

With him loosened up at my expense, I dive in headfirst. "Look, I'm not saying I like you, but you did a great job with this party."

"Me?" His brow rises.

"Don't be dumb. We all know you are the one who does the heavy lifting."

A grin creeps from his bottom lip. He walks toward the coat check, and a young woman with mousy hair scrambles as she sees him approach.

"Give me a tag." He snaps his fingers when she doesn't move as quickly as he would like.

She hands him the empty paper and the pen and writes the name of the guest who launched the bag at my head. As I watch his hands move, the curl of the letters slams into my gut. I recognize that handwriting.

"I, uh, need to find a bathroom," I say.

He points to an orange door to his left. I rush inside to catch my breath. I wish I could think more clearly but despite the purple fog in my head, I know now who wrote the note for Ms. Aubergine. *Alberta sees you.*

Two has known every place I have been since the moment I first met him. I compose myself and step back out.

"I'm going on break. Follow me," Two says.

We walk back into the party, but into a "sober shack" with '90s hip-hop playing and glow-in-the-dark jewelry. Definitely the most rhythmic dance party I have seen in the massive space yet. He hops onto a stool, then orders a round of mocktails and a hit of oxygen for each of us. It's probably psychosomatic, but the oxygen sobers the rest of me up. The drink, a grapefruit-lime slushy with candied-ginger Pop Rocks, deserves a Michelin star.

"Do you ever wonder what it would be like to be on your own? Not working under Bettina's oppressive thumb? You could be in there, just enjoying the party," I ask.

"No. I couldn't." Two rises after downing his drink and weaves through the party again, past the pink room and the scarf tent, past a room covered in polka dots where a small group rages at a silent rave. We push past a wine cellar with a sommelier.

"What are you looking for?" I ask him.

"Here."

We turn a corner to a hall with a door and a sign that says ROOM OF REFLECTION. He puts his hand on the knob but doesn't twist it.

"Bettina isn't who people think she is."

"What do you mean?" I ask.

He opens the door. Reflection, not the kind offered in the halls of a church or mosque. Reflection, like a room full of mirrors. One thousand Twos walk to the center of the room and sit in the lone wood chair.

"What is this place?" I ask.

"It was supposed to be a meditative experience, but the spiritual leader we booked had some trouble with customs, and then the vibe just seemed a bit off, so Bettina decided to hang the mirrors. She said if anyone stumbled into the space, they would get what they needed out of it."

"What do *you* need, Two?"

All the Twos stare back at me. He knows how pretty he is, so he can't help but smile at the sight of himself. He stands.

"I'm a straight white boy trying to get into the fashion scene. I have no real family connections, no scandals. My parents are normal, mostly good people who have generational wealth. I'm boring. I have no edge. I need her to bring me into the fold."

His teeth grind. Finally, the weak spot showing where I need to push him.

"Bettina has no real power unless you let her. Estella knew that, and it pissed Bettina off. Bettina uses you."

"You think I don't know that? I'm letting her."

"Why?" I push.

"Because it was working! Bettina finally saw she was better off without Estella."

His mouth screams from every inch of room.

"Two, if Bettina did something, if she hurt Estella, you have to tell me. I can help you. I know you think I'm your enemy, but I'm not. I hate seeing the way she treats you. I know something is going on. I know you left that note to scare Ms. Aubergine."

"I was protecting Bettina!" Two steps away from me. "The minute Estella started reeling her back in, I could tell she was going to go to the dark side again. So I did what no one else could. I found the truth."

"What are you talking about?" The fear in my face covers the walls.

"Do you think for one second that I don't know you are trying to weasel into the spot that opened up in her friend group? Get in line. Some of us have been waiting, and I have what it takes to make someone disappear."

His eyes are redder than his hair. They burn into me.

"You asked me what I want. I want you gone!"

Two lunges at me, and there is nothing to grab but the chair. I can tell by the grooves the only wood that could make this is *Schinopsis brasiliensis*, and the thing about *Schinopsis brasiliensis* is, it might as well be stone.

The room knows what I need.

I raise the chair up, and he jumps back as I swing. The first mirror is a piñata beneath my hands, exploding into hundreds of pieces, each one a different shrill in its landing. The second smash sends a tremor through the remaining mirrors, ragged and twirling defeat. The room becomes an ice rink warmed by springy tongues spitting glass. One shard for each disappointment, one sliver for every tear, and the next one and the next one until the ground is a broken mirror. The door opens, and people stream in. Thousands of eyes stare back at me from the now-reflective floor, including the hostess herself.

Like in the pink room, the whispers about me start.

"What is she doing? She's completely lost it. How embarrassing."

"Who even is she?"

"How mid."

Their judgments hammer into me as I swing the chair into the walls. I can't meet their eyes; I can't breathe. Between the shattering of the mirrors and the beating in my head, I can't think. I can't tell them to fuck off. I can't be sorry for myself. Not when I see the black-hooded coat standing across from me, far enough behind the crowd they don't notice. But I learned my lesson more than once. They are not getting away, not this time. I throw the chair and scream so loud, glass splinters again.

"GRAB THEM!" I shout and point to the empty space where the hooded figure was, but has disappeared just like Estella.

The glass shards bite everyone's ankles and toes as half the party runs and the other half grits their teeth and bears the sting, too enthralled by my behavior. People willing to suffer to record my social demise. The hungry bees vying to suck the life out of me move in to get the right shot when Bettina tackles me. I see Mo standing above me, watching as Bettina forces me down. The contact with the floor rips my skin all over, but he doesn't help me. No one helps. They all stand behind her and wait to see what I do.

"What did you do to Estella?" I say quietly enough that only she can hear me.

She grabs me, eyes round and hurt.

"DO TO HER? The only thing I did was love that girl! I'm basically having this party in her honor. If she can disappear, anyone can. So we might as well make something out of it. We are celebrating the opportunity to still be here. The chance to rethink our futures, reimagine who we want to be."

The room is enraptured. I am becoming a popularity boost. Her stepping stone to being an iconic trailblazer. Rather than bringing her speech home, Bettina bends to my ear from where she crouches over me. "I know what you are doing. You will never replace me in her world."

"Yeah, well, I know you lied to the police. You saw Estella the day before she disappeared. You got that Balenciaga bag back." I lead with the facts Bidi told me.

Bettina's face tilts, caught.

"I only saw her to get my bag and closure. I knew about the birth certificate. I knew she needed answers. I offered to help, but she refused."

"And that is why you went to the counselor?"

She throws her head up to laugh.

"I have a therapist, a shaman, and a psychic on speed dial. I don't need that rent-a-doc."

"There is footage of you at Beaumont that same day! We caught you, Bettina. You were there!" I push.

"No, I wasn't!"

Bettina takes me by my flower collar, and the spray-painted petals crumble beneath her hands.

"You have no clue what you just did, but good luck ever finding success again once I'm done with you."

Security guards make their way through the mess and collect me. I scream at Bettina's back as they carry me away. I scream through the stream of comments from her guests and the irony that now that they've thrown me out onto the curb like the trash, my face will be in everyone's minds and trending on their feeds, not Bettina's, not even Estella's. Mine.

"Pippa!"

Mo pushes through the mass of people blocking the door just before it slams shut. He helps me up from the ground, but I shove him away.

"Are you okay? That was out of control—you need to go to the hospital." His hands move up and down my arms, and he brushes away any remnants of glass.

"You told me I could do this. You said I was the only one who could!"

I use all the power in me to slam my hands into his chest, but he catches my wrists. He looks into my eyes.

"I'm sorry, Pippa. I tried to get to you."

He lets go to cup my cheek. The electric shocks in our skin are almost enough to forget what just happened. But his thumb runs over a scratch from the glass, and it all comes back.

"Go back inside, Mo. I'm not your people; they are." I push him off and get into the first car waiting in a line to take guests home.

CHAPTER 34

Mo

The burn inside me spreads, the rage she inspires eats me alive. The curve of her neck makes me want to scream. The pinks and reds and orange-yellows from the flowers that float in the air in her wake make it so that I can still feel her even after she's gone. How can someone so perfect make me want to explode?

Dread that I've missed my one chance to finally tell Pippa how I feel every time that I look at her overtakes me.

My phone buzzes with a text that interrupts my pity-fest.

Unknown Number:

third car.

I walk past cars stationed outside to take people home once they come staggering out of Bettina's black hole of a party.

A black SUV is the third down the line. The door opens for

me as I approach, and I hop in beside the long black hoodie. "I need to get to a computer, I've almost got what we need."

"Let's go."

The driver follows their command, pulls out of the line, and drives down the street.

CHAPTER 35

Pippa

If this disaster of a night went down in a movie, I would hail a cab, and a greasy middle-aged man would pick me up. He'd ask, "Where to?" and I'd tell him, "Just drive." He'd be curt but sage, and I would go on an adventure where he'd show me all the things I've taken for granted, and I would arrive late to my destination but better—enlightened, even.

But this isn't a movie.

Instead, shortly after I am thrown out of Bettina's party and into Mo's arms for probably the last time, a college kid drenched in cigarette smoke pulls up to take me home. In the car, I let the techno music he blasts and the breeze from the open window and the waves in my stomach put me to sleep. In my dreams, I block out the sound of Mamãe's phantom heart, so I don't have to fight the itch, the need for answers. I don't have to convince myself that I am worthy of seeds.

In my dreams, I am a butterfly. I am luck. I am the sparkle in a child's eye. I live off the flowers. I am the honey voice behind the perfect song in the shower. I am the first time I learned beauty does not always equal symmetry.

In dreams, when I get lost, I just keep going, and the pieces that need to be picked up and sorted and put back together—they turn to precious gems floating in a river until someone finds them and gives them a new story.

In dreams, I don't fumble with my keys trying to get into the store to get a snack and a Gatorade because the purple pill keeps sneaking back up to the surface. I don't notice that the bell usually hanging above the door is knocked over until I take a few steps inside to find Jo's body on the floor, and I am reminded that dreams, like lives, are fickle, fragile glass houses.

I use my whole might to try to wake her, to flip her over, purple and blue as a newborn struggling to taste its first oxygen. I scream in her ear. I pinch her wrist to detect life and find it as empty as her eyes. I reach around her neck, the closest thing to a hug we have shared in years, unable to enjoy it as this is our last embrace.

This is not the first time I've found myself in this position, standing over her lifeless body. There were times when she would pass out so hard from drinking, I had to pour a bucket of ice water on her head to bring her back. This is not the first time I have had to wait to hear her breathe, but this is the first time in my life her breath never comes.

Sirens appear after what feels like forever, and they rush in and pump her bare chest like a beaten-up bike tire. I hear them shout words like "gone" and "time of death" and "what a shame." A cop with a goatee blocks me from watching any more. There's more to do, like ask me questions:

"Do you know where you are? Do you know who you are?"

"Do you know why you are here?"

I look back to him and say, "Aren't we all asking ourselves those the questions?"

I am still floating, only now through a fog.

Unamused, he asks:

"A drug habit?"

"Money problems?"

"How's the neighborhood been lately? Rough? It seems rough."

I do not confirm the story he has already written—that my aunt was poor and stressed with a kid she couldn't afford and didn't ask for so she drank like everyone else without resources does. I only shake my head and try to avoid the smell of rank eggs and burnt coffee on his teeth. There might be a time when that's all I remember from this day, the terrible breath on this beast of a man who keeps checking his phone like his time is being wasted on another statistic, but right now I feel everything. The nighttime cloaks my grief, the less than ten minutes he spends inside to gather evidence, each second a lifetime.

"A formal report will be written, but the examiner saw blunt force trauma to the head," he says. "Did she have enemies?"

My mother turned into Jo's enemy. At times, I was too. She didn't have many others, besides a bottle and a credit card. I do, though. *The hooded jacket,* I think, but I can't speak as her body slams against the gurney. Once she has been officially pronounced dead, and I've identified her, the cop speaks again.

"Because you are seventeen, San Francisco law says that CPS won't become involved unless you cannot locate a guardian or we detect you are in danger. You do need to report to the station to meet with a social worker by midweek. Do you understand?"

"Mm-hmm." I nod. The wheels sting as they nip at my toes on the way out the door as Jo leaves the Bahia Padaria for the last time.

A Working Eulogy for Jo(sefina) Santos Vas Santos

Jo saved every penny she could find to leave Brazil and come to California to start a new life. Her plan was to go to business school and start a Brazilian food empire. She had just begun when her twin sister showed up and left her with her newborn niece, whom she had no clue what to do with. Jo worked by night cleaning buildings, hands burned by the chemicals, and by day at the shop, which, after ten years, she took over and turned into the Bahia Padaria.

Jo got her wisdom teeth taken out a couple years ago. The dentist said she should do it in two shifts, first one side, then the other. They said the pain was easier to manage that way, but she refused. She told them there was no point in suffering twice if she could get it over with in one fell swoop.

She kept to herself, a walking sack of unrealized potential.

Jo used to say, *Art is for people who can afford to waste time* and

Pippa, you are so focused on the tip of your nose, you can't even see what's ten feet in front of you; that's how people fall and

Leave me alone; I'm tired. And

Leave me alone; I'm hurting.

She didn't actually say that last one, but her eyes did.

She worked hard when she could. She was trying. And she was always around; you could count on that. The neighborhood counted on that.

CHAPTER 36

Pippa

I don't know what time it was when the police left, but since they did, I have been awake. No word from Bidi or Mo. When I call, their phones go straight to voicemail. No one has been here to put rice and beans into my mouth or hand me a cup with a straw to drink ice-cold water.

No one comes around to help me through the last waves of the purple pill, or to hear me when I tell them that the trip up wasn't worth what has happened coming down.

No one helps me clean up the store, so I sit on my knees and scrub the smell of death lemon fresh. At dusk, I go outside. The whole front of the store has been caution-taped off, but beyond the yellow warning, white candles rest in the hands of the neighborhood. The flicker of the flames looks just like San Francisco at night, just like Rio at night, surrounded by a wall of twinkling lights.

Mamãe's and Jo's sister cities in standing vigil.

CHAPTER 37

Bidi

I look at Mo in the back seat of the car. “This better work,” I warn.

While I now see he had good reason to do so, he did literally have me kidnapped yesterday, and I’m not going to just let that slide. He rolls his eyes and bounces his leg, his nerves still getting the best of him despite the brave face.

I don’t have the energy to be worried about this plan. I’m worried about Pippa. Our phones have been locked up and placed on airplane mode since yesterday. That way we can’t be tracked. But it also means we have no clue what is going on out there and Pippa doesn’t know where we are. Mo filled me in on how the party went. She must be a wreck.

“Please, can we just send her a text?” I ask.

Mo considers it but shakes his head.

“It’s to keep her safe,” he whispers.

He’s down bad for Pippa. I don’t know how I never saw it, but now that I can, it’s been there the whole time.

She will understand, I tell myself. We exit the car and head to Beaumont.

Henry the security guard greets us, smiling at Mo. "Mr. Mo."

"Hey, Henry!" Mo flashes his own smile, then daps him up and compliments Henry's fade and new sneakers. The man, all gassed up by Mo, glows so much he doesn't notice me pull the key off the wall for the main office.

"I'll catch you later, Henry," Mo says. We walk around the corner and out of sight.

"Come on," he says. We race to the main office, where I stand guard as Mo searches for something on the security footage. Fifteen minutes later, we are on our way to the library.

"Well?" I ask.

"At the party, when Pippa confronted Bettina, she refused to admit it was her in that tape. She said she did see Estella, but she didn't go to the school," Mo says.

"Well, she's lying," I tell him. "She had the purse the day of the confrontation."

"Well, she definitely got the purse back from Estella. But what if she handed it off to someone to get it home?"

It clicks. "Two."

Mo grins. "Ding, ding, ding."

CHAPTER 38

Pippa

How do you care for a bleeding heart?

Lamprocapnos spectabilis, otherwise known as the bleeding-heart flower, is quite needy. The plant requires frequent hydration and does better in the shade. Working compost into the regularly fertilized soil encourages a bolder bloom. If the sun gets too hot, its foliage may begin to yellow and dry. If this happens, carefully remove all withered segments, but do not remove anything until you are sure it has died. It would be a shame to write it off before it has had a chance to self-revive.

The morning keeps bursting through the windows in the apartment like the universe is saying, "Shove it down, keep it moving." It's too quiet to sleep anyway. No mayhem trailing the kitchen to the TV. No disdain shooting from the corner of Jo's eye.

I open the shop because that's what Jo would have done. The bell on the door rings for each person "checking in" and "just making sure." They stream in and out with handholding and kind words and "stay strongs." I stand at the front for as long as I can through their tears and memories of drunk nights and rough mornings. I receive their nods and platitudes, which is more than Bidi has offered. She hasn't even sent a text.

"You represent her house now, you hear?"

"You hold her up."

"Don't take for granted what she gave you."

Stories of the way Jo came into the neighborhood hit like a tsunami. The way she fed them bolinho de bacalhau and goiabada e queijo. The way she would putter around at night out front kicking the cans and the empty promises from the door.

"She never changed, bitter to the very end."

They reminisce and chuckle over her disposition.

"But she sure could party!" Jimmy holds his flask up and throws his head back with a gulp.

I sift through the community's grief, as thick as it is salty. I sink lower and lower into it until my phone rings. I pull myself free and walk to the back.

"Hello?"

"Is this Philippa Santos?"

I can smell his breath through the phone. The cop with the goatee. Sour and tepid. "Yes."

"This is Officer Barnum. We received the preliminary toxicology report. Do you have the file number associated with the case we gave you to confirm?"

"Her name was Josefina Santos," I tell him.

"Yes, but do you have the case file number?"

I pull the phone away from my ear so I can search the Notes app and see if I thought to write anything down.

“Um, yes. It’s 7845667.”

“Thank you for confirming. We don’t have the extensive toxicology, but the preliminary report looks like something led to her heart stopping.”

I hear a stapler bang down, papers shuffle. He’s multitasking as he delivers news about my dead aunt.

“But you said it was a head injury when you were here.”

“Her skull was cracked in three places, likely from the fall after whatever she took. Was she a frequent drug user?”

“No.”

“What about alcohol?”

“I mean, she—she—she wasn’t addicted. She just needed to relax sometimes, like most people,” I lie.

“Mm-hmm. If she drank regularly and took Tylenol, that could lead to this condition. Or she might have just taken it a bit too far last night. It’s a common way to choose to go.” Papers crunch in the background; he’s already moved on to the next case.

“No! She didn’t do this on purpose,” I push.

“We see it all the time. Sometimes it’s an accident, sometimes a cry for help.”

“But things were finally getting better! She was trying,” I shout.

“Miss, I know it’s not fun to stare at the truth, but there was no evidence of foul play. No other fingerprints. Now that it sounds like you are saying she did have an alcohol problem, that lends itself even more to our theory.”

“That is not what I said!” I shout.

“Miss—”

“She wanted to renovate the store. Why would she do this?

Why would she fall back so far when she was so close to being free?"

He sighs. "Relapse happens all the time, more than you'd think."

"Can you just look into it a little more?" I beg him, though I don't know why I'm bothering; they haven't even been able to find Estella.

"Miss, I've got sixteen other cases on my desk today. I'm sorry for your loss, but there's nothing I can do."

"Please. She's my only family," I beg.

"We have to wait until the complete toxicology is back, but we are expecting the report to support our current diagnosis of accidental overdose. Unless something damning comes to light, the case is going to be closed."

My head is heavy, too heavy to think, so I say my last thank-you and close the shop, and then I head to Jo's office. My wrist nudges the mouse of the brand-new computer I persuaded her to buy to make bills and my homework easier. I empty my brain and fill the search bar with questions, ones it can answer:

What happens when someone dies?

What do you do after someone dies?

What do you do with a lifetime of things? How do you handle someone's affairs?

How do you have someone cremated? Should you have someone cremated?

What happens when someone is cremated?

How much does it cost to have someone cremated versus buried?

Do you have to have a memorial?

How much do memorials cost?

And ones with no definitive answer.

Do people ever come back? How long does grief last?

What does it mean if you feel nothing? Why does everyone leave me?

I ask all the questions. I let them out one after another, released, and then I click to erase the history of this evening. It's only fair that I get a chance to evaporate too. I delete any proof I was here until my history is gone and Jo's is right in front of me.

Job posting: Part-time store clerk

Bahia, Brazil, flights

How to not give up

How do you stay sober

How long until you stop craving alcohol

How to repair relationship with daughter

How to make amends

What I know is that ten thousand metal bobby pins stabbing my heart wouldn't hurt as bad as knowing she died with guilt so strong it cracked her skull. The desk falls apart under my fingers; her papers fly all over, her innermost secrets scattering. The "scribblings you write when you're sad" type of secrets. The "no one is smiling in these childhood photos and don't ask me why" type of secrets. The "antacids to relieve the pain she never complained about" type of secrets. The "coupons, Groupons, and other new expenses she'd begun to pile up despite our fresh start" type of secrets.

The cop is right. The weight of secrets is what killed her.

Bang. Bang. Bang. The knocks keep coming until I drag myself toward the door.

"We're clo—" I stop when I see Ms. Aubergine through the glass.

My chest flies open as I rush forward.

"Ms. Aubergine!" I open the door and leap into her arms. "What are you doing here?" I ask. She never leaves the estate.

"I had to go to the station." She speaks slowly. "It's about to be on the news. The rest of the lab work came back. The blood on the shirt, it's hers. She's gone, my Stella. While I was there, I heard your name over the radio. I heard about your aunt."

Guilt seeps into me. Here she was getting the worst news of her life, and she decided to come check on me. If she weren't holding me in a hug, I would rush to the wall and give her back the necklace. I would come clean about everything. But she squeezes me tighter.

"Why don't you come stay with me for a little while?" she whispers. "You shouldn't be here alone."

There's nothing I want more. Ms. Aubergine is stable. Maternal. She's lonely too. I nod. "Yes, please."

The car lulls me, free of Jo's baggage, her burdens, her breaking points. I'm free to drift into the farthest place, where the ocean plays tamaracas around my feet, and Jo and Mamãe bob just above the surface on either side of me. Sisters reunited, they are too overcome with each other to notice the way I sink lower and lower, my lungs filling with liquid, unable to pull any more oxygen in. I wake to a gasp, free to suffer the reminder that with each inhale, grief is just drowning in the air.

The car stops in front of the estate. Ms. Aubergine gave me a chance once; maybe she will do it again when I tell her the truth.

Forget-me-nots are low-care plants that often live short lives, but *Myosotis sylvatica* are self-sown seeds and replenish themselves before anyone ever notices.

"Can I work today, Ms. Aubergine? The final patches are prepped. It would only take me half a day to finish."

"Of course you can. I'll take your things," she says, and walks inside with my bags.

I might as well go one more time into the greenhouse. The flowers under the lights have begun to bud, so I transfer them one by one. I use my knuckles to churn the soil into a divot and place the flowers down beside each other to grow. One more moment to pretend all I need is the whisper of the sun and the call of a dahlia. When the last pocket of the garden is planted, I put tiny flags the same shade as the flowers in the gaps so she can get a preview of the color scheme before they start to grow.

"Oh, Pippa," Ms. Aubergine says from behind me.

I don't need to turn to see her face. I know she gets it, what I was hoping to create—a home, no matter who lives here. She takes me inside for tea and mixes carefully, measuring the bags with precision—this is a recipe; she isn't improvising. I lift the cup to my lips. The bitter notes of licorice and soil make me cough.

"It's supposed to be an effective antioxidant. The only thing we can do is move forward, you know, filter out what we don't need, since those tend to be the things we hold on to the tightest."

"You were right. Jo . . . she couldn't do it. She couldn't keep it together. She's gone. I have no more family. I barely ever did. Bidi left me too."

Ms. Aubergine's body tenses. "She was never a good friend to you, always making you small. You aren't alone anymore."

I will be as soon as she learns about the necklace.

"I have to tell you something—" The calm on my tongue is fuzzy and the teacup starts to feel like a brick in my hand. My body finally feels safe enough to shut down and rest. Ms. Aubergine leans forward to steady me.

"Shh, shh." Ms. Aubergine bends down to remove my shoes for me.

She rises and helps me off the chair. She guides me up the stairs through the halls and under some covers, then puts her hand on my head. *This is love,* I think.

"Ms. Auber—" I try again, but my tongue won't move.

"Shh. We'll talk soon," Ms. Aubergine whispers.

Sleep comes, and I sink into the down cover on the mattress. I release myself and float.

CHAPTER 39

Bidi

The library door cracks open and I turn to Mo.

"You ready for this?" I ask, and though the answer is stained in sweat on his shirt, Mo nods and winks.

"Let's do this."

I crane my neck out to catch a glimpse of Two's indigo jeans, which clash with the maroon rug.

Two clocks Mo beside me but doesn't give him the courtesy of a full greeting.

"I don't know how you got my number—" He fidgets with his hands.

"We wanted to give you a chance." I step forward.

"A chance . . . ?" Two asks. "Look, Bettina has been invited to two underground fashion shows, and I've got to pick up outfits from three separate boutiques. So whatever this is—"

"Don't play games, Two. Give us Estella's birth certificate."

Two smirks. "Or what, public school? You're gonna write an Instagram post about it?"

"Or we could out you and make you the number one suspect in Estella's murder. Come see for yourself," Mo taunts.

He walks over. Mo plays him the evidence. First, the fight at the door that we originally thought was Bettina, then the smoking gun we just pulled from the security footage of Two sneaking into Brodsky's office and leaving with the paper files.

"How did you get the files out of the desk without the key?" I ask.

"I waited until the librarian went to the bathroom to snatch the key. Are we done here?" Two yawns dramatically.

Count to ten and take ten deep breaths. That is what we tell Caroline to do when she feels angry, or someone is unkind. I'd love to punch his front tooth out, but what I've got is going to hurt more.

"Oh, we also have this whole montage of you parading around town with Bettina's ultra-exclusive Balenciaga purse like it was yours. So either you tell us everything or this goes directly to your boss."

"And if I give it to you?" he asks through his teeth.

"You can watch us delete the footage, and no one, including Bettina, will ever know."

Two's face turns redder than the carpet. He weighs his options.

"Why'd you do it, Two?"

"Bettina and Estella had broken up for the millionth time, but Bettina still couldn't get over her. She thought if she solved Estella's problems, they would get back together again. Bettina knew Estella wanted her birth certificate, so I decided to contact Brodsky for the files and make a deal for the swap. When I got there, though, Brodsky decided to ask for double what we agreed."

Brodsky got greedy.

"She said that Estella had complained of emotional abuse at the hands of Bettina, and to uphold the code of ethics, she threatened to report Bettina to the school administration and then leak it. She was going to ruin her reputation unless I paid her what she wanted. I obviously couldn't trust her. So yes, I took that file without paying a dollar. And if Estella wanted it, she was going to have to agree to leave Bettina alone—which was what I was planning to tell her before she disappeared into thin air."

Two smirks again, proud of the chaos he has caused. "I don't care what they say on the news about a bloody shirt. Estella is out there, I've always known that, which is why I left her agoraphobic mother that note. I wanted her to know that I was onto her, onto both of them, her and her weird mom."

Two reaches into his bag and pulls out a document, holding it just out of my grasp.

"Delete it." He snarls through his teeth and waits for Mo to capture the video evidence and drop it into the trash. I snatch the papers from Two's hands before he can try anything else.

"See you around, Public School." Two sneers and marches out.

Mo types and clicks, and the footage he deleted is back on the screen. He drags it into an email and sends it off.

"What just happened?" I ask him.

"I sent it to Bettina," he says with a smile. "No one talks to my cousin like that."

I place the birth certificate on the table for us to inspect.

FATHER'S NAME: FELIPE DA SILVA. BIRTHPLACE: SÃO PAULO, BRAZIL.

When I search his name on my phone, an old newspaper article comes up about his death. Apparently, he was seen harassing a woman and was then attacked by men defending her.

Ms. Aubergine said he was a bad person. That she was protecting Estella from who he truly was. "I think Ms. Aubergine was telling the truth," I say.

The walking hoodie, but fashion, steps into the library.

Ms. Magwitch pulls down her hood.

"Well done, you two," she says, and takes the certificate.

"Will you finally explain what is going on? You said it would all make sense if we figured out who had the certificate. I did that, and it still doesn't! Does it even matter now that she's gone?" Mo shouts, frustrated. When Ms. Magwitch grabbed me yesterday, she and Mo promised everything would be okay, but no one involved in this mess is okay. Estella is dead. Everyone at this school seems guilty of something. My instincts start to waver. I don't know who I can trust anymore.

Magwitch points to the certificate, and her unpatched eye scans it excitedly. "Look more closely," she urges.

Mo does. His eyebrows perk up when he sees the discrepancy. He turns to me, and I read what he points to. "'Mother's birthplace: Alberta, Minnesota'—Hey, wait, that's not Amelia Aubergine's name—"

The librarian sighs. "You both have been so helpful and patient. There's a bit more I never told you for your protection, but you deserve the whole truth. We don't have a lot of time, but let me explain."

CHAPTER 40

Pippa

The scent of the honeysuckles wakes me from outside the window. Groggy, I rise into the sweet air. If I get too comfortable, I will never confess.

The hallway is quiet, no movement in the windows as I walk through the house and land at Ms. Aubergine's office. I can't look her in her eye and tell her the truth, but I can leave her a note and walk away. Inside, every surface is a locked box; there is nothing for me to use to write, not a pencil or a Post-it.

Velvet blinds cover the windows, and I pull them open to find a flowerpot on the windowsill filled with pink flowers, their genus on the tip of my tongue. I brush the windmill-shaped petals between my fingers. My brain feels so heavy from sleep, I can't make it work to recall their name. I pinch the flowers in frustration.

"You shouldn't do that." Ms. Aubergine's voice grates my ear.

Almost immediately, my palms twitch and an itchy burn runs across them.

"I'm so sorry, Ms. Aubergine—"

"You should be," she says, then holds her palm out.

The cool of the necklace slides onto her desk. The gold peony shines bright against the cherrywood.

"I told you once that I know when I'm being betrayed," Ms. Aubergine says, shedding her skin.

She pads past me to the window, where she draws the blinds shut again so only the slightest sliver of the early morning light can come through. Ms. Aubergine pulls a plastic zip tie from her pocket and quickly binds my hands.

"What are you doing?" I shout.

Ms. Aubergine collects the flowerpot in one arm, careful to avoid the flowers growing from it. Now that she knows, I fill in the gaps. I spill everything in one breath.

"I can explain. Someone has been following me, and they left that necklace. I was afraid that if I told you, you wouldn't believe me. I was afraid you would blame me."

"Of course I blame you!" Ms. Aubergine takes my elbow with her free hand and walks me to the hallway and down the stairs.

"Ms. Aubergine, please. I never meant to lie," I beg.

The truth just got bigger and hotter like my reddening, burning hands, like these itchy fingers I can't seem to satiate. We enter the kitchen, and she sits me down on the ground, my back to the legs of a chair. She swaps the flowerpot for some rope on the counter and ties me to the heavy furniture. She spits insults under her breath as she works.

"You could have left! You could have avoided this! You did this to yourself!"

"But you saved the store so I could stay!" I remind her.

"I didn't save your little business, but you were so sure I did that you became even more devoted to me, and I'm not one to argue with a gift, dear. Like I said, you did this to yourself."

The words she says jumble together. They make no sense. Along with the fire raging on the surface of my palms. The rash seems to be worsening by the moment.

"Please, Ms. Aubergine. I don't know what you are talking about! I just wanted to help you," I cry.

"Sticking to your story, huh? Well, how about this? You want to hear the story of how your aunt looked before she took her last breath?"

The truth dawns on me through the searing across my knuckles, a bubbling burn. Jo didn't hurt herself. She was trying. I blubber and rock as Ms. Aubergine watches with delight until I catch my breath, snot-covered and swollen.

The teapot screams. She walks over to silence it. Ms. Aubergine dons gloves and begins to snip flower heads from the pot from her office whose name I still can't place. She plops them into the teapot to steep.

"Ms. Aubergine, please," I beg.

"How about I tell you the story of Estella and how she came to be?"

Ms. Aubergine grins, but evil finds its way out of the cracks, proof of what Bidi knew all along. My blood stops. Not cold, just blocked, the room in my heart I believed was for her turns hard and the valves, once functional, begin to die. Her eyes get dim.

"I'll start at the beginning. My parents, they wanted me to be a certain type of person. They wanted to control me, but I wanted to be free. I wanted to see the world. I was young and naive and thought nothing bad could happen to me. I convinced them to let me go for a semester abroad, but the only program they allowed me to attend was in Argentina my senior year of high school. A program that catered to the wealthy elite and had a reputation for high levels of monitoring and security. The car picked me up at the airport in Argentina and dropped me off at the castle. That would be my living quarters and school for the next few months. I remember when I pulled up to that castle, I was paralyzed by its beauty, but I knew the sprawling building would keep me from the only real chance I had to be out in the world. The internet wasn't what it is now. Back then, people could be erased entirely. Before I could be checked in for orientation, I ran to a neighboring country with nothing more than my luggage and a purse. It was a different life. I was a different person. Speaking of which, before I go any further, I should properly introduce myself. My name is Melissa. Well, some people knew me as Missy, but you can call me Miss Havisham." The twinkle in her eye is red and bloody.

"Please, I don't understand." I cry.

"Hush, you foolish girl. You will. Just listen."

Then

The End, for Real

Amelia and Missy had gotten back on track. Amelia didn't need a man to raise this baby. She needed a family, and Missy was her family. She was more of a sister to her than her own sister had been. Missy had stayed after Felipe had run upon learning the news of the baby.

One afternoon, Amelia was craving something salty, but the baby was doing somersaults in her belly and the aches were killing her. Missy had begun to feel a twinge of jealousy at the massive belly Amelia now carried. All Amelia did was complain and groan. She didn't appreciate the work Missy was doing to care for her. Missy offered to go get some salgadinhos. Food was the only thing that made Amelia smile these days, and Missy needed the reset. *A nice walk in the fresh air would calm her irritation,* she thought. But when she walked into their building's lobby, Felipe was standing there.

"How is she?" he asked.

"That's not your business," Missy snapped, and tried to walk around him. He blocked her.

"I know I hurt her. I want to fix it," he said.

Missy started to march out of the building, but he followed her.

"Please, listen. When she told me about the baby, it was like the world opened up before me. The first time I saw her wasn't at the bar that night. It was the first day I moved here, I walked down the block and saw you both here in the lobby cleaning and singing. I couldn't stop listening to her voice. Her laugh felt like a ribbon, smooth and cool. Binding. The more I got to know her, the more I knew we needed each other. I dreamed of a long life and a family, but it happened so quickly. I have nothing, no money, no security. I ran because I was scared. I ran to talk to my sister. She is coming to help. We are going to make it work. I just need Amelia to forgive me."

He sounded just like Amelia, Missy thought. A perfect match for her magic. Missy knew what would happen if he went up there and Amelia saw him all desperate and in love with her. Felipe's story was good enough to trick a hormonal woman already saturated with his spell, but not Missy. She would never let that happen, not after what he'd put them through. Missy knew she had to deal with him, but to do that, she had to get him as far away from Amelia as possible.

"This really isn't a good time. I need to run to the market." Missy trudged out into the hot Brazilian sun.

"I can go with you, carry your bags," Felipe said, running after her.

He wasn't going to leave her alone. They walked in silence, him trying to think of more ways to prove his worthiness and her coming up with a way to make him go away for good.

"I'm glad you made up," Felipe said after a few moments. "She spent so much time talking about you. She loves you like a sister. I would never get in the way of you two."

Felipe stopped to collect himself, overtaken by the magnitude of Amelia.

"Our love came on as sudden as the flu, disorienting at first. But once the fog broke, everything that had once been a barrier became clear. Just knowing she was at home was enough to get me through the day. I want her to be happy."

All Missy heard were the things men always say to women to make them believe they know better. She'd seen her father do it to her mother her whole life. They stopped in front of a clock tower in a quiet square. Missy had been taking turns and loops, heading as far away from their home as possible.

"Right now, what she needs is calm. We have that. I am her calm," she said.

"Missy. Please." Felipe gripped her wrist.

On instinct, she screamed, "Let go of me!"

Felipe threw his hands up to release her. "Sorry, I didn't mean to hurt you—"

A group of young men nearby called out to see if she was okay. From their angle, it seemed to have looked like Felipe pushed her. She could tell when they started to walk over that they were agitated. Hungry for someplace to put their anger. Felipe stood beside her. So when they approached, they told him to leave her alone.

"We know each other. This is just a misunderstanding—" Felipe explained, eyes jumping to Missy for confirmation and backup. When she didn't offer it, they pounced.

"Please!" His voice was drowned out as their feet cracked his bones.

When his head met the cobblestone, Missy backed away and let the universe correct itself. She stopped at the market for the snacks she had promised to buy, then took the long way home. Missy shook herself off before she finally stepped inside her apartment building, ready with excuses for what had taken her so long. But when she got back, Missy heard a scream from the lobby.

Now

CHAPTER 41

Pippa

My fingers roar under the spreading, burning rash as Missy Havisham continues her story.

"The scream I heard in our building lobby was violent. The image of Felipe somehow surviving the attack and crawling back to the apartment to tell Amelia what happened with those men flashed before me. But when I heard the scream again, I rushed up the stairs to our apartment, and I found Amelia almost passed out in a river of blood. The baby lying on the floor had called for me. I couldn't carry both of them. I couldn't get the neighbors in the building involved. They knew Felipe too. When word got out of what happened in that park, it could come back to me. People saw me with him, after all.

"I stood over her and saw that Amelia appeared to be dying if she wasn't already dead. But the baby seemed okay, so I took her, and I ran. I didn't let Estella out of my sight, and I vowed to protect her forever. My daughter. My everything."

Missy is crazed, eyes sharp and pointed.

"When I made it back home to Alberta, I expected a joyful reunion, but instead, my Black, fatherless baby and I were shunned. My parents said they had already held a funeral for me. I was dead to them. I could feel the walls closing in again!" Missy shouts.

"What did you do?" I sob.

"I had no choice, I did what needed to be done. I always do," she snaps.

She killed Estella's parents; she killed her own. Missy's narration accents the moving images in my head as this horror story plays out. I just need to keep her talking. The longer she is occupied, the longer I have to get out of here.

"I took the fake name, Amelia, in honor of my friend giving me Estella."

"She didn't give her to you; you took her!" I correct her.

Missy didn't just take Estella from her mother; she took Amelia's story too. She took her name and her history; she glued cloth petals to an empty stem. This whole time I thought I was protecting Ms. Aubergine from the world, but I'm the one who needed protection from her. My anger elicits a wider smile. She's enjoying this, all of it.

"Aubergine was my mother's maiden name—no one ever pays attention to the mother."

Missy turns her head sharply. "Estella and I were doing great in our new life, until six months later, when the real Amelia showed up right here at that gate."

Blisters form on my fingers, the pain distracts me from the itch, the insatiable, clawing itch. Missy swims in nostalgia.

"Estella and I couldn't have her making a scene or drumming

up curiosity with these nosy neighbors. So I invited Amelia in, and I offered her tea. We were old friends, after all. We had been through so much. She said she forgave me for taking Estella. She understood why I had done it, thinking she'd died on that sad apartment floor. But now that Amelia had found us, she wanted Estella back, but we couldn't have that, could we? I had to protect my child. Don't worry—it was peaceful; the tea worked quickly. Amelia fell asleep, and then I took her to the garden and placed her in a hole I dug under my willow tree. Missy and Amelia's final adventure together."

She walks around the counter and pours the tea she brewed into a mug, then walks it toward me. My body turns to that moment when freezing starts to burn. Even with the soul-crushing clang in my brain. Even with my hands knotted and blistered, tied behind me, I'm still here. Even as Missy approaches, I clamp my jaw shut, tighter than a crocus flower at night.

Bidi says when you protect your spirit, they have no power, no matter what they do to you. Too bad she'll never get the chance to read me to filth over this.

Missy's bony hand grasps my chin, and she pinches either side to force my jaws to part. Her nails push so hard they draw blood from my cheek as she pours a trickle of the liquid she brewed down my throat. The pain in my hands finds its peak, a sharp bolt that runs from the tip of my fingers to the top of my head all at once. The screaming, the burn, the lies.

"Why are you doing this?" I try to spit the remaining tea out, but I feel the warm liquid run down my esophagus. "You should be appalled at your lack of basic gardening knowledge, by the way. Honestly, it's embarrassing, Pippa. Even I know you never touch an oleander." Ms. Aubergine taunts me with the name of the poisonous flower I couldn't remember in her office.

Missy stops, then pouts, pitying me. "Oh, Pippa, no one even knew you existed. Even at that point. That's what I'm trying to explain to you. Amelia could have just lived a happy life with you. Grateful for one healthy child, but she got greedy. Just like you. You couldn't stay away from my doorstep. You kept coming back, kept digging."

Her words melt through me. Nothing makes sense. The only Amelia I have ever known was Missy, and even that was a lie. "What—what do you mean?"

"Pippa, come now. Don't fight. It's been quick with all the rest. It will be quick with you too. Don't you want to see her again?"

"Who?" I cry.

"Amelia, you blubbering fool! Or perhaps I should call her by her real name: Sofia Santos." Missy's glee makes my stomach turn.

Footsteps clack on the marble floor behind me. But the way I am tied, I can't turn to see who it is. Missy rises, eyes trained on the doorway, like she's expecting someone. Whoever is here to help her finish me off. I open my mouth to scream, but then Estella is next to me, the opposite of dead.

"Our mother," Estella says.

"Our . . . mother?" I repeat, though the heaviness in my head is starting to deepen. The oleander moves fast.

This whole time I was looking for a mother, and mine was here, screaming to me from beneath the garden I brought back to life.

The honeysuckles.

Mamãe was shooting her signal out into the air, a call to the lifelines forced to dead ends on the map through Missy's bloody nexus. They shielded her secrets from the rest of the city. They filled the holes where sin burrowed. "Our mother," I whisper, eyes locked on Estella's like that first morning we found ourselves outside this house. Our beginning, our end.

Linnaea borealis is a descendant of the honeysuckle family. The narrow stem sprouts evergreen leaves, waxy, as if laminated. They sit at the center of the stalk and balance the split at the top. Two flower cups, ombre from pink to white.

Linnaea borealis, also known as the twinflower.

CHAPTER 42

Estella

For so long Missy told me she was just trying to protect me, but a cage is still a cage, even with ten-thousand-thread-count sheets.

She held on to me like I was going to be torn away. Like I was a commodity she couldn't risk losing. Missy played up her love to hide fear. Crocodile tears to distract from her sharp teeth. I was the lie that couldn't be, not the way she made it, trimmed, mowed, and cultivated. But lies, like gardens, are easily plucked if you know where to look. So how do you hold on to a feeling before it slips from your fingers? How do you hunt when you don't know what it is you need to find?

When I released myself from Missy's grasp, I started to hear the truth begging to be uncovered. Missy held her cards close, but once I caught wind, I grasped on tighter.

Pippa has always been nearby. The dull beat on my temple—I felt her before I saw her. Every time she held her breath, my heart stopped too. I just didn't know half the pain was hers. I never saw her until I saw her, that same morning I stepped out of this house ready to disappear. From that point on, I couldn't get her out of my head, but I couldn't bring her in, either, not until it was time. Now that the barrier between us is shattered, I can't think of the right words.

Missy does what she does best, though, and butts into my thoughts. She takes over the moment.

"Welcome home, Stell." She stands at the island, towering over my sister.

"Surprised?" I taunt.

"Surprised? Oh no, not surprised. I'm thrilled, honey. I am so glad you are back. Once I realized what was going on, I knew you just needed some space. I ran away, too, when I was your age. I decided to let you have your fun."

Beside me, Pippa groans. Steam still wafts from the teacup on the counter. She couldn't have ingested the poison that long ago. We have a little bit of time.

"Let me? You thought you could keep this lie up forever? You got lucky pulling your little life swap and moving back to America before the internet and social media took off. You could still reinvent yourself without anyone knowing. You could hide behind your mysterious wealth."

I throw my real birth certificate into her face just as Jaggers enters, looming over me. Missy sidesteps in his direction.

"Jaggers! Perfect timing. I think it would be best for you to walk Estella upstairs to her room. She can stay there until I send for her. And honey, your feelings are valid. One day you will understand that everything I did was for you."

Missy waits for him to move toward me. Instead, he takes her by the shoulders.

"Jaggers, what are you doing?" Missy yells.

Unfortunately for her, there was no way I was going to go into this without some backup.

"Daughters shouldn't be taken from their mothers," I say.

"Estella, I am your mother. Do you think you would have had the life you have now if you had stayed there, with them? Do you think you would be who you are today if it weren't for me?" Missy snarls.

"Sisters shouldn't be taken from their sisters," Pippa whispers from behind me.

I turn my back to Missy and undo the knots tied around Pippa. She falls onto me, still breathing, but lightly enough that I move my ear to her mouth to keep track of the inhales. Jaggers pulls a chair out with one hand and pushes Missy into it. He gags her with a silk scarf and pulls zip ties from his pocket to tie her ankles to the legs of the chair so she can't run. He does the same to her wrists, then walks to the front door.

"Pippa!" Mo and Bidi cry out. They rush into the room and to either side of Pippa. "Shit, she is barely breathing. We have to get her help!" Mo lifts her up, frantic.

"It took us long enough to find each other; don't leave just yet," I whisper into Pippa's ear as they pass.

"Bidi, let's go!" Mo shouts, but her eyes are trained on Missy.

She shakes her head. "Nah, I'm staying."

From what I've seen of her online, Bidi seems intense—accomplished and high achieving. Confident. Being a savage bitch is my love language. I'm glad Pippa has had her all this time. Maybe I'm not mad that this means she's going to be around me all the time now too.

"You still don't see your mistake? How I finally figured out who you really are?" I ask.

Missy attempts to berate me while her tongue is tied flat to the bottom of her mouth with the scarf.

"You got sloppy, Missy." Missy's eyes expand. Her nostrils flare.

"You thought the certificate would keep your secret? My father, Felipe, had a sister. A sister who loved him very much and whom he told everything to—*everything.* Who would walk to the end of the earth for him. For justice. For her nieces."

More footsteps come from the archway, the floor-length coat, her black hood.

Magwitch steps into the light without the patch across her face. She wears the same birthmark etched around her eye socket as I do, hers a deep brown set on her beige skin while mine is the inverse. All Missy's bad decisions face her, ghosts and poison alike.

"I'll go with Pippa to the hospital," Magwitch says. "You call the police and let them handle Missy," she reminds me, squeezing my wrist.

"Of course, Tia." Within seconds, the tires screech outside. Silence befalls us, and Bidi breaks her death glare with Missy to face me.

"So, Estella, what is the plan?"

CHAPTER 43

Pippa

I figured when I died, I would be scared, or that my life would flash before me in some curated slideshow with snapshots of treasured memories, my darkest moments, my ascension . . . but all I see is the leaf on the London plane tree that was planted by the city just outside the window of the shop. It's barely a tree, a stick with a single leaf. The runt of some public initiative to spruce up the neighborhood. And yet, somehow, this leaf figured out a way to thrive.

How long has it been? I swear that leaf has been mid-flutter for hours.

I feel cold, like the cold is now becoming my natural state. Like I've been bathed in metal or wrapping paper. Like it's covering me whole. Maybe that's how death works. On the outside, you disappear, but the essence of you remains encapsulated in some cold mist, and you just are, like that leaf, waiting for what comes next.

There is a tree called the Bennett Juniper in the Stanislaus

National Forest thought to be four thousand years old. Imagine standing in one place for so long with no measure of time but the sun in the sky. The shift in birds' songs etched into your skin, a living memorial to their dying species. Imagine stillness forty centuries long. The call of the wind, a permanent white-noise machine. Juniper trees are evergreen, as in, retaining the color in their leaves year-round. As in, enduring. As in, never changing. As in, stuck.

I'm stuck, too, somewhere between alive and not.

The weight on my head makes it impossible to open my eyes. All I have are snapshots of the last time I remember my eyes being open and a sour taste in my mouth. Large hands under my knees and my neck. All I have is the beeping to my left that feels like a hammer. My eyes still won't open, but the energy it takes to try knocks me back out.

"Good morning, sweetie. Today is a good day to wake up."

Light slides between the tiny crease in my eyelids, the first success at cracking back into life. A nurse with black hair leans over my body to adjust and untangle the cords growing out of me like a bougainvillea vine. She breathes out the remnants of the cigarette she had on her way to work. I blink again. She holds my hand and gives me the smile teachers give when you finally get the math problem right after trying so many times.

Doctors stream in and announce my progress. My systems are stabilizing from the oleander poisoning, but they need to keep me for another night to monitor an irregular pulse. My throat is dry and cracked from the tubes. But if I could, I would tell them the skipping pulse might not be medical. None of the women in my life have ever been regular with their hearts.

Seconds after they walk out, the door opens, and Bidi runs in. She hops onto the bed and hugs me.

"You were right about Missy. You were right about everything," I say.

"I love that song," Bidi croons, chuckling. "I'm glad you're still alive."

The door opens again, and Estella walks in, black boots, riding pants, a vintage tee. The girl dancing in the corner of my dreams—it was her all along. Her looking for me. Not Mamãe. My sister. This whole time, she was less than an hour away.

"What is going on?" I ask.

"There's someone you need to meet," my twin says. Estella nods at Bidi, who leaves the room. The black hooded jacket sails in, but the hood, round and high, is pulled down.

"Ms. Magwitch?"

I try to sit up too quickly, and every injury I've sustained cries out. They all rush over to me. Estella's hand fits into mine. She sits on the bed with me.

"Be careful, Pippa."

I look over at Ms. Magwitch again. The crescent moon encasing the eye she had covered with the eye patch would have to have been sliced off Estella's face and Gorilla Glued for it to be more of a perfect match.

"What—"

"Oh, Pippa—" Ms. Magwitch rushes to me.

"How—"

"I never thought I would find you—" Tears run down her face.

"Why—"

"When I did, I wanted to say something—" she cries.

"Who—"

"But we had to catch her—"

"We?" I ask.

"There is so much to explain. So much for us to catch up on," Estella interjects, breaking our rhythm.

"My brother, Felipe, was your father," Ms. Magwitch says, pulling out a photo of a man whose eyes burn into me from the picture. When she unfolds the other half, I see Mamãe. A photo of my parents together for the first time.

"He wanted to be a musician. He changed his last name from our father's British name, Magwitch, to Da Silva, our Brazilian mother's maiden name, to appeal to the market. Your father was a romantic. He fell in love a lot. Well, he always thought he was in love, and then your mother walked into his world. Soon she was at his place whenever I called. When she found out she was pregnant, it was your mother who wrote to me, distraught at the fact that Felipe was pulling away. My brother showed up on my doorstep months later. He'd run away because he was afraid to ruin the best thing he'd ever had."

Magwitch's eyes tear up.

"I've never seen anyone so scared. Of course he should have handled it differently, but he was a teenager, a child about to have a child. He didn't know better. I told Felipe I would love him no matter what; if he chose to stay away, that was his choice. He was my brother, and I loved him, but *I* was going to be in that baby's life. In your lives. Felipe was fraught for months. We strategized about how to reconnect with Amelia—Sofia. And then finally he decided, no matter what happened with your mother and him, whether they made it or not, we were going to give you a good life.

"We returned to Rio together. Every day since that one, I have wished I had gone to that apartment building with him, but my baby brother, he was resolute that he needed to speak to your mother alone. When he didn't come back, I rushed to their apartment and found Sofia alone on the floor, drowning in her own blood. We went to the hospital, where she had you, Pippa.

"She hadn't been to the doctor throughout the pregnancy. No insurance and no money, so no one knew she had twins until your mother got some IV fluids and woke up, shouting for her other baby. We know now that Missy had taken Estella before I got to their apartment. Your mother was so distraught, she couldn't explain what happened. She was confused, but she knew Estella was out there. Sofia was so traumatized and disoriented. No one believed there was another baby, not without proof of one. I'm guilty of that too."

Estella squeezes my arm when our aunt hangs her head.

"I held you, Pippa, at the hospital. I asked her if she had heard from Felipe, but she just sat there crying for her lost baby, the one that, as far as we all knew, didn't exist. Doctors made me leave after a while, and I promised her I would come back in the morning. I hurried to the hostel, but instead of finding my brother, the police were waiting for me in the room. They told me he died from random street violence—wrong place at the wrong time. When I returned to the hospital to tell your mother, she had already discharged herself. She vanished with you, and I was left alone carrying the weight of the life you all were supposed to live together.

"When I got back home in São Paulo, I tried to move on. But after a while, I couldn't face the gaping hole. I left Brazil, I lived and learned abroad, I got my degree in library science. I let my accent disappear but nothing made up for what I had lost. The only thing I kept from my old life was the stack of letters your mother had written."

"Letters?" I whisper.

"Seventeen years later, I was working at a library in Vancouver, and some of the kids who came by after school used Estella's image from a viral post of hers in a mood board. Suddenly, I was looking at my brother, but she looked nothing like the baby I had held in the hospital. I remembered all those years ago, the way your mother claimed there was another baby. It all came back. Her pain, the confusion."

Ms. Magwitch stops to collect herself, then goes on. "I left the next day for California. Estella was easy to find. I showed up to the house, expecting a tearful reunion with Sofia, but when I saw Missy through the gate, I knew something was wrong.

"I waited to approach Estella alone. I showed her the letters your mother sent me. She picked up on details, places and names that she had heard in passing throughout her childhood. Secrets

Missy let slip over the last seventeen years, secrets she had only ever trusted your mother with. We followed the breadcrumbs and found this."

Estella hands over an old newspaper. The *Alberta Gazette* from years ago. The headline stands out.

Missing Girl Found with a Baby Days Before Parents Die in Tragic Cardiac Event

Beneath is a photo of a younger Missy holding baby Estella.

My aunt continues, "When a position at Beaumont came up through the librarian job board, I took it. Estella and I could speak freely at school. And we started putting the rest of the story together. We decided on a plan to use Estella's disappearance to shake Missy up."

I can still see the purple mandrake from across the street. Mamãe's soul reaching out to me from her grave beneath the flowers. Magwitch interrupts my thought.

"We didn't know who you were yet, Pippa, but then there you were, a vision of your mother standing there on the corner, right as I drove Estella away that morning. I thought I had seen a ghost! And a few days later, you walked into my library.

"Pippa, once we found you, we wanted to keep you safe—that's the only reason we didn't come to you sooner. Ignorance is bliss. We tried to distract you with the necklace, the flowers. Move you off the scent of Missy. But you found your way to her anyway. When you all pulled that stunt breaking into the counselor's office, we realized we needed someone on the inside. The day we all got caught by Pummel and Brodsky, I brought Mo in so we could keep an eye on you. He was willing to do anything to keep you safe."

I feel the blush in my cheeks rise. Something clicks. I jump in.

"Wait. The check for the shop? That was . . . you?" I ask.

My aunt and my sister nod in tandem. They had so much time to plan and get to know each other, without me.

"We were so close to catching Missy and holding her responsible for the deaths of our parents, her own parents too. We wanted to tell you everything right then, but you kept putting yourself in danger! We barely had time to move forward with the plan without you derailing it. Somehow, stalking you didn't scare you enough to stop," Estella explains as Bidi walks back into the room.

"It's too bad they didn't just fill me in from the jump. I could've told them that the more outlandish and reckless the idea is, the more drawn to it you would be. Also, I held the nurse off for as long as I could, but she's about to come in. You need to rest, Pippa. You are still seventy-two hours out from being almost murdered."

"Sorry about the poison. We had to let her keep talking. Mo got this ultrasensitive microphone from the school, and we recorded her whole confession," Estella adds.

My aunt kisses my forehead on the way out. Estella and Bidi flank me through the nurse checkup, the testing, the blood work. My keepers, old and new. When the nurse leaves, the question I have been holding in spills out.

"Where's Missy—"

Bidi's and Estella's eyes meet. The twinge of jealousy I feel at their newfound silent language is matched with joy. My two most important people don't hate each other, at least not yet.

"What happened?" I ask again.

"She's not going to stop until you tell her," Bidi translates for my sister.

"She's right," I confirm, "so start talking."

CHAPTER 44

Estella

We agreed that I would be the one to tell Pippa when the time came. Bidi collects her things, but she doesn't leave when she gets to the door—she turns around and walks back over to Pippa and sits beside her. I look away to give them a moment.

"Before I go, you should know we are doing an interview. The idea is to pivot the attention from this to my campaign, ya know . . . now that you have returned to the land of the living."

Her assertiveness is so powerful. I love a woman unafraid to take up space.

"Of course that's the idea." Pippa laughs at her best friend.

"And, like, get some rest because the sooner you're well, the better to keep up the momentum for the campaign now that we've solved the case!"

Bidi gestures to me, all "found" and shit.

"I had a chance to chat with someone from the mayor's team, and they said this is the time to build the foundation. So when I am eighteen, I can hit the ground running—"

"Ahem," I cough, interrupting her political-ascension plans.

"Yes, okay, we'll figure out the details later. I'll be back soon, Pippa."

Bidi walks to the door. "Wait." I rush to give her a hug. Bidi smells like jasmine oil and Starbursts.

"Thank you." My lips brush her ear with the whisper.

Electricity runs through us both, but we lock it up. Not now. Whatever that charge was has to wait until another day. I wait for the door to shut. Bidi's not used to sharing Pippa. I don't want to shove it in her face. Once she's out of view, I kick off my shoes and climb into the narrow hospital bed.

"All right, are you going to tell me now or what?" Pippa whines.

"Don't panic," I start.

"Has saying that before anything ever helped? Like, are there psychological studies to explain why any human would utter those words before delivering any kind of news?" Pippa's blood pressure cuff goes off after her rant.

"Can you not have a stroke right now? Please!"

"Fine." Pippa sips water and takes slow deep breaths. "Ready," she says, eyes closed.

"Missy's gone, she got away."

"What!" Pippa shouts.

"Don't panic," I repeat, and this time it's an order. "The cops came, and they took her. They put her in the back seat of an unmarked car and left in a procession, which is apparently a safety precaution. Each car had instructions to peel off into their respective routes so no one could follow or injure the suspect in custody. Since all the cars were identical, no one would know which had Missy. But somehow, the car she was in never made it to the police station."

I pull out my phone to show her the most recent headline.

Melissa Havisham on the Run After Daughter, Estella, Returns

The photo shows a car with Missy cuffed in the back seat, and the driver is blurred, unable to be identified.

"Explain to me why I shouldn't be panicking?" Pippa asks. The excitement pulls what remaining energy she has from her body. She lies back.

"All eyes are on her. She isn't coming anywhere near us. She's got to stay hidden, and while she does that, I'm on it."

"You're on it?" Pippa asks me.

"I found you, didn't I?" I remind her.

"Um, not really! I literally walked onto your street as you were running away," Pippa corrects me.

Bidi wasn't lying; she's maddening.

I put a pillow on my shoulder so she can lay her head there and place my fingers next to hers. Pippa's hands are so much better, just red marks where the blisters from the oleander poison had been.

Neither of us knows where to start or how to make up for lost time or to catch up on all the secrets that got us here. All we can do is jump in.

"How did you find me?" Pippa asks.

"Missy hired Jaggers to tie up her loose ends once I started sniffing around for information about my father. But she didn't know I had already hired him on my own to do some digging when she wouldn't let me see the birth certificate. When I left, he was already inside. And thank God, he kept tabs on you . . ."

"Where were you?" she asks.

"Not far, Magwitch's house in Daly City."

"You've been here the whole time?"

"I wasn't going to leave you," I tell her.

"What about that bloody shirt?" she asks.

I hold up my arm to show her the tiny, bruised pinprick in the crease of my elbow.

"A distraction. I thought if you thought I was dead, if I gave you an ending to your investigation, you might back down for ten seconds."

Pippa's eyes squint. "I can't tell if you are a supremely evil genius or just a genius."

"Thank you." I nudge her with my shoulder. You only do snarky-ass honest with people you really love, and I have never felt a love like this. So instant. So easy. So bruised and ready to heal.

"Pippa, I am so sorry about Jo. Missy had figured out I was still around and who you were, but you still had no clue. So much was going on, she had the perfect window to go to the store in secret. We would have done something. We would have given the whole thing up to save Jo."

Pippa has lost almost everyone who should have loved her. But not me.

"It's not your fault; it's mine. I told Missy all about Jo. Missy must've thought Jo was a liability. Maybe she just wanted me to feel more alone than ever. So I'm the reason she's gone." Pippa cries, "Missy made me feel like no one truly cared about me but her."

"Missy was good at making people think what she wanted them to think," I say.

The reminder of who isn't here sits bittersweet between us.

"What do you think she was like?" I ask.

"Mamãe—I mean, Sofia?" Pippa clarifies, and I nod.

"I want to think she was like a brain freeze from ice cream, shocking and sweet and a little bit of pain," Pippa says.

"What do you think her hair smelled like?" I ask.

"Like seashells and incense. Gardenias and cinnamon. Like orange and dark chocolate. All the things you thought wouldn't go together, but do," Pippa imagines out loud.

"Sounds overwhelming," I say.

"She should have been, but I think she was soft. Easy to be around. The type of person you wanted to be loved by. Trust me."

"I do trust you, Pippa."

The bellow of an orca gurgles out of Pippa's stomach. It overwhelms the chaos with an immediate truth: My sister is hungry. That is something I can fix.

"You must be starved! All you've had is tube food for days." My feet slide into my sneakers. "Let me go grab us something. There's a to-die-for hand roll place around the corner. What do you like? You know what? I'll grab everything. No food allergies, right? Me either. I'll be right ba—"

I get to the door and freeze. I reverse. I take my shoes off and climb back into bed.

"What are you doing?" Pippa asks me.

"I'm getting it delivered," I say, and pull up the Caviar app. I'm not missing another second with my sister.

Without a Trace Interview Transcript: Martina Abreu with Estella Aubergine, Pippa Santos, and Elizabeth Jones

Martina Abreu: Missy Havisham was, until recently, known as Amelia Aubergine but now dons the titles kidnapper, murderer, and fugitive. Missy went to great and devastating lengths to keep her crimes a secret, but it turned out there was an even bigger scandal brewing that Missy was unaware of . . .

It was revealed that Estella's secret twin sister, Pippa, lived just a few miles away. They lived wholly different lives, socially and economically. Filled with more twists than a Shonda Rhimes Netflix binge, Estella Aubergine and Pippa Santos's story is meaty. The young women have agreed to sit down for an exclusive interview about their lives and their future. Later, we will be joined by Elizabeth Jones, who was instrumental in the reunion.

Thank you both so much for joining us. I know this is a complicated time, but I do want to start off by expressing my condolences. I am so sorry for your losses.

Estella: Our birth mother left a hole. That's what you say when people die, right? "They left a human-sized hole in the universe," like her death peeled away a sixty-four-inch layer. That's a pretty big hole, but I'd expect nothing less. We never got to know her, but we are pretty sure she never did anything small.

Martina: Weeks ago, you two had never met. But now you are here, sitting side by side. How has it been reuniting?

Estella: I've gotten to know a lot about my sister recently. I'd say we are like two sides of the same coin: one you bet on and the other surprises you.

Pippa: [*laughs*] What does that even mean?

Estella: Um, are you kidding? That was extremely profound.

Martina: Well, it certainly didn't take you long to get sisterly bickering down!

Elizabeth: Get it together, both of you! Martina, they can fix this in post, right?

Martina: Um, yes.

Pippa: Well, I always knew something was missing. I thought it was my mom. I mean, it is—she has been missing, but she's gone. Estella isn't, and maybe I could feel that. I used to dream of her, the idea of this person I needed. I never thought I would find her. I never thought there would be someone whom I would know better than anyone, even myself.

Martina: I have heard that twin bonds are unbreakable.

Estella: We read that after twins are born, they can't sleep unless they are close to each other. It's like we are catching up on seventeen years of sleep.

Pippa: Except we have so many questions, so much time to catch up on, that we just lie in bed asking them until we drift off and then wake up and start all over.

A doorbell rings.

Estella: Sorry, one second. I have to let the movers in.

Elizabeth: She should have let me schedule the movers. I'm the organized one; Pippa's the dreamer.

Pippa: What does THAT mean?

Elizabeth: Is this a good time to pivot to the investigation? Or, you know what, why don't we just pause, yeah? Pippa, you are rich now. Can we order Sugarfish? Martina, let's cut it.

Muffled voices. The mic cuts out.

Elizabeth: We good, you sure? Everyone's settled and had their emotional support beverage? Great, please, let's get this done. Are we back? Test, test. Great. Martina, take it away–

Martina: Ahem, yes, thank you. Well, we are joined here by Elizabeth Jones, who led the charge to find Estella.

Elizabeth: Hi, yes, hello, thank you for having me.

Martina: What are you allowed to share about the investigation?

Elizabeth: I can tell you what we know about Melissa "Missy" Havisham. Her parents, Mortimer Havisham and Celia Aubergine, came into unexpected money in their late thirties. It was the type of money most people never hear about because it stays in some small town like the one they lived in in rural Minnesota. As a result, Missy was isolated; she had tutors and etiquette classes until she was high school age. She was a day student at a strict boarding school.

From what we have uncovered, it sounds like she struggled socially. Just after her eighteenth birthday, Missy left to go to an international exchange program in Argentina, but she never arrived. Her parents spent hundreds of thousands of dollars searching for their only child, but after a year, they had a funeral, and then the couple died suddenly, six months after that.

Martina: What caused her parents' deaths?

Bidi: The reports say random cardiac events, but Missy confessed to Pippa before trying to kill her that she went home to her parents after she kidnapped Estella at birth, just before they died. She said they rejected her and Estella and she did what she had to do.

Martina: That sounds like a motive.

Bidi: Yes, and the physical causes of death are also very similar to the rest of her victims'. We suspect she poisoned them all. Before her parents' bodies were discovered, we believe she posed as her mother and emptied their bank accounts. After that, Missy was never seen again.

Martina: You mean, not until she appeared in the Bay Area, under the name Amelia Aubergine.

Bidi: That's correct.

Martina: Diabolical. Do you have any updates about the ongoing case to find her after she escaped police custody?

Elizabeth: That's a good question for what appears to be an incompetent police force that somehow receives the largest portion of our city budget.
But I can tell you that we are following every lead possible.

Estella: This is what Missy does; she disappears. I'm very grateful to Elizabeth and to her cousin Maurice for everything they did to help us. Everyone is entitled to the opportunity to be found. They worked tirelessly to uncover how and why I disappeared.
If not for their investigation, Beaumont's former principal and counselor would also still be employed after blackmailing me and countless others.

Martina: Very true, and I believe you have an official announcement for us today. Is that right, Elizabeth?

Elizabeth: It is. Thank you for giving me this platform, Martina. I am thrilled to announce that I am running to be the youngest person ever in San Francisco history on the city council. You won't be surprised to hear that I plan to propose a program to address the imbalanced response missing persons receive from the police and media based on their race and socioeconomic status. Estella has clout and an expensive zip code, but what about Marshai Williams and Selena Ruiz, who are still actively missing?

In honor of my best friend's late aunt, I am also planning to propose city-run day care facilities and small-business loan incentives that benefit the city as much as small-business owners.

Estella: And as executor of the Aubergine estate, I am really proud to help fund what I believe will be a revolutionary campaign.

Martina: Well, from all of us over at KRON4 SF, we wish you the best of luck.

Elizabeth: Thank you. I hope everyone tunes in more to our local stations. The place we can make the most progress is right here at home. We have the power to make this city better for everyone.

Martina: Thank you, and we look forward to following your campaign. So, Estella, Pippa, what's next?

Estella: We're going to Brazil.

Pippa: For the summer—we're going for the summer. Well, she's leaving immediately. I am sticking around to take care of some things at home—my aunt left behind her business, and I have to finish all the paperwork for my senior year at Beaumont. I'm transferring to be closer to my sister.

Estella & Elizabeth: And Mo.

Pippa: I hate you both.

Martina: Brazil is where both your parents were from?

Pippa: Yes. Our mother was from Bahia, and our father was from São Paulo. They met in Rio, so we are going to start there.

Estella: It's going to be an adventure. Missy took both our parents from us as well as our aunt, but we have a whole history waiting. We have a family.

Martina: You know, as we have been sitting here, I have noticed how frequently you keep taking each other's hands.

Pippa: Do you know what it's like to live for seventeen years feeling like half your heart was cut out? Functioning at half capacity because the other part is mourning something it doesn't even know or understand?

Martina: No, I don't.

Estella: If you did, you wouldn't let go either.

Martina: Mmm. Now that you have each other, is there anything you wish you had known when you were younger?

Pippa: That just because you don't see something, that doesn't mean it isn't there. Sometimes you just have to keep looking.

Estella: Okay, sis, I'll give you that one, a lil corny but hashtaggable.

Martina: I love that. Well, this has been quite an enlightening conversation. Thank you both. For a story with such a devastating start, these sisters who were quite literally ripped apart at birth, Estella and Pippa get to pick up their story from exactly where they began, beside one another.

As for the hunt for Missy Havisham, tips from all over the world have come in with sightings, but so far, nothing has been deemed credible. Her case remains an open investigation.

Elizabeth: As do the cases for missing people like Marshai and Selena and Lena and Latisha and Francesca. Photos and information can be found at FindThemAll.org.

Martina: Thank you, Elizabeth. Thank you, Estella and Pippa. Good night.

CHAPTER 45

Pippa

Estella's voice bounces on the other end of the phone. "Three weeks flew by."

"They really did. I can't believe the contractors you hired turned this place around so quickly."

I walk through the space formerly known as the Bahia Padaria. The smell of fresh paint is so strong it gives me a headache.

"Whoever said money can't buy happiness never knew it was for sale, honey." Estella cackles at herself. "Do you like steak? I booked reservations for dinner."

"Yes. I like steak, Estella."

"Can you dance? Like, did you also get rhythm, or did that all go to me?"

Estella shoots out questions one after another. It's what we have done over text or FaceTime every day, all day while we have been apart, until tomorrow. The windows of the space are covered with parchment paper because everyone in the neighborhood is always trying to get a peek inside. We got one of those huge bows and scissors, but it's not time for that, not yet. There's a knock, and through the paper I can see their outlines, Mo and Bidi.

"Stell, I've gotta go. They're here."

"She's going to love it, Pippa." Estella hangs up, and I step outside.

"What's going on?! Why did you text me 'SOS'?" Bidi shouts.

"Everything is fine. I, um, well . . ."

A couple of people stop a few feet away to listen in to our conversation, but that's what I'm banking on. I need a nosy crowd. I focus on Mo and his crooked smile. He winks and pulls the ribbon from his pocket and starts to tie it up.

"Mo? Wait, what is happening?"

I take Bidi's hand.

"Jo would want me to keep the shop alive, whatever that means. So I started thinking, what was the Padaria, you know? The traditional definition is about the food and the stuff. But here, in this neighborhood, this place has always been where people help each other."

The ever-growing crowd murmurs, while Jimmy and Jerrod, Malika and Caroline all nod. Mo pulls out a stepladder and opens it for me. He holds his hand out so I can take it to steady myself as I climb. Bidi is the one who gives the speeches, but for once, it's my turn.

"A group of cities is called a conurbation. A group of polar bears is called a celebration. When atoms join together, they become a molecule. All the petals of a flower are called the corolla. Derived from the word 'corona,' as in: wreath, crown, chaplet. 'Corolla' means 'little crown.' In Portuguese, we would say 'A Pequena

Coroa,' and we welcome the little crown on the head of this corner. An ode to this little world we made, to the roots we fought to keep alive. To the act of building a life as resistance, living in joy as though it is our right, too.

"A group of elephants is called a memory. A retinue is the group of people who advise someone with power. A group of caterpillars is called an army. A Pequena Coroa, formerly Bahia Padaria, is a community garden and food co-op, a place where you will be nourished. The apartment above is now a campaign office for grassroots local government. We all know the true royalty here, the head deserving of the little crown. Bidi Jones, may you don your crown well and walk around knowing we got you. Your retinue will always be here to catch you if you need a break."

Cheers fill the street as I grab an ornate crown of pink roses and wildflowers and place it onto her braided head before we stream inside. Jo stares from the wall, her picture blown up and framed. She hangs in the same spot she would have stood and stares down with a look that asks, "What the hell do you think you are doing, and how can we help you?"

"It's so bougie."

"Oh, you fancy."

"Okay, Pippa! I see you."

"Bidi's a big bawse!"

"Don't get lost in the sauce."

"Stay humble."

"Stay close."

Bidi pulls me into the back, to Jo's office, which is now a

temperature-controlled pantry for anyone in the neighborhood who is down and out and in need of something to eat.

"I can't believe you did this!" The excitement flies out of her.

"Of course we did. It's yours, whenever you want it. We have to sit down and talk about logistics. I don't want you to take on too much. We can hire people—no, sorry, we have to hire people. But Ms. Magwitch—I mean, my aunt—she's going to help run it while you do school. She has some literacy program ideas—she is good in the garden. Turns out gardening's a genetic skill."

"Pippa, are you coming back?" Bidi stops me to ask.

"What? Of course I am!"

"Where are you going to live?" Bidi asks.

"We sold the estate. We're going to buy someplace nearby."

"Wow, look at you, in your gentrifying era." Bidi laughs, but it wanes. "Pippa. This is—it's all—it's just too much."

"It's not, Bidi. It's what you deserve, my way of saying thank you for being my ride or die."

Something is different now between us, with Estella in the picture. I am doing things on my own, and Bidi is freer to focus on herself. Almost like we had to break apart to find a new way to fit together. The door opens, and Mo walks in.

I wrap myself around Bidi for a hug and say, "I'll see you when I get back in a few weeks."

"Thank you, Pippa." Bidi swallows.

I know accepting help isn't easy for her, but she deserves it, and for once, I am happy to be the one to offer it instead of being on the receiving end. She walks out of the room, and the four walls vibrate around Mo and me. Our breath sends static everywhere. "I feel like I haven't seen you in ages," I gasp.

A smile spreads across Mo's whole body. He makes his way around a stack of rice sacks. His hand cups my cheek, and I throw mine around his neck. I pull myself up closer to kiss him, and we stay that way, no need to come up for air, until the door slams open.

"Mo, you need to help me with Caroline! Wow! Oh!" Bidi stands facing our direction, but her eyes jump around, careful not to land on us, "No rush . . . but, like . . . do you have an estimate of when you will be, um . . . done?"

"When's your flight?" he asks me.

"Six a.m.," I answer.

"I'm busy until six a.m., Bidi," Mo says, and pushes the door closed.

CHAPTER 46

Bidi

I rush into the shop and through the crowd. I don't need to hear whatever is happening in there.

My phone buzzes.

Estella:

How was it? Were you surprised? Do you like the paint? I picked the wood for the floor.

Every time her name pops up on my phone, the thrill sizzles in my chest. I can't be doing this, falling for my best friend's secret twin sister. But it's hard to avoid Estella when she sets her sights on something. She gets what she wants; it's sort of her thing.

Buzz.

Estella:

wow, leaving me on read . . .

I duck into a corner to take a photo of the space, but a green maxi Skims tank dress fills the screen. Bettina's new intern, a girl with two tight buns on the top of her head, blocks my shot. Behind her, Bettina smirks.

"What happened to Two, Bettina? Fired?" I smirk back.

"Oh no. I promoted him. A mastermind like that is someone you want in your corner." She steps in front of her intern, right in my face.

I try to shift her out of my way.

"It feels good, doesn't it?" Bettina steps with me.

"Excuse me?" I ask her.

"When she acknowledges you. When she makes you think she loves you." Bettina's eyes point to my phone. I put it away.

"I don't know what you are talking about." I try to slide past them toward the door, but the new intern boxes me in. The place is too crowded right now for me to run.

"She did the same thing with me. She made it seem like she was enamored and interested in every single detail of my life, but Estella was just digging for information. She was building a narrative to trick me into falling for her over and over. To keep me under her thumb, to use me for what I could offer her. Pretty convenient, isn't it? That you get this building? I don't know; it seems like payment for your loyalty?"

I step up to Bettina.

"You have something to say to me, Bettina Drummle?"

"You don't know what Estella's capable of," Bettina warns me. "She's going to drag you down with her if you aren't careful."

"This is pathetic," I say, and begin to walk away. Bettina follows me.

"There is no way Missy just escaped." Bettina's voice cuts through the celebration. "You think you all are going to get away with this? Letting a murderer go?"

"You are delusional; why would we want to help the person who almost killed Pippa? I was standing with Estella when the cops drove her away. Missy has disappeared before; she's being consistent. If anything, we relied too much on a system we knew wouldn't take a rich white woman seriously as a threat. They didn't even put her in cuffs! They gave her In-N-Out before the ride to the station!"

Bettina bristles. She shifts her tune, the next in a line of excuses she has planned for this moment. "The public loves a scandal, and you've got your little campaign coming up. Do you think you're going to just waltz away from all of this with no consequences?"

"Oh, Bettina, honey, I already have."

Her threats explode before her, a mushroom cloud of her own demise. The shock weighs on the corners of her lips. They drop past her chin as I walk out the door, adrenaline pumping through my whole body. I walk a few blocks and then make the call.

"Hey!" Estella answers on the second ring. "Miss me already?"

"Bettina was here."

Estella catches her breath. "What did she do?"

"She thinks you're trying to lure me in. I think she's jealous."

"Hmm," Estella says, "I don't know, Bidi. Maybe you should follow that lead, see where you end up."

Even through the phone I can see her face, the flirty eye spark, the perfect smile. I push the Pop Rocks down in my gut.

"No, Estella. I mean it. She's out for blood. She is going to be a problem. She's coming for my campaign."

I just escaped chaos; I can't handle more.

Estella sighs. "I promise, Bettina Drummle is nothing to be worried about, okay? She's a sad, spoiled brat. Now that that's settled, let's get back to me luring you in."

Brazil

CHAPTER 47

Pippa

Humidity sticks to my neck like muscle memory, and I know before I have taken my first open-air breath off the plane that this is home. The Padaria is my home. The library is my home. The neighborhood is my home. The beaches of Rio de Janeiro are my home. My aunt's arms were my home. The steam off a fresh pot of feijões is my home. My mother's womb was my home. The smooth stem between the thorns is my home. My mother's secrets are my home. The last bite of a brigadeiro is my home. The space between Mo's shoulder and neck where I have begun to lay my head is my home. The coils that spring from my head are my home. The corner covered in cigarette smoke and potato-chip bags is my home. The smile the middle-aged couple share as they dance zouk on the beach is my home. The sun covering my body already covered in sand is my home. The garden is my home. The soil is my home. The machete beheading agua de coco in a single slash is my home. The crumpled family photo taped to my cabdriver's car ceiling on the way to Estella's apartment in Leblon from the airport is my home.

It's absurd—the idea you can come from only one place, the idea that you should be only one thing. Please, I have two heart-beats. I have a sister.

As long as I have her, I am home.

CHAPTER 48

Estella

The seventeen years apart hurt less than the past thirty days. Phantom pain where we had just begun to heal. Pippa made it in time for us to start our birthday celebration. Officially eighteen, adults. The first birthday together since the first one together.

"Are you hungry?" I ask as soon as her bags are dropped upstairs. It's two in the morning, but that doesn't mean anything, not in a city like Rio.

"I'm always hungry," Pippa says.

"Good, come on."

The old man at a twenty-four-hour salgadinho shop whispers a common phrase to me every time I come in, and today is no different.

"Chute o pau para da barraca."

The man speaks slowly so I can use Google Translate.

"What did he say?" Pippa asks.

"Kick the stick out of the tent."

I use Google to find the meaning: "to lose patience or give up."

I pull up my Notes app and hand my phone to Pippa to read the rest of the phrases while we wait for our order.

Fazer uma coisa com o pé nas costas.
Translation: "To do something with your foot on your own back."
Meaning: When you complete a simple task.
Vingança é um prato que se come frio.
Translation: "Revenge is a dish to be eaten cold."
Meaning: Revenge is more satisfying with a slow burn.
Quem tem boca vai a Roma.
Translation: "Who has a mouth can go to Rome."
Meaning: When you ask for help, you can go anywhere.
Querer abraçar o mundo.
Translation: "Hug the world."
Meaning: Welcome new experiences. Do everything; live as much life as possible.

I return with a paper bag filled to the top with various fried, salty snacks.

"Will you come with me somewhere?" I ask.

"Of course," Pippa says.

We eat on the way to the entrance to the Jardim Botânico. A security guard walks from the inside and unlocks it. No flashlights, no streetlights, just the moon hopping from his bald head, off his key ring, onto the ground between us.

"What is this, Estella?" Pippa whispers, but she'll see soon enough. I turn to the man and hand him the rest of the food.

"Boa noite, Marcellus."

"Sem pressa, take your time. Querer abraçar o mundo."

CHAPTER 49

Pippa

Goldenrods are underappreciated, mistaken for weeds, disregarded as allergens. They get literally no credit for attracting the bad bugs away from the other flowers so the bees and butterflies can feed from them. Everyone is out here judging them based on their looks, and all the while they protect the entire ecosystem. They keep the world spinning. They stay unbothered because they know people see what they want to see and that has nothing to do with them.

I mean, Missy underestimated us and look what happened. She's in hiding, and here I am with Estella.

A botanical garden in the dark might not make sense to most, but that's why they're not my twin sister. It's the way the trees whisper. Creatures break through ponds at their surface, foraging, eyes waiting to crack under a sky of shade. Stingless bees vibrating to their own lullaby that they made it through another day with no dagger, no bullet, no fight. Right now, I can hear the whole world at night. It's a miracle anyone gets any sleep when they could be here, lungs open, arms out, oxygen in abundance. Standing in a forest in the center of a city with twinkling fireflies crawling up its walls, a perimeter of watch light from here to the Bay.

Rio de Janeiro is the sister city of San Francisco, Jo said.

And here we are bridging the gap among the cacti and the bonsai, the brazilwoods and the capirona. We face the magnitude of how much stays alive despite the inherent vulnerability of being. This is it. The perfect time for a wish.

"Hey, Stell? There is something I've been wanting to do with you, but I didn't know when, so I've been just carrying this stuff around."

"Okay . . ." She indulges me.

I reach inside my purse to pull out my Post-its and a pencil, a small steel cup, and a lighter. "Write down a wish for Mamãe. We have to let her go," I say.

Estella didn't grow up with this tradition, but she doesn't need me to explain. She takes the pencil and a Post-it and writes. I do the same. When we finish, we fold the Post-its up and find a corner away from the flowers on a cement path to place them into the cup. I bend down to light the Bic and watch the notes catch fire. Estella and I hold hands as the flames crackle, and Mamãe rips through the night, free to fly, to rest, to enter our dreams without consequence. Our mamãe, a lightning bolt. The fire behind the sun. The only one.

And her girls standing in a garden, ready to hug the world.

CHAPTER 50

Estella

"Want some tea?" I ask Pippa soon as we walk into the apartment. Some habits die hard.

"Um, yes, something simple, maybe ginger?" Pippa suggests.

I return with her mug ten minutes later, but she is already asleep. The cup is warm in my hands, one of the few comforts from my childhood that I don't want to let go of, even though I try to push the rest of Missy away. I walk to the window to stare out at the city my sister and I came from but have never known.

Ordem e Progresso, the Brazilian flag, hangs outside and beats at the early morning sky with untamed measure. Rio de Janeiro has the sound of a beginning. I have whispered the words every night I have been here until they lived inside me, to free myself from what I've done. But most nights, the memory flicks on, and I haven't figured out how to make it stop. My punishment is I have to sit in the truth until I've lived it all over again.

Bidi and I stand in front of the gate. We watch until Missy is inside the car, and they drive off down my street one by one. A car

I ordered pulls up for us, and we race to the hospital. Outside, Jaggers stands waiting.

"Pippa just got transferred to the ICU," he says.

"Bidi, you go to her. I just have to run to the station to fill out paperwork."

Bidi looks at me, afraid to see Pippa that way, broken and likely comatose. I wrap her in my arms.

"I'll be back as soon as I can," I whisper. I watch her step into the hospital, and the automatic doors close behind her.

"Let's go," I say to Jaggers.

He drives me to the same soundproof cabin in the woods he hired his associate to drive Missy to after he veered away from the procession of cops at a busy intersection.

Missy sits tied to the chair beside the only other furniture in the room, a fold-up table. She makes muffled sounds in my direction.

"Do you have the tea?" I ask Jaggers.

He pulls out a thermos and pours a mug. He hands me the full cup.

"Untie her mouth," I say to Jaggers. "Let's see how she likes the Missy Havisham special."

The moment Missy's tongue is free, she starts. "You don't have it in you."

I hold the cup up to her nose so she can smell the scent of her own poison. Missy doesn't flinch. She doesn't move a nostril. I dump the tea at her feet.

"You're right; that's not my style. Jaggers?"

For someone as large as a downtown condo, Jaggers moves unnaturally fast. He pulls the blade from his pocket and brings it down to free Missy's arms. She twists her wrists and places her hands onto the table to stretch out her fingers. I give Jaggers another nod, and he brings the blade down again in one motion. Two of her fingers roll onto the floor.

Missy's scream is bloody. It pours out of her, a wail that fills the whole padded room. She screams until her throat is raw. After she's stopped, I hand her a dish towel to wrap around her injury.

"I was wrong; you do have it in you." Missy is ashen, but wonder fills her eyes.

"No, you were right. I'm absolutely nothing like you. I'd never get caught," I prod.

She looks up at me from her seat, the towel already tie-dyed with her blood. I crouch. I am nothing if not stubborn. I always finish things, so she's going to have to sit in what she started until I say we're done.

"You know, Missy, now that we have these digits of yours, I have a feeling the police are going to find some fingerprints at the shop. There won't be any question about the truth of who killed our Tia Jo."

Missy looks up at Jaggers, who collects her pointer and thumb with gloves and a baggie.

"She looks thirsty; give her something to drink," I instruct.

He hands her a bottle of water, and she chugs the whole thing down in seconds.

"Estella, you're going to regre—" Missy stops midsentence, her mutilated hand scratching at her throat.

"What was that?" I cup my ear.

"Estella?" Missy croaks at me.

I smile. "It wasn't a total lie. Oleander isn't my thing. I went for hemlock, which works much quicker. I couldn't risk you figuring out a way to weasel yourself out of here. Sorry, Missy."

Missy turns blue. She claws at the table, and her chair rocks side to side and threatens to tip over but steadies once she is gone.

The ginger tea is still too hot to drink, but I sip it anyway and let the burn dissolve the remainder of the memory. The police are so busy analyzing the fingerprints they uncovered once I demanded a more thorough investigation, they haven't even considered that she's not on the run. By the time they find her body, she will have decomposed. Rotted, the same as my mother. I've made sure of that.

My phone buzzes—unknown number. I walk to the other side of the apartment into a bathroom, then close the door and turn on the faucet for a buffer before I answer.

"Jaggers?" I ask.

"Yes, miss."

"You can't do this to me!" Bettina's scream cracks my eardrum.

"Do I proceed?" he asks.

There is more of Missy in me than I want to admit. More than Pippa or Bidi can ever know, but I am just doing what she taught me—protecting my family at all costs.

"Yes—just a warning, though," I say, and hang up before I change my mind. I wonder how she would like it if I threw my own rebirth party in honor of *her* disappearance.

Pippa is curled up like a snail's shell on the couch, so I fit myself beside her and cover us both with a blanket. It is my job to keep her safe even though the world will try to hurt her, and I can do that, even with the evil Missy left behind inside me.

Pippa once told me that we all come broken like granules of freshly laid soil, unpacked, air streaming down and up, breathing to make room for a whole life. She said, before trees climbed the sky, sunrays and raindrops had to find their seeds deep down, so they could grow.

I can grow, too, I remind myself, and hold her tighter. *I just had to be found.*

ACKNOWLEDGMENTS

The idea for *What Lies Beneath the Flowers* came to me at a time in my life I think of as B.M. (before motherhood) but was written in the A.M. (after motherhood) chapter. If I'm being honest, when the time came to actually write this book, I didn't think I could do it. I spent years struggling to get my brain to settle into the creative mode I need to effectively put words on the page. I would wait for the story to burst from me the way it has so many times before, but there was nothing. I had to learn to wear this new mother skin while keeping my children alive and safe from the global pandemic. With every free second I had away from caregiving, I searched for the person I used to be, but for years, I could not find her. Then one day, she popped up in my mirror. I have so many people to thank for supporting me through this process, but I'mma start right here.

To me, I say, go on now, girl, you really did it with two babies and a pandemic and a double mastectomy and hysterectomy—you finished this damned book.

Thank you to my Woos for the constant emotional and drafting support. I would not have found me again without your assurance that I was still in there.

I am so blessed to know and be a part of the WGAE writers

group we formed. This community of brilliant minds has been such a burst of joy and inspiration. Thanks for taking on a messy manuscript and giving such thoughtful feedback. You are all stars.

Sacha and Nikki, y'all really are the best and always read the dirty first draft, and then the second. Thank you endlessly; your notes make me so much better.

This book would not exist without the generosity of Nicki and Aditya and Ilona and Daniel. Thank you for offering me your homes to work from, and sorry for the random pages of stream-of-consciousness notes I often left in my wake.

One of the best things to come out of the artist formerly known as Twitter was my friendship with Ashley Woodfolk. Thank you for keeping me sane in this double job of mother and writer. You are such a gift to me.

Thank you so much to my managers, Jermaine and Richard, for giving me patience as I crawled from the fogs of motherhood and multiple surgeries.

To my sister-in-law, Carla, who took a break from her own brilliant writing to give me a full developmental edit on this book, I am so grateful to have gotten you as a bonus sister in this life. Your generosity, in spirit and practice, is so beautiful.

To Beverly, you believed in my voice and my life changed. I am forever grateful you gave me the chance.

Bria, thank you so much for coming in halfway through this process and helping me across the finish line. Taking on a retelling and a mystery thriller for the first time was overwhelming, and your insight and notes were the guiding light I needed.

Mommy and Daddy, I watched you hold tight to your creative

callings despite financial stresses and divorce. I believe I accomplish what I do now because I bore witness to both of you refusing to let go of your passions amid the chaos of life. I gave up on this book so many times, but I came back to it because that's what you taught me to do, so thank you.

Lastly, I want to say thank you to my husband, Matthew, who makes it possible for me to do this work. Thank you for betting on me since 2009. Thank you for this life we have built for our girls. You make waking up even better than the dream.

ABOUT THE AUTHOR

NATASHA DÍAZ is an award-winning author and screenwriter living in Brooklyn, New York. She has contributed stories to several novels, including the *USA Today* bestselling *Black Girl Power, The Grimoire of Grave Fates,* and *House Party. Color Me In* was her debut novel; this is her second.

natashaerikadiaz.com
@tashidiaz

READ ON FOR A LOOK AT NATASHA DÍAZ'S DEBUT NOVEL!

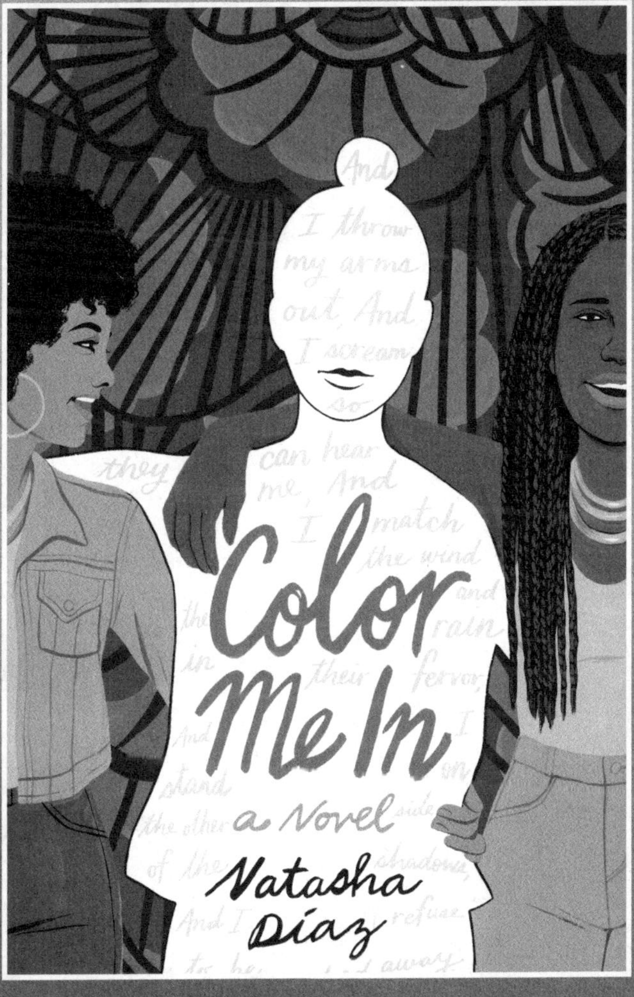

"An emotional roller coaster you won't want to get off of. Absolutely outstanding!"

—Nic Stone, *New York Times* bestselling author of *Dear Justyce*

Prologue

One. Two. Three. Four. Six. Seven.

Squirrels dart back and forth across the park, so I count them, anything to distract myself from how bad I have to pee. The line is taking forever, but I'm not going to have an accident, not when we finally made it up to the front.

"Excuse me?" a syrup-sweet voice asks my mom as we shuffle an inch closer to the tire swing. "My daughter is riding the swing alone too, and I've got to take the roast out of the slow cooker. . . . I was wondering if they could go together."

"Sure," my mom agrees.

The lady bends down to me, meeting my gaze with Cinderella-ball-gown-blue eyes.

"Well, aren't you just the prettiest thing?" she says. "How old are you?"

I look up at my mom for permission to talk to a stranger. She nods.

"Six," I say, holding up the fingers to confirm.

"Five," my mom corrects.

The woman laughs like we told the best joke in the whole wide world.

"They're such a riot at this age, aren't they?" she says.

"Sure are," my mom says, remaining friendly enough not to be rude, but monosyllabic so as not to invite further conversation.

The lady points at her daughter. "That's my Samantha," she says. I see a small, pale girl whose light yellow hair is so fine it looks like silver thread in the sun.

"They're only a year apart. Maybe I could get your number for a playdate? I so need a break sometimes. How long have you been nannying? She is so well behaved; her parents must love you."

The lady talks a mile a minute as she rummages through her bag, unearthing pacifiers and baggies filled with Cheerios.

"Aha!" She holds up an index card with crayon all over it and writes her name and number before handing it to my mom.

The line of exhausted parents waiting behind us starts to grumble; it is our turn. The woman hoists Samantha onto her shoulder like a rag doll and walks past us to put her on the tire.

My mom crumples the index card and it hits the ground like a dry leaf. She begins to walk toward the swing, but I don't move. This isn't the first time someone has said my mom is my nanny. In fact, it happens so often that I have begun to get concerned.

"Mommy, are you really my mommy?" I ask, distressed.

My voice projects much louder than I intended, and everyone in the park turns to stare, even the blue-eyed lady. Their eyes burn through my sweater like angry moths and I lose the last bit of control I had over my bladder. Hot pee trails down my legs as I shake, terrified as to what my mom's answer will be.

My mother's golden-brown skin glows, illuminated by the sun that streams through the branches of the trees overhead. When she bends down, I see her lips quiver. She cups my face and her thumbs rub my soft, whitish cheeks, as if the gentle sweeping motion is all I need to clear the pain away.

"I'm your mommy," she says.

And then she drags me out of the park before I get a chance to ride the swing.

Chapter 1

I have lived trapped in that moment ever since.
In the dreaded ambiguity
That follows me everywhere I go.
Even here,
In this grimy mirror,
and bitter fluorescent glow.

The electric hiss, like bees caught in a plastic casing, sends shock waves from the sterile lightbulbs in the bathroom of Mount Olivene Baptist Church. The sound travels over the damp off-white tiles, back to my reflection in a mirror so streaked and blurred with soap scum my skin almost blends into the walls behind me. If it weren't for the burst of brown freckles that swarm around my nose and across my cheekbones, I'd be the way I am most of the time: invisible—swallowed up whole by the imaginary bugs and the all-encompassing beige.

Cloudy Pepto-Bismol-pink gel squirts onto me like projectile vomit from the rusted soap dispenser and sends a foamy streak across my light yellow shirt. I go to grab a handful of waxy paper towels piled up on the side of the sink and bump my phone and church program, which I've covered with poetry scribbles, sending them to the ground.

"Damn it!"

My shout echoes through the empty space and I stand with my eyes pinched shut, ready for Jesus Christ to float into the ladies' room and smite me for using foul language in his house. But no one comes. The organ upstairs begins to play, accompanied by the choir. They drag these hymns out for like, twenty minutes. Four sentences that repeat over and over and over, gaining in volume and excitement and conviction with each go-around.

Take me to the water
Take me to the water
Take me to the water
There to be baptized

This is the song before closing remarks. I need to get moving before the Gray Lady Gang rushes in here for their weekly gossip session, which, for the record, is way scarier than the reincarnation of the lord and savior.

Every Sunday, the posse of eighty- to one-hundred-year-old ladies shows up in matching skirt suits and refined wigs, ready to talk shit and bully folks in the name of Christ. The whole congregation knows that they kick out anyone who dares use the bathroom during their regularly scheduled meeting with a swat of a cane and a glare so rigid that their victim is liable to cross over right here in the bathroom.

"Did you see what she had the nerve to wear today, Eveline?

She's a two-bit hussy, if you ask me. Stuffed into that getup like a breakfast sausage . . ."

Their raspy voices rush under the bathroom door with the breeze from the fans in the hallway. I'm too late.

Currently, the talk of the town is Miss Clarisse, a woman in her sixties who owns a clothing boutique that specializes in form-fitting, outlandish attire best reserved for '90s Lil' Kim videos. She is back on the prowl for love after her fling with Pastor Davis ended abruptly a few weeks ago—the Grays threatened to circulate a petition for his retirement, deeming it inappropriate for a community leader to be seen with her in public. Miss Clarisse isn't exactly helping her case, showing up to church every Sunday in outfits so tight it's a miracle when she doesn't pop right out of them.

Their murmurs move closer, so eager to dive into the juicy updates that they can't even wait to get inside the room. The pounding from their thick heels against the floor counts down to our impending faceoff. I have to save myself.

I burst through the door just before they arrive and walk past them without making eye contact as I rush to the stairs.

"Humph!" grunts the oldest and roughest GLG member, Miss Eveline. Her straight, chin-length black wig sways ever so slightly under a wide-brimmed lavender hat adorned with netting and an embroidered silver rose.

"They can't be satisfied takin' our houses, now these white folks got to come up here into our churches too?" Oretha, a light-skinned woman who is the tallest and spriteliest in the bunch, asks.

Miss Eveline smacks Oretha's hand with a guttural "Shush!"

"That there is Nevaeh, Pastor Paire's granddaughter," Miss Eveline says. "The Jewish one," I hear, before the bathroom door closes behind them with a sharp click.

Chapter 2

I quietly enter our row with my arms crossed over my chest to cover the gigantic wet spot. Anything to avoid attracting attention.

Stand. Clap. Praise. Sit.

Every week it's the same. I could handle the idea of church on special occasions, but every Sunday? My dad believes organized religion is for people who are weak and lazy, which is why they would rather listen to burning bushes and holy ghosts for direction than to logic. For the most part, Daddy only claims his Jewishness as an excuse to avoid spending time with my mom's religious Baptist family or to get his own mother, who goes by "Bubby," and tries to force us to go to temple all the time—sometimes under threat of death—off his back.

"It's not about being Jewish, honey. It's about being a Levitz," he says after he pulls Bubby off the proverbial ledge and sends her home in a cab. I always try to ask him, "What does that mean? How can I be a Levitz without being Jewish?" But he just shakes his head and changes the subject. After a while, it got easier to not even try to figure it out.

My phone lights up in my lap. The screensaver I set up is a slideshow of photos chosen at random. This one is from a year ago. I should have deleted it. We were barbecuing, and my dad teased my mother by waving a chicken wing in her face. (She hates them, but I can't understand why—they are so delicious.) He chased her around with it and we were all laughing.

"Ow!"

Clawlike nails plunge into the back of my arm. I put pressure on the angry half-moon indents on my pale skin, punishment for having my phone out during services. Sundays used to be fun and easy and dependable, but that's all in the past now. Since my parents' separation, nothing is the same.

Stand. Clap. Praise. Sit.

Done.

A sharp voice accosts me.

"Nevaeh, are you hungry? I *said,* are you hungry?" my auntie Anita yells, repeating herself for the power effect.

Auntie Anita is bossy. She has three kids and says if you aren't direct, nothing gets done, but I think it's just in her nature to tell people what to do. She and my mom couldn't look less like siblings if they tried. Anita's skin is darker than my mom's golden brown, and she is almost five inches taller, not to mention the half foot added by the pile of twists that sit in a perfect heap on top of her head.

"Corinne?"

The natural crevices that outline each muscle under my aunt's deep brown skin are on display as she grabs my mom's shoulder.

My mom sits beside us with her head in the clouds. She's petite, only five foot three, but regal. Her hair is pulled into a tight ballerina bun without so much as a baby hair out of place. Her eyes keep wandering down to her hand, where she fumbles with her wedding ring. I get it. I had braces for a few years, and mid-conversation my tongue would just drift over them like a magnet—there's something about that mixture of metal and rubber covered in slimy spit. It's weird, but the constant motion soothed me.

"Girl!" my aunt yells, failing to pop whatever bubble my mom is lost in.

Death would be less painful than the embarrassment from the glare of every person in the church as my aunt, irritated, sucks her teeth so loudly that the angels in the stained-glass windows join in on the judgment.

"Come on, let's get Pa out of here before these old ladies smother him to death with their questions. It's not like he's got a direct line to Jesus. Nevaeh, go find your cousins and walk back to the house. It's our turn to drive Miss Eveline home, and Lord knows we won't have room for you all with her electric wheelchair in there." She charges through the parishioners, dragging my mom along toward Pa's shiny smooth head.

My grandfather stands out among the wide-brimmed Sunday hats and colorful silk scarves donned by the gaggle of women who listlessly wave paper fans around their faces, fighting off the deadly forces of menopause and global warming.

"Nevaeh, how you doin' this Sunday?" Miss Clarisse intercepts me in her bright red pleather pantsuit. Her unseemly character was no doubt the cause of my aunt's quick departure.

I smile and silently fight my urge to look down at her cleavage, which jiggles with each word that rumbles out of her.

"I'm fine," I whisper.

"Damn, you're quiet!" she yells through a wave of people who shake their heads as they walk by.

She takes me by the shoulder and spins me around.

"Why don't you come down to my shop? We'll get you into some fine dresses and have you look real nice for church next Sunday. Your mama's taste is a little . . . dry after living in the suburbs with all those white folks for so long. Bring her with you and we'll get you both some attention from a brotha."

She smiles, but her voice betrays her desperation. Her shop is thirty years old, and the storefronts around here are getting picked off and sold one-by-one to the H&Ms and Zaras of the world.

"All right," I say, and allow myself to get caught up in the crowd.

I've got to keep moving. My cousins, Janae, Jordan, and Jericho, always sit with the youth group on Sundays, at the farthest end of the room.

"Nevaeh!"

Jericho, who goes by Jerry, is always excited to see me, as if I didn't just move in with him a couple months ago. His mini-fro bobs along with him as he makes his way toward me to give me a hug. I squeeze his cheek. Jerry recently went through a preteen growth spurt, but it turned out to be horizontal rather than vertical.

"Jerry, can you get Jordan and Janae?" I ask. "We have to walk back."

We turn to the crowd of kids who orbit around my older fraternal-twin cousins, protecting them like keepers in a quidditch match. Jerry looks at me, terrified.

"Fine, I'll do it. Stay here," I say, irritated and anxious as I walk toward them.

Janae looks up and nods at me as I approach. She sees

everything, a skill she likely gets from Anita, although that's about it in terms of their similarities. Janae has this avant-garde vibe that makes her both intimidating and alluring at the same time. She takes after her father, with eyes so big and brown you're likely to get lost in them. Janae rarely pipes up unless she really has something to say, unlike Jordan, who has something to say at all times about everything.

"Ever heard of an iron?" Jordan says judgily, tugging on my wrinkled shirt. "You remember everyone, right?"

Her friends nod. We've done this every week—the same song and dance around Jordan and Janae having to explain to their friends why I only just started coming to church, why I'm not in youth group, why I can't tan, and why my last name sounds like a brand of matzo ball soup.

"Your mom said we have to walk back. They don't have any room in the car," I explain sheepishly.

Jordan sucks her teeth as loudly as Anita, so I back up a few steps to give her and Janae space to say bye to their friends.

Jordan is Anita's carbon copy, the younger twin by a whole fifteen minutes—a fact she will never let Janae forget (like either of them had a conscious choice in the matter when they were barreling toward the birth canal).